HEAL
For Me

Ebook ISBN: 978-1-957959-04-7 Print: 978-1-957959-05-4

Cover Design: Coffin Print Designs

Editor: Dee's Notes: Proofreading and Editing Service

Formatting: KB. Formatting

HEAL For Me

KB. Row

To the readers

This is a continuation story that must be read in order, starting with *Break For You*

By now, you know how this couple works. While Heal For Me itself is not triggering, there is mention of past triggers. If You made it through Break For You and Leave Me Broken you will find this book is light on triggers.

- Grief

- Alcohol use

- Talk about infertility

- Happy tears

Happy Reading,

—KB

"Healing isn't a destination, it's a journey." –Payson

"Your heart has to be my absolute favorite part about you. First broken, now bandaged, but not quite healed. A journey so beautiful it hurts." –Ash

To you—the readers, for sticking with me through it all.

1

"ARE YOU READY, DARLING?" Mum pokes her head into my room.

I stare out the window at the winter-gray skies. My stomach is in knots, and the last place I want to be today is a funeral, but I know she would want me there. I can't let her down . . . again.

"Yes." My voice cracks, and Mum steps in, closing the door behind her, and stops once she is by my side. She wraps her soft hand around mine and squeezes, like she's done my entire life. It doesn't matter that my hand is nearly twice the size of hers; I'll always be four years old to her. "It doesn't feel real."

"Sometimes, the people you just met make the biggest impacts."

Isn't that the truth. If moving to Bayshore has taught me anything, it's that someone doesn't need to be in your life for long to make years-long impact.

She squeezes me one more time before flipping her wrist to check her gold watch. "It's quarter-to. We better get going."

I peel my eyes from the snow-covered trees and pull my phone from my pocket. I've since changed the inappropriate photo of Payson's *underage* body to one of me kissing her cheek. It's sweet, and her smile is huge,

I

something you don't see a lot from her. A familiar sadness shines in her eyes, one I'm not sure will ever go away, especially now.

"Have you spoken with Henry?'

"Yes, everything is fine, Ashley. He promised he would text or call if anything happened."

I sigh, not wanting to think too hard on how I'm trusting him with her as we head for the door.

I pull into the church parking lot but don't get out. The weight of Mum's stare burns my face, but I can't find the motivation to move from my seat. It doesn't feel right saying goodbye to Paul without Payson. She should be here. Her granddad was her favorite person, and she will miss his funeral because she couldn't stand the thought of living someplace where he didn't.

"It's going to be okay, Ashley." My mother's voice is something I will always find comforting. I'm beyond thankful she flew in for this. Dad will be here at the end of this week for Thanksgiving, but Mum and Henry came early to be here for me; they got in late last night. I wish Dad would have come instead of my brother, though. I love my brother, but I'd much rather Dad be sitting with Payson. I don't trust him to water plants for me, let alone look after my girl. He's not responsible for her, that's what the doctors and nurses are for, but I'd feel better about being apart if Henry wasn't such a wanker.

Walking into the church, holding the door for Mum, I mumble, "I just can't believe she's not here. It's going to crush her when she wakes, Mum."

Mum taps my hand gently. "I know. That is why you will be there for her."

My eyes burn, but I'm not sure if it's knowing what I'm about to walk in to, or that I will have to relive this moment when Payson wakes up. The devastation will fill every part of her when she realizes she missed her granddad's funeral because of a choice she made.

Mum and I are sitting in the back of the church. Luckily, we were a tad early because we wouldn't have been able to get a seat if we had been any later. The church is nearly bursting at the seams with people. I bet Paul is smiling down knowing all these people are here to remember him and pay their respects to his family. Payson's aunt starts the service, and someone silently slips into the seat next to me. I'm a big guy and may have been taking up as much room as I could so no one would sit there, but Jethro doesn't care. This guy is such a—*church, Ashley, remember?*

"Nice of you to show up," I mutter just loud enough for him to hear—and apparently, my mum too because she nudges me.

Jethro narrows his eyes at me, then leans forward to see my mum. I think he's trying to smile, but it looks more like a grimace. Either way, my mum smiles at him and takes his extended hand.

"Jethro, Payson's Uncle."

Hardly.

"Beverly, Ashley's mum."

He dips his head and drops her hand. "Nice to meet you. Wish it was under better circumstances."

The funeral goes by brilliantly—for a funeral, I suppose. There wasn't a dry eye in the audience the entire time. Even saw Jethro shifting in his seat at the especially heart-wrenching parts. I didn't cry, but there was a burn behind my eyes. Partly for Paul, but also for Payson's aunt crying in the front row. Losing your sister and father within a short time would be so hard. Too hard for the average person, and Payson is not an average person. She refers to herself as a robot often, but I think she is the opposite. She's so empathetic, and I worry about her well-being once she allows herself to feel everything.

Like Mum said, though, I will be there for her. No matter what.

The time comes for everyone to say goodbye, and because we are in the last row, we are the last to get in line.

"Paul went all out," I comment, standing in front of the champagne-colored casket with gold accents.

"It's beautiful." Mum sniffles. Seeing everyone else crying had her choked up the entire service, even though she never met Paul. Especially when Payson's aunt sang "Amazing Grace." She's an amazing singer. It makes me wonder if Payson can sing. That's hereditary, right?

"Paul always was a humble man, but it doesn't surprise me," Jethro says. "He would want the best to meet God—or whatever."

I can't believe this frail man lying in front of me is the man I spent hours with for weeks and hardly saw sit still for longer than it took to have a cup of coffee or tea. He was looking rough toward the end, but he seems so breakable now. Which, I guess he would be. It'll never not amaze me how fast time flies by. He is ninety something, and while I have no idea what it's like to live that long, I know what it is like to live as long as I have, and it feels like days but also centuries since I was young. I can imagine the same will be true once I am older.

That unfamiliar burn spreads in the back of my eyes once again. I lay my hand on top of his and drop my voice. "I promise to look after our girl."

A sharp noise comes from Jethro, but I ignore him, say another goodbye in my head, and then move along. I hug or shake hands with each of Payson's family members, and they thank me for coming. I'm not interested in hanging around sad people anymore, and my anxiety is through the fucking roof not seeing Payson, so we won't be attending the wake.

I throw open the church door and suck in a deep breath of the frigid winter air. The sun is out, but it's still freezing.

"I'll meet you at the hospital. I have some things to do before heading up," Jethro says as we head toward our respective vehicles.

I leave him and Mum to say goodbye so I can start my truck and get the heat going. The ground has a thick layer of snow over it now. Snow was definitely something I had to get used to when I moved to America, but after living in Colorado, I learned to love it.

Mum opens the door a second later. She drops into the seat and rubs her hands together, her jewelry clinking as she does.

5

"That was a beautiful service."

I nod as I back out of my spot. Cars are lined down the street, and I'm pretty sure it's a no parking street. That's how much Paul was loved.

"It was everything he deserved."

2

Ash

THE ELEVATOR DINGS, ALERTING us we've reached our desired level. The walk from the elevator to her room is one hundred and three steps. You start to lose your mind the more time you spend here, so counting my footsteps is just something to pass the time. A nurse greets us on the way, and Mum pauses to speak with her because she can't bear not to find out the life story of everyone she comes in contact with.

I don't wait for her, she can find her way to room 404, or the nurse can show her, but I've been apart from my girl long enough.

Opening the door to her room, I sigh in relief seeing her lying there, which is confusing because I would love nothing more for her to be up, walking around, or even just awake. I crave seeing her big green eyes on me again, but I also know what could happen when I do. Brain damage, memory loss. It's all a worry. They say her brain is functioning how it should, and they've told me how lucky she is for that. Payson lost three quarts of blood and died officially for three minutes on the way to the hospital. I know what could happen when she wakes up, but I still hope she does. An alive and alert Payson who might not remember me is better than a Payson in this vegetative state.

I'm so busy looking her over I don't even notice it's not my brother next to her.

"How is she?" Janelle mutters while stroking her hand.

I clear my throat of every emotion from the funeral and seeing her here. I made the call to her a few days after the incident, but her mum had already filled her in. She struggled to get a flight here, and I forgot she mentioned she would be up today.

"The same."

Janelle stands when I stop next to her, then hugs me. My white T-shirt is damp when she pulls away. I removed my suit jacket, tie, and dress shirt before coming in here. My change of clothes is in the bag I dropped by the door.

Janelle doesn't meet my eyes when we pull away, and guilt rips through me. I promised I would keep Payson safe, and I failed. The conversation in the hallway of the hotel comes barreling back in my mind. We should have listened to Janelle. I should have listened. Payson was so far down the delusion of "cutting is helping," but I should have known better. *I* did know better and still allowed myself to be pulled into the delusion as well.

I was so mad at her, and looking back, I had every right to be mad. Pills? What the hell was she thinking? I still don't know, but I know now I should have looked at the bigger picture. *Why* was she taking the pills? Was it because her knee? Maybe, at first, but I think she found out the numbness didn't just stick to her knee. It left her feeling numb everywhere. How I didn't see it, I don't know. I was blinded and missed the warning signs. That alone will haunt me forever.

And when she opens her big beautiful eyes, I will never let my anger or need for her blind me from her suffering again.

As we stare at Payson, I don't know what Janelle is thinking, but all I see is Payson wet, bloody, and lifeless in my arms.

"Ronni is here too."

I glance around, then to the connected bathroom, but the door is open.

"She is showing your brother the cafeteria." She flicks a puzzled look my way. "He's—"

"I know." She flattens her lips the same as mine. "Why did he need her to show him?"

"He didn't."

I don't know what the hell Henry is thinking, probably saw Ronni, heard she's a model, and . . . it doesn't matter. He's definitely not getting involved with one of Payson's best friends.

Janelle's weak smile fades, and tears fill her eyes. She turns her attention back to Payson and strokes the back of her hand.

"Why isn't she awake yet, Coach?"

The thickness forms in my throat again. Some coach I am. Fucked a player prior to the season, even if I didn't know, it'll never not bother me. Then I went and fell in love with another and did unspeakable things to her. I never thought about her playing or her future. I was so worried about getting my needs filled I considered nothing else. That's not what a good coach does, not even close.

"They don't know."

"I feel so guilty."

"Why do *you* feel guilty?" Janelle is not even on the list of people who led to this very moment, it makes no sense for her to feel guilty.

She drags her sleeve under her eyes. "I left her and look what happened."

"You have no reason to feel guilty, Janelle." I grab and hug her, hoping it's more comforting than I feel. I exert all my energy on Payson and being here ready for anything that I have little to spare. "You are doing what is best for you, exactly what Payson would want, you know that."

"Doesn't stop the guilt, though." Her voice is soft.

I swallow against the permanent lump in my throat. "Trust me, I know."

I let go, Janelle grabs hold of Payson's hand, and strokes the back side. "You shouldn't feel guilty either. We all could have seen this coming, but no one looked hard enough. Payson is a master at hiding what is happening in her head."

From the moment I noticed the signs of self-harm, I was anxious for that call. But somehow, she made me forget the horrified feelings regarding the situation and shifted them into something sinister. Payson looks like an angel, but her demons are persuasive. Unfortunately, I let them talk me into doing ghastly things. If anyone is to blame for Payson lying here today, it's me for encouraging her cutting. It's me for thinking I was handling it when I wasn't. Not even close.

"I didn't think it was this bad," I admit in a hushed tone.

"No one cuts themselves for fun, Ash." Janelle grips Payson's wrist and flips her arm over, exposing the cuts. Including the word *beautiful* I carved after Janelle and Payson's fight. I look away, unable to handle the sight any longer. "*You've convinced him that this helps you*," Janelle once said. Payson convinced me, but it didn't take much. What? One pleading look and I sliced her open. I caved so easily, not once thinking about the repercussions or what the future would look like. Did I really believe she would outgrow this? Like it was some phase or some shit? Or maybe it would always be something we did. And when we have kids, we would need to explain why Mum is always bandaged? Fuck no. I don't bloody know what I was thinking. All I know is that another blade will never touch Payson's skin. Ever.

Janelle, Mum, and I are sitting around Payson, softly discussing various things—mostly Janelle's time in California—when Henry and Ronni walk in. He holds the door for her and bows when she walks past.

"My lady."

Ronni giggles, and I shoot a look at Mum, then Janelle, who is already crossing her arms over her chest, like a disapproving parent who caught their child doing something they shouldn't do. *Like flirting with a man you don't know while your best friend lies in a coma.* I'm glad I'm not the only one who doesn't approve. I think we disapprove for different reasons, because there is no way she could know Henry is an even bigger player than I was and is completely cut off from real love. But no matter what, this isn't the bloody time.

"Where have you been?" Janelle's tone is harsher than I expected. We've only been sitting here maybe twenty minutes after I changed, so I'm not sure how long they were gone before I got here but must have been long enough to piss her off.

"I told you we were—"

"You forget why we are here?" Janelle snaps.

Ronni darts her eyes to Payson but is quick to look away. She catches my glare for a moment, and something like disgust passes over her face, but she lowers her eyes to the ground before I can get a good look.

"No."

"Could have fooled me. Payson would *never* leave your side if roles were reversed. But she always was the better friend. Wasn't she, Ron?"

She says nothing. Her shoulders tense, but she keeps her mouth shut and head pointed down.

"Whatever." Janelle falls back into her seat and takes Payson's hand once again. Anger burns around her like an abandoned flame.

The room fills with heavy tension, and Henry walks to my side.

"I told you to stay with her." I keep my voice low but firm.

"I did, but I got hungry, and Janelle was here."

"You could have asked a nurse to bring you something." I'm doing my best to keep my chill, but seeing how careless Henry is about this is exactly why I hated the thought of him sitting with Payson. Mum assured me everything would be okay, and I guess it is, but it doesn't change the fact he left when I told him not to. "Some things never change," I growl.

He scoffs. "You expect me to just sit here and what? Watch her breathe for hours?"

"Henry," Mum scolds but it's too late. Within three seconds, I'm on my feet with my little brother pinned against the hospital wall.

"That's exactly what I expected." Paul's funeral was longer than most because so many people had nice things to say about him, but it still wasn't long enough for him to leave. "What part of *she is everything to me* don't you bloody understand? I trusted you to just sit here, and you couldn't even do that."

He struggles against my grip, but I'm bigger and he's not really trying to get out. I can see the guilt written on his face. Henry has always been a loose cannon, so I don't know why I thought something being important to me would matter to him at all.

"I would have done the same for you with—"

Henry's chest rumbles with a growl. "Don't bloody go there."

"You know it's true."

His cold eyes harden. "But you didn't, because where were you, huh? While I was watching the love of my life die, where was *my* big brother?"

"That is enough!" Mum snaps, and stomps her heel against the hard ground.

I shove away from Henry and shake my head, trying to rid the guilt ripping at my insides. When it was him, I wasn't even in the same country. I was at the peak of my career playing a game while he lost the most important person to him. Being in my situation now, I'll never forgive myself for that.

Payson's door opens and Ronni ducks out. Henry isn't far behind her, storming his way from the room. Jethro walks through with a single eyebrow raised. "I take it that was your brother?"

I grumble but shake it off because being worked up helps no one. Mum taps me on the shoulder, and I fall into the chair across from Janelle and grab Payson's other hand. Dropping my head to her hand, I kiss her knuckles and soak up the relief only she can give me. It's been a fucking headache today, and it's all catching up to me now. I'd love nothing more than to talk to Payson.

"Your brother," she whispers for only me to hear since Mum and Jethro are busy chatting away. "I didn't think anyone could be a bigger asshole than you, but then he strolls in. Is it an English thing?"

I lift my head, cock my eyebrow, and scowl, but she doesn't back down. "Well, is it?"

"No." I roll my eyes. "Maybe. I don't fucking know, but I'm glad I'm less of an asshole than him."

"Yeah, well, you didn't flirt with both Payson and I when we first met, did you?"

Fucking hell, Henry. I might be the older brother but he should not follow in my footsteps. He's still older than these girls by a lot. Pot-kettle but still. We need not make it a family trait of going after girls nearly half our age. It's not a great look.

I shouldn't be surprised, and I guess I'm not if I really think about it—I'd just rather not. If there is a pussy nearby, he will flirt with it. Part of his "charm." What doesn't make sense is why Ronni was entertaining it.

"Isn't Ronni dating a photographer or something?"

Janelle shrugs. "Guess not. Ronni isn't a cheater, just a liar and a bad friend, apparently."

Hearing Janelle's harsh attitude toward someone meant to be the third of their trio surprises me. It's not my business, but that's never stopped me from digging into Payson's affairs anyway, so I ask about it.

Sadness flashes across her face, and she bites on her bottom lip. "I thought when I moved to California, Ronni and I would be close again. Like me and Pay are, but that's not at all what happened. I called her a few times before school picked up, but she was either always busy or just didn't answer. Then school started and I got busy. We chatted with Pay, and that's the only time I we spoke."

"I had no idea. I'm sorry."

"Yeah, I didn't want to complain to Payson because she obviously had her own shit going on, but yeah. It was *jarring*, as you would say, for a while. I don't even know why she flew back with me."

The obvious answer is to see Payson, but here we sit and where is she? Even with the fight between Janelle and her, if she cared, she would put it behind her and be here right alongside us.

"What do you think is going on?"

"I don't know, and I don't know if I want to."

"Meaning?"

Janelle meets my eyes with a serious look. "Ronni isn't the friend we once knew. She has secrets now."

The way she says that sends an uneasy feeling throughout my body. I can't explain it, but I'm not sure I trust Ronni, and I definitely don't want her around Payson while she goes through whatever she is going through. It's selfish, but I'm not anything if not selfish when it comes to Payson. I probably can't make my feelings known to Payson when she awakens, but I'll figure out something if it comes to it. She can't worry about others while she is healing.

Ronni rubbed me the wrong way in California, and not just because she disapproved of my relationship with Payson—most would. It was something else, like Janelle said, she has secrets. She's not who she seems on the outside, and I caught onto it. Maybe it was the small conversation I had with Monica, I'm unsure, but something didn't sit right. And now, her disappearing is leaving behind a bitter taste.

"How is she?" Jethro asks, stepping to my side and eyeing his niece.

Letting everything else fall off my shoulders, I focus on what's important right now and always.

"The same."

3

"Thanks for letting me crash here. Mom and Brette should be back in a few days, and I really hate being alone."

I dip my chin, too tired to do much more, as I set her three bags in my last spare room. "No problem. When do you have to head back to school?"

"Not until after Thanksgiving. I explained everything to the dean and my teachers. Most of them told me we would figure it out once I got back and the others are emailing any assignments I might miss out on, but it's not much, given the holiday and such."

"You are welcome to stay as long as you need."

The door behind me opens, and Parker steps out of his room and snaps his mouth shut as a mix of guilt and anger flash over his face. I didn't consider their short history when I offered her a place, but even if I had, what would I have told her? No, you can't stay here because my son cheated on you? No. Payson would want her here, and if I'm being honest, Janelle reminds me of her, and I enjoy having her around.

The door behind me slams, and she rolls her lips between her teeth.

"I think I'll just stay until they're back."

"Brilliant. I better go talk to him. Let me know if you need anything."

"Gotcha. Thanks, Coach."

I pause before closing her door. "You know, you can call me Ash. I'm not your coach anymore."

"Yeah, I know."

Well, okay. Her door closes behind me, and I suck in another deep breath before heading into Parker's room. I knock as I open the door.

He's sitting on his bed, spinning a football on his finger, and doesn't bother looking my way.

"She's only here for a few days, Park. She had nowhere else to go." Not quite true but true enough.

"Not even a big house on the other side of town?" He scoffs and curses in Italian. If I was a better dad, I would tell him not to curse, but he's allowed to be upset. Even if he was the one to ruin the relationship by cheating, he's young and emotions are hard to handle. It's not an excuse, and he knows how I feel about his infidelity, but I can't change the past. No matter the mistakes Parker makes, he is still my son, and I will love him regardless.

"Her parents aren't home, and she doesn't like being alone."

His harsh exterior softens a hair.

"I'm sorry if it is awkward for you. But I couldn't tell her no. It's not an easy time for anyone."

"Yes, I know. Payson being in the hospital, not waking up. I know, Papa. Okay? You don't need to explain it to me again how difficult it is."

"Parker," I bite out, more with shock than anything. "What is going on with you?"

He tosses the football, drops his head back onto his bed, and sighs. "Nothing. I'm fine. How was the funeral?"

I don't believe him, but I'm barely able to keep my eyes open at this point. I will ask him about his outburst later when I'm thinking more clearly.

"It was fine, but I am going to shower and take a nap before dinner. Your nonna offered to cook tonight, so at least we won't be eating takeout again."

My joke goes unacknowledged, and I sigh. "I love you, Parker."

"I know you do, Papa."

At least he knows.

I don't know how much guilt one person can hold before they break, but I might be close.

Paul

"Nana, look!"

Payson holds up the poor little frog she caught, nearly squeezing it to death. I'm close to taking it to ensure she doesn't when Joy grabs it and cradles it in her dainty hands.

Payson looks up to me with bright, excited eyes. "Nana is holding it!"

Joy winks and bends down, slower than she used to, but that comes with old age. After Payson goes home, we will most likely fall asleep on the couch. We love having her over but appreciate sleep a little more once she's gone.

"Can we keep it, Nana? Can we?"

"What did Grandpa say?"

I hold back my grin, letting Payson break the news that she needed to ask her nana. My granddaughter has me wrapped around her little four-year-old pinky, and it's impossible for me to tell her no.

"Did he now?" She lifts a challenging eyebrow. "Well, if we keep it, it can't go home to its family."

Payson thinks over her words for a moment. "What if it doesn't have a family?"

Wise beyond her years, this one.

"It does," I assure her, it's the least I can do since I got Joy in this predicament.

"But what if it would rather stay here with me?"

Joy softens her face and grabs Payson's hand lovingly. "I bet it would love to stay with you. But it probably has a mommy and daddy that misses it."

"Well . . . okay, if you're sure."

"I am," Joy says, standing.

She grabs Payson's hand and leads her to the woods behind our place to release the frog. Payson is rubbing her eyes when they return and walks right into my arms. She sniffles, and I pick her up. "What do you say we go inside and grab a couple fudgsicles before your daddy gets here."

She perks up at fudgsicles, and I chuckle.

I wrap my arm around Joy as we wave to Hunter and Payson. He rolls the window down, letting her yell to us. "I love you, Nana and Grandpa!"

I love being a father, but being a grandfather might be even better.

"We love you more!" Joy yells as they disappear down the road. Then she sags against me and chuckles. "I don't remember four-year-olds having so much energy."

I press my lips to the side of her head. "We weren't seventy years old back when we had a four-year-old, dear."

"True." She sighs. "Do you think we will be around a good while? You know, just to see her grow up."

That's one thing you worry about as a grandparent—dying before you get to see your grandbabies grow. I'm not afraid of death, I know where I'm going, but I fear leaving my family behind. Especially little Payson and Jason who look up to us so much. I know things aren't great in my daughter's house, and our place is a nice break for them. It's one of the main things I pray weekly about.

"I don't know, I hope so."

Joy nods against my shoulder. "I just want to see her happy. Them—I mean."

I hold back my grin, knowing what she means. We love all our grand-children, but those two hold a special place. Especially little Payson, with her being so young. So full of joy and life. It makes you step back and appreciate the small things, like a toad in your yard again.

She's brought new life into our old bones.

I wake from the phone ringing, but Joy gets to it before I can. It's not until I hear my wife's worried tone that I put the foot of my chair down and climb out, grunting and groaning as I do.

"Okay, okay. We will be right there."

"I know, dear. We are on our way right now." She points across the room to our keys, and I grab them. I have a feeling I know exactly where we are going.

"Is he coming back?"

Joy wipes her eyes and reaches into the glove compartment for another tissue. "She doesn't think so. He took everything.

"What are we going to do, Paul? What about the kids? I could hear little Payson crying for her daddy."

Joy sobs into her tissue, and I place a hand on her lap, hoping to comfort her in some way. I pray to myself, and I know Joy is doing the same. That's the only thing I know to do right now.

"They will be okay, Joy. We will make sure of it."

4

"YOU CHEATED ON ME!"

I shoot out of bed and throw my door open to see what the commotion is. It's still dark out, so I know it must be early. The hallway is a stark contrast of bright lights and yelling to the calm of the night, or early morning, I'm guessing.

Janelle stands in her doorway with her arms thrown out to the side while Parker is in her face with his arms crossed over his chest.

"Only because you were in your bedroom with your ex. What was I meant to think?"

I feel Janelle's anger from here. "That, uh, I don't know, I don't automatically fuck someone just because they are in my bedroom?"

Parker's jaw locks. *Is this how I look when I'm angry?*

"You didn't have to fuck my uncle."

Janelle snaps her mouth shut, and her arms fall. Defeat written all over her face. "You fucked *Alyssa*. The girl that fucked my ex who knows how many times behind my back. The girl that has made it a mission to ruin my life since third grade." Janelle flicks her eyes my way and stiffens. "And the same girl your dad fucked before Payson."

31

And with that, she backs into her room and slams the door behind her. A second later, the lock clicks.

Parker stares after her for a while, then slowly turns to his room but stops when he sees me. So many emotions pass over his face, and I watch as his respect for me, what little he had, dwindles.

"Park—"

He raises his hand and shakes his head. "I need to get ready for school."

Good fucking morning. I hope this isn't an omen to how the day will go.

Payson's beauty never ceases to amaze me. I've been staring at her for the better part of these few weeks, and I'm positive I could draw her down to the little freckle on the side of her mouth—if I could draw, that is. She's not been in the sun recently, so her golden skin is paler than I've seen, but it only makes her freckles pop. Her dark hair is in a plait to keep from knotting, making it easy to see her whole face.

I'm able to see everything, but what I want to see is her big, beautiful eyes. I crave to see her green irises. The way they dilate only for me. The way she searches me out in any room she's in. The fear that comes at realizing the last time I saw her do that may be the last time, is nearly crippling, but it will be something we work through like everything else in our path since the beginning.

Payson's door opens, and low chatter fills the room.

"I think we should paint it blue," Janelle says to Jethro.

"Paint what?"

Janelle twists her lips and looks to Jethro, as if she's waiting for him to answer me. Whatever they were talking about obviously isn't a conversation I will enjoy if she is acting like this.

"Payson's bedroom . . . at my place."

My guard is up immediately. We discussed what happens with her after she gets out of here, but neither of us could come to a conclusion we both liked. I said she would live with me, but he didn't like that, and I wasn't on board with her at his place. Last I knew, we agreed to not agree on anything and decide when she woke up. Even letting her decide if she is capable.

"She's not living with you." I release Payson's hand before standing. I'm pissed, and the last thing I need to do is squeeze her too hard.

"I spoke with Vicky this morning. She's in no state to take in a teenage girl, especially one like Payson." He levels his stare, as if I don't know what he's talking about. I know exactly what he is talking about, and I know exactly what she needs. Me. "She signed Payson's guardianship to me."

I wasn't thrilled about Vicky being assigned her guardian, but since she was the only family in the area, it made sense. Knowing she would not support our relationship and I couldn't ask Payson to sneak, I figured she turned eighteen soon enough and our relationship could pick back up. Now, if Jethro is her guardian, I know he will do whatever he can to keep us apart.

"Over my dead fucking body."

"You don't have a choice, *Coach*." He's taunting me, and I'm in just enough of a bad mood to feed into it, so I'm in his face in a second.

"Don't bloody act like that's all I am to her. We both know when she wakes up, she's choosing my house."

Anger burns deep in his eyes that resemble Payson's yet hold a darkness hers don't.

"She won't have a choice. Payson is seventeen for nine more months. As long as she is living under my roof, she will not be *seeing* her thirty-three-year-old coach."

"Say it."

He shifts, and I know I don't have to explain what I mean. He knows. Not once has he admitted to Payson and me dating. He always had a stupid word to put in place of dating, like *seeing*. What the fuck does that even mean. He's acting as if he can stop her from seeing me, but he can't because I am her coach as well as her boyfriend. She will see me one way or another.

"Say it," I demand, inching closer so we are nearly nose to nose. "Say it. Girlfriend. Soulmate. Future wife. Because she's all that." I inch closer. "She's. Mine."

He raises his fist, but I am expecting it and able to dodge it before it connects with my face. I grab his stupid collar and slam him against the wall, but he flips us and does the same to me. I sputter as the air drains from my lungs, but I don't let up on my grip and neither does he.

"I kill men for doing the same shit you are, and the only reason you're not dead and I'm not turning you in is because she's lost enough recently."

"Enough!" Janelle shouts, her voice bouncing off the walls. "You think what Payson needs right now is two Neanderthals fighting over what they believe is best for her?"

Neither Jethro nor I say anything or loosen our grips.

"You're going to have to accept their relationship, Mr. Gilbert. But Ash—" She sighs and drops her eyes to her best friend. "I don't think your house is the place for her." I'm not able to open my mouth before she continues. "Parker is having a rough time, and I don't think bringing a broken Payson into that mix will help anyone. Including her."

Parker *is* having a rough time, and I'm glad I'm not the only one who picked up on it, but I wish there was nothing to pick up on. My son has been with me for a few months, and how much of that time have I spent focusing on him and his needs? Hardly any.

I shove Jethro as he backs away. I straighten my shirt, not looking at anyone as I take my place next to Payson.

"What are you suggesting?" Jethro's voice is as unsure as I feel myself.

"Well, I have been looking up places that help with . . ." She doesn't want to say it, but we all know where she's going. "And there is one right near me. The reviews are amazing. I was waiting to bring it up at a better time, but when's a better time than you two about to rip out each other's throats?"

"What is the name?" Jethro asks.

"It's called Blue Gate Help Center."

I gawk at the two of them. "You're not actually considering sending her away, are you?"

But the look on his face says it all.

"Sending her away won't change our relationship." *I hope.*

He rolls his eyes. "My feelings toward you and Payson's *relationship* has nothing to do with the fact that Janelle is right. Payson needs help." He holds up a hand to keep me from speaking. "Help that neither of us can give her."

"Bullshit," I hiss.

"Ash," Janelle mutters, dragging my gaze to her. Jethro turns and heads from the room with his phone to his ear. "I love how much you love my best friend." Tears fill her eyes, and I look away, a new heaviness weighing down my chest. "But she needs help from someone whose beliefs can't be swayed with feelings. Look what happened with just a little convincing."

Her fingers drag over Payson's visible cuts, and I feel a make-believe blade cutting apart my insides as she does.

"I'd never let that happen again." I lift my eyes to her so hopefully she can see how serious I am about never letting another blade touch Payson's skin.

"I know." She lays a hand on mine. "But think about it, Ash. You were so against it and then . . . I can't lose my best friend, Ash."

I can handle Payson; I know I can. I can give her all the help she needs. Convince her of proper care instead of succumbing to what she *thinks* she needs. I had a moment of weakness before, it caused a big lapse in judgment, but I would never let it happen again.

But what if I did?

Staring into the tearful blue eyes of maybe the only other person on earth that loves Payson as much as I do, I know she's right. My love for Payson outweighs everything, including my morals.

"No one wants to see Payson get better more than us. If I really thought she didn't need something like this, you know I would have never brought it up, but I really think it will be the best thing for her."

It may be, but what if it's not.

And what if it destroys us? Payson doesn't do well with space. Her abandonment trauma will come roaring back until it swallows her whole.

"Just think about it," she adds before settling into her seat and pulling out her phone. She mentions something about reading on it, but I don't know how you read on a phone. Either way, with her distracted, it gives me time to think. You'd think I would have had a lot of time to do just that with my girlfriend in a coma, but it's been the opposite. Since Payson has been here, my life has become even more chaotic.

Almost as if the universe doesn't want us apart.

I am dropping my head to the back of the couch when I hear the bus outside. Thankfully, I was able to get Parker signed up for the bus so late into the year. It saves him from being stuck at school if I'm running late from the hospital and Luca from having to be here at a specific time.

I wait, patiently, for the familiar creak, then I stand and plod toward the front room to meet him.

"How was school?"

He jumps as he slips from his shoes and tosses his bag to the side.

"I didn't think you would be home yet."

His cool tone doesn't anger me, it only saddens me and makes me realize Janelle was right, and I have been ignoring Parker and his needs for far too long.

"Janelle is staying the evening with Payson. I thought we could head to the gym together."

His hazel eyes narrow, but eventually he shrugs, and I let out a small, relieved breath that he's not interrogating me.

"Go get changed. I will wait for you here."

His footfalls are a little more perky as he bounds up the steps toward his room. I grab the gym bag I packed for us and throw it over my shoulder. It's basketball and wrestling season at Bayshore, so we won't be heading to the school but to the gym Luca uses when he wants to workout outside the house. It's a little outside town, but he says it's nice and has a full-length indoor football-soccer field for Parker to practice.

I know he's been itching to get on a field, and while there is nothing like an outside field, an indoor field is better than nothing.

"I thought you went with Mum to pick up Dad."

Henry stops in the kitchen doorway, an apple raised to his mouth, and scowls. "No, Luca wanted to go, not me."

Luca wanted to go pick up my dad? I shake my head; it probably has more to do with Luca getting antsy. He doesn't often stay in one place for too long. I know he's been thinking about visiting Italy this summer. I think that will be good for him, but I worry if things don't improve with Parker, he will ask to go back and stay there. I could force him to stay with me. I am his father and have the rights, but I'd never do that to my son. I want him to want to live with me, not be forced to.

Parker hits the steps and spots Henry next to me.

"Are you coming to the gym, Zio Henry?"

Henry waits for me to answer before he does. With both of them looking at me like a lost puppy, I roll my eyes and sigh. "Hurry up, we haven't got all night."

Things haven't been the best between us since the hospital after Paul's funeral. We've mostly been able to avoid each other, since I'm at the hospital so often, but I can't hold a grudge forever. While I still need to talk to him about flirting with Payson's friends, it would be nice to spend the night with my son and brother just fucking around and not thinking about anything serious.

5

"It's bloody hard being good at everything." I throw a sweaty arm over Parker's shoulders, tug him into my side—despite him fighting me—and drop a sloppy kiss to his sweaty hair. "I haven't played football in years and you two just lost."

Henry snorts. "We only lost because we took it easy on you, old man."

I release Parker and punch Henry's arm. He dodges it, but I'm too exhausted to chase after him. Maybe I am an old man. Lately, I feel sixty-three not thirty-three, but I chalk it up to stress and lack of sleep.

It did feel good to get in a good workout. Weights are nice and what I prefer, but a night like this is refreshing.

We are heading for the showers when Henry slaps my chest, pointing across the mostly empty weight room. Two girls stand there, one against the wall and the other in front of her. They aren't touching but their stance is intimate. I glance at my brother, and he pumps his eyebrows twice.

"You are disgusting."

I plan to just walk past the girls, let them continue whatever they are doing, but as we pass, the one not on the wall turns, then I stop dead in my tracks.

Ronni stares back at me, wide-eyed and lips parted. I glance at the girl in front of her on the wall. Before, all I could see was a bit of blonde over Ronni's shoulder, but seeing her face I, unfortunately, recognize her too.

"Well, hey, *Coach*." Alyssa licks her lips, checking me out with fake interest. She's more jittery than normal, looking at Ronni in a panic, then us. It takes her a moment to calm down, but she does and then smiles. The same smile I've grown to hate, because I know it's the same one she wears right before she says or does something jarring. It grows when she sees Parker, and even more when she notices Henry. "I didn't know you had a brother, Ash. A hot brother too."

My chest rumbles when she extends her hand to him, a flirty grin stretching her face. He glances at me before taking it hesitantly after picking up on the tension in the air.

I haven't seen her since the end of the season and was just fine with it. Alyssa Burton has caused more issues in my life than necessary. She's like poison ivy on your life—a bitch to get rid of.

"Henry," he tells her, weariness in his voice.

"Alyssa."

Recognition smacks him in the face, and then he drops her hand. It only makes her chuckle.

"So, you've heard about me." She steps closer, between me and Parker. Ronni comes back into view, but she's avoiding making eye contact, guilt heavy in her body language. Alyssa's bitchiness almost made me forget how close they were when we walked up to them. They were close, nearly kissing I might even say. Are they dating? As far as I know, they are straight, but it's not like I know either of them personally, so it's possible they are together. I wonder if Janelle is aware of their relationship. Since they flew in together and she couldn't stand to be in the same room as Ronni, I will assume not.

"Which one has been talking?" She pokes Parker in the chest. "Son." She moves closer, but the look on my face must keep her from touching me. She's lucky she doesn't, I am in no mood for her and her games. "Or *daddy*?"

My insides revolt at her words and the fact she can even say them. Once again, Alyssa may be my biggest regret in this lifetime. If I could go back to that first night, I never would have drank.

Ignoring Alyssa, because I've learned that is the best way to get her to back off—not play whatever game she wants you to—I lean over to see Ronni.

"You been up to see Payson today?"

Ronni freezes. Even Alyssa stumbles as she backs up. Anger filling her face, she crosses her arms over her chest and looks to Ronni.

"No." She shakes her head, still staring at the floor.

"Shame you came all this way to see your *best friend*, only to not see her." I lay the best-friend card on thick, hoping to get through to her. I don't know her deal or the secrets Janelle mentioned, maybe it's her relationship with Alyssa, but I know Payson loves Ronni, obviously more than Ronni loves Payson and that pisses me off. It pisses me off more that she is here with Alyssa rather than being by her best friend's side.

"Well." I look around and clap, and both girls flinch. "We need to get home. Have a good night."

Henry falls into step with me. "That is the Alyssa that Janelle was shouting about?"

I dip my chin.

"I cannot believe he chose her over Janelle."

Looking over my shoulder, Parker is following, with his head hung low, but he's far enough away not to hear his uncle.

"Me either," I mutter, and my own regret rears its ugly head.

"Or that Payson is threatened by her. Payson is Gucci, Alyssa is Pound Land. Quick, easily accessible but not as rewarding."

"If only drunk Ash saw the same."

Henry claps me on the shoulder and squeezes. "None of the Pearson boys make great decisions when intoxicated. Remember when Dad thought it would be a good idea to paint the living room while liquored?"

I snort at the memory. "That color was awful."

"Yes, it was, and Mum was pissed."

For whatever reason, Dad thought a great anniversary present idea was to paint the living room pink. He says it was mauve when he picked it out, but it wasn't. We woke up to pink walls and paint basically everywhere else in the room. Dad never touched a paint brush or tequila again. These are the moments I appreciate with Henry, reliving dumb stuff from our past, but it doesn't change what was said in the hospital. It's been weighing heavy in the back of my mind ever since.

We reach the locker rooms, and I pause, causing Henry to look at me.

"I've been thinking about what you said in the hospital room."

"Don't, I was a wanker."

"Yes, you were," I joke. "But so was I. And what you said about me not being there when Bridget was in the hospital is true. I should have been there, and I'm sorry."

Henry's face fills with equal parts acceptance and agony. He taps my arm on his way to the shower, and I know that's his way of accepting my apology. Henry loves to talk, but not when it comes to Bridget. What happened with Bridget isn't something he likes to relive. It was a difficult time for the entire family. Mum used to cry every night worried about Henry and his mental state. I didn't know that at the time, but Grace filled me in after the fact. It only sucked more knowing everyone was struggling and I was completely unaware. I knew about Bridget and the whole situation, but not about the aftereffect. If I wasn't so selfish, I could have assumed, but I was at the peak of my career, young and blind to anything outside of what was directly in front of me. I'll never forgive myself for not being there for my family, and I'll never miss a big moment like that again.

For the first time in a while, hope blooms in my chest. I'm trying to not let it become overpowering, but the more the doctor speaks on Payson's tests and the positive results, it's difficult. He's saying everything looks good from a medical perspective, the only thing to do now is wait for her to wake up and see what they are working with.

"Can we help her wake up?" Janelle asks the question that's been simmering in the back of my mind.

The doctor purses his lips. "Kind of. There have been more studies lately that show coma patients are more likely to react to pleasant things from their life. Familiar smells, voices, touches."

"Like her favorite lotion and song?"

"Yes, that, and holding her hand." He gestures to Payson's hand in hers. I dropped her hand when he walked in, like I do every time. I'm trying to come across as a caring coach, it's difficult, but I think I have them fooled. Well, besides the nurse I had to give a hundred to, to keep quiet after she caught me kissing Payson on the lips. It was a simple peck, and I didn't notice her behind me, but she saw and looked surprised. I doubt she would have blabbed, but money can be an extra incentive to not do that. "Favorite television show or movie. Candles, food."

We mutter to ourselves, planning to get things that Payson loves and bring them here. Jethro offers to bring Janelle by Paul's place to grab a few of Payson things; it's probably best we get most of her stuff out of there anyway, the less Payson has to go there when she wakes, the better. I'll bring her by whenever, especially since Paul left it to her in his will, but it's best we do it when she wants to, and not when she needs a hairbrush or something similar.

"Can you sit with her for a moment?" I ask Mum.

"Of course." She picks up her knitting needles and moves closer to Payson's head where Janelle was. I kiss Payson's knuckles before following after the doctor. I find him at the nurses' station scratching away on the clipboard, probably charting all the stuff he discussed with us.

"Doctor?"

He glances up and pulls his glasses off. "Yes?"

I suck in a breath, not sure how to word this. "What is it really going to look like when she wakes?"

He swallows and flattens his lips, hopefully not about to sugarcoat it for me. That's not what I want. I want to be prepared for the worst, so if it doesn't happen, it won't feel so bad. He lowers the clipboard and gestures for me to follow a few feet down the hall where there is no foot traffic.

"This is the easy part. Payson's tests have all come back good, but that's just the medical side of it. She was dead for three minutes, in a coma for the past couple weeks. There is going to be some kind of lasting effect, we just can't be sure what it will be until she's awake."

"What are the possibilities?"

"Well, there are so many—"

"What are the odds she wakes up and remembers everything and it's just like she left off?"

He flattens his lips, and my stomach plummets. "It's not likely. Her mind will most likely make her forget what landed her here, the brain has a funny way of protecting us during the hard moments. She could remember everything up to the point she decided to . . ." He pauses, leveling his stare, and I nod, signaling he doesn't need to finish. "But we won't know until she wakes.

"Then there is the mental side of things that will need to be discussed."

"Like?" I ask, confused on what he could mean since he said everything is okay.

47

"Rehab. A help center. Payson has serious issues that need to be addressed and handled before she ends up here again for the same reason. Or somewhere else for a worse reason."

There are those words again. *Help center*. I don't get it; he doesn't know *I* am her help center.

"I know this isn't something anyone wants to think about, but I suggest you do because she could be awake any day now, and the ball will need to be rolling as soon as she is. We take suicidal patients very seriously. Sorry, Coach, but she might miss a few practices."

If only that was my main concern. "Thank you."

He dips his chin before walking away.

Thinking of Payson as a suicide patient is difficult and sends my body into a frenzy. She is, I know she is, but I guess it is hard to think of her that way. Since meeting Payson, I've known she was broken. It was obvious, even in the highlight reels, but seeing her in person—that sadness and the disconnect from everyone around her is so prominent in her eyes. Payson is beautiful and broken. I often wondered how she's never dated before me, how she doesn't have blokes following her around school and asking her out, but it makes sense now. Payson comes with baggage that high school guys are not looking to carry. They wouldn't know how to handle all her quirks, not really, anyway. Payson needs an authority figure who isn't afraid to tell her what to do, within reason, of course. She needs guidance.

She needs me.

The more I think about it, if Payson and I weren't together, I have no doubts she would have ended up with an older man still. She craves that power play, knowing she is cared for in only the way we can. The way *I* can. No other man would understand her like I do. I know that for sure.

I only wish I understood her enough to not have let what happened, happen. I should have never ghosted her for those few days. I shouldn't have fucked her that day in my office and left. I've made mistakes in our relationship, more than most in such a short amount of time, but no more. When she opens those big beautiful eyes, I will be there with open arms, ready to protect her from the world.

Mum drags a finger behind Payson's ear, probably pushing a stray hair away. Plaiting her hair was a difficult task, and it's not my best work, but at least it's out of her face. I move closer, and Mum's familiar humming fills my ears; a song she used to hum when I was a young boy. Memories flood my mind as I take a seat.

"I haven't heard that song in a long time."

A gentle smile dusts over her lips. "You used to love Elvis."

"I think I loved him because you did, Mum."

She mirrors my smile before continuing. She was nearly done by the time I walked in. I take Payson's hand between mine and lay my head down. The lack of sleep is catching up to me. It's not like I don't have time to sleep—I'm here a lot and could sleep, but I'm also home more than enough hours to sleep a proper time—it's what happens when I close my eyes.

Images of Payson wet and bloody are the perfect things to keep sleep at bay. I have to wait until I'm about to pass out and just pray dreams don't interrupt me once I do. Nightmares are more like it. Ones where I don't get to her in time. I didn't pick up the phone and she died all alone in that bloody field.

I almost didn't answer, I was still mad at her and wanted a minute to breathe, but something told me I needed to. Now I know why.

That conversation is one I will never forget, even if I wanted to.

"Payson?" I know it's her, she's the only one with that ringtone, but I don't know what else to say. I'm not happy with her.

"Do you want to get married in the afternoon or evening."

My hand pauses from cutting the carrot in front of me, my eyebrows pinched. "What?"

"I think during the sunset, you think that would be pretty?"

We haven't talked in days, and the last time I saw her, I fucked her and left, now she's calling to talk about our wedding?

I listen harder and recognize the loud noise in the background as the same noise as the rain pounding against my tin roof. What the fuck is she doing outside in the rain?

"Payson, where are you?" I dry my hands against the towel on my shoulder and toss it onto the counter.

"I think a spring wedding would have been nice."

Would have.

"Payson." The phone complains against my tightening grip. "Where are you?"

"I love you, Ash, I always have, you know? You were the only consistent thing in my life when I needed it most."

I pull the phone away and pull up her location. Thank fuck she didn't shut it off. But where the . . .

The field.

The field I took her to after the fashion show where I tied her up and fucked with her head. Pushed her to her limits.

Yelled at her about how fucked she is.

"Why are you there?" I growl. "Go home, Jailbird. Come here, just—just get out of there."

There's a pregnant pause as I rush to grab a shirt and throw shoes on, but I don't like that she is silent. If I couldn't hear the rain pounding in my ears, I'd have thought she hung up.

This is the phone call I've been dreading since day one of knowing Payson. I feel it deep inside me that something isn't right. Something in her carefree voice and the fact she's discussing our wedding in past tense, like it's not going to happen.

"I'm on my way, okay? Just hang out, and I'll be right there."

"I love you, Ash. Please don't ever think I didn't."

"Payson," I beg, unable to help it now.

"And . . . just know that I was already too gone by the time you came into my life. You were a good distraction, but—" A shaky breath filters through my ear. "You should have left me broken."

Not enough.

"Jailbird." A tightness forms in my throat. The line goes dead, and I choke on my next breath.

"Fuck!" I throw the front door open, and Luca stands with his hand out as if he was about to open it.

"What is going on?"

"Payson" is all I'm able to get out. I hurry by him and head to my truck. The rain pellets at my back, but I can hardly feel it with the pounding inside of me. "Call her granddad's! See what is going on," I shout to him over the rain.

He holds up a thumb, and I slam my door.

Hang in there, babygirl.

She says she was too broken, but she's so far from the truth. I'll make it my life's mission to show her there is more to her than the shattered pieces.

I blink back to the present and drag a hand under my eyes. No tears fell, but it doesn't stop the emotions from choking me.

Mum stares at me, so many unasked questions cross her face, but she stays silent.

"Dad coming up soon?"

"Yes. He was just showering last we spoke."

The time change has been difficult for Dad to get used to. I've only seen him here and there since he got in because all he seems to do is sleep. I guess that's what happens when you age. Mum did just fine, though, so I think he is milking it.

"She's so beautiful, Ashley."

I drag my eyes back up to Payson's face, admiring the same thing Mum is. "I know."

Mum grabs my hand, brings it up, and kisses it softly. "I'm proud of you. A girl like Payson isn't an easy task to take on." She regards Payson again and smiles softly. "But they are aways worth it."

"She is everything to me, Mum. I know our ages and her mental state are things that need to be considered, but I know if she would just wake up, we could do it. We can figure it all out together. I just need her to wake up."

"It's going to be a long road for Payson's healing, Ashley. One that will require heaps of patience."

"I know."

She taps my hand, stands, and presses a motherly kiss to Payson's forehead, then mine before disappearing to the bathroom.

"I need you to wake up, babygirl. I know I failed you before—several times—but I will never do it again. You just have to open your eyes."

"Here." Mum returns and holds a hand out to me. Inside of it is a small blue velvet box I immediately recognize. I shoot a look up to Mum. "You asked me to bring it, and I did. I've just been waiting for the right moment."

My hand shakes as I grab it from her and pry it open to reveal what's inside. "You think now is the right time?"

"I think so. But you will need to properly propose once she is awake. You can't let her miss out on a proper proposal when she has missed out on so many proper things in her short life."

Payson's past upset Mum, like it should most people, but especially Mum who is more empathetic than anyone I know. She is also the best mum, and knowing Payson missed out on the privilege of having a proper mum hurts her. I'm glad I'm able to not only give Payson myself but also a reliable family to call her own.

Taking the ring between my fingers, I hold it up, and emotions swirl inside. "I don't know what to say, but I guess I don't need to say much. You knew this day was coming." I let a faint smile break through. "I doubt you will even be surprised when you wake up with an engagement ring on your finger."

Taking her hand in mine, I straighten her ring finger enough that I'm able to slip the ring on with ease. I let Mum know her size, and thankfully, she got it resized before coming here, so it fits like a glove.

"Perfect," Mum says, her voice shaking.

She is. I cup Payson's face and ever so gently press my lips to hers. They're rougher than normal, but I soak them in anyway. I'd give anything to feel her kissing me back though.

When I take her hand again, her fingers twitch, and I freeze.

"Mum."

"What?" She moves closer, probably hearing the urgency in my voice.

"She . . . she moved. Her fingers, when I grabbed them, they moved inside of my hand."

I lay her hand in mine, and we watch and wait for it to happen again.

"Come on, Jailbird."

The moment that nickname spills from my lips, they twitch again, and I know I'm not the only one who saw because Mum gasps.

The biggest, and probably goofiest, grin I've ever had pulls on my face. "I'll never believe you when you say you hate that name again, *Jailbird*."

Once again, her first two fingers move. Emotions flood me, and I don't even care how big of a pussy I look right now. My girl moved. For the first time in weeks. I've finally gotten a reaction from her. Even if it was just fingers. Today, it's fingers, tomorrow, I get to see her eyes.

I lay another rough kiss against her lips and pull away just enough to see her entire face.

"Open your eyes, babygirl. Our story is just beginning."

Payson

Squeaky shoes fill the gymnasium as the players run from the locker rooms. The crowd roars with cheers, and my stomach flutters. Searching for him, *I scan the gym, and a smile stretches across my face as I spot him. I feel thirteen smiling over a boy, but he's not just any boy, or a boy at all, really, he's a man. A tall athletic, hot man. Ash Pearson, number two on the Colorado Wildcats male volleyball team. The way his white and red jersey fits his lean body is mouthwatering. The first time I saw him, I got butterflies, and it's no different to right now, even though it's been years. There is a difference today—I'm eighteen. Finally legal, and the day I will approach him. It doesn't matter he is twice my age, I know there is a connection between us. I don't know how I know since we've not spoken, but I felt it that first day.*

"He looks good," Janelle says beside me.

I nod feverishly. "As always."

"Alright, keep it in your pants." She shoves me. "At least until after the game. Then go wild."

I roll my eyes. I have no interest in losing my virginity—today. Might not say no if the meetup goes well, but I can't think about it because if I do, I'll panic, and I don't want to be sweaty when I approach him.

He's as amazing as I remember. Even better than watching him on TV. He's up for serve this time. On the edge of my seat, my heart races watching him warm up for his infamous jump serve. No one in the league, hell, no one in the sport serves like Ash Pearson.

"Let's go two!" The gym isn't quiet, but my voice carries enough for him to glance my way. He smiles, and I lose all ability to function. "Did he . . ."

"Shut the fuck up, he just smiled at you!"

I didn't imagine it if Janelle saw it too. Ash tosses the ball and performs a perfect jump serve as always, but who cares, because Ash Pearson smiled at me!

"You are so losing your virginity tonight."

I couldn't focus the rest of the game. He didn't look back up at me, but the excitement from when he did never went away.

Even now, the game ended thirty minutes ago, and my heart is still racing remembering his perfect smile flash in my direction. It could also be because nearly the entire team has come out of the locker room and I'm anxious there is another door he might have left out of and I missed him, but I'm trying not to think like that.

"Where is he?"

"Maybe he is jerking off in the shower thinking about the girl in the audience he smiled at."

Janelle has never been one to help pull me back from a full-blown obsession, that's Ronni's job. She usually keeps me grounded, but she's not here right now.

"You're not helping my nerves."

"I'm not trying to."

I shove her, and she giggles. "I'm just saying. Guys have huge egos, he will love that you can't even speak when he's in front of you."

"You might be more delusional than I am. You know that, right?"

"Maybe." She shrugs, not giving a shit. "But Collins likes it."

I lean against the wall and cross my arms, pouting. If only everyone was as lucky as Janelle and was basically gifted the love of her life on a silver platter when her mom married his dad. It was weird at first, but they've been together nearly four years and everyone is beyond happy for them. He plans on proposing soon, but that's still a secret.

"He should almost be out, and we will be right there."

Janelle and I glance toward the feminine voice to see a tall blonde heading our way with a phone pressed against her ear. Her dress is tight and hugs her slim body like it was made for it. The black accents her sun-kissed skin and bright-blonde hair perfectly. She looks oddly familiar, maybe a model or something. Definitely has the body for one. She's in heels, but when she stops in the hallway across from us, I know she would still tower over me without them.

"I think he is proposing, so I went home and changed." Her gaze flicks our way, but it leaves just as quick. "Yes. I found the ring. Silver, huge diamond."

Janelle nudges my arm, and we swap looks.

"Of course I'm going to say yes. He's amazing in bed."

I have to bite my lip to keep from laughing out loud. What a wild con-versation to have in front of people; only marrying someone because they are fantastic in bed is a little odd, but I've never even dated anyone, so what do I know?

Not that I didn't have guys who wanted to, but I turned them all down, and eventually, they stopped trying. My heart has belonged to one man and one man alone since I was eight.

"Okay, I need to go. He should be out any minute. Bye, Mom. Love you."

She was telling her mom how good her boyfriend—soon-to-be fiancé, apparently—is in bed? Her and I have completely different relationships with our moms, that's for sure.

She drops the phone into a tiny silver clutch. Then her cold eyes flick to us, and she scowls but says nothing, and neither do we. The hallway fills with a weird awkwardness, but it's gone when the locker-room door opens and he walks out.

Ash Pearson, in the flesh and less than twenty feet away. Janelle grabs my hand and lets out the faintest of a squeal. Luca Berutii wanders out after, quickly catching up with Ash, and they fall into easy conversation. My stomach tightens to an uncomfortable level seeing them. I'm not obsessed with Luca like I am Ash, but he's still amazing. Incredibly handsome in more of a high-fashion way. Sharp jaw and nose. Intense eyebrows and high cheekbones; he could be on the cover of some magazine. Ash is . . . sexier. Boy next door maybe when he was younger, but the only thought that comes to mind right now seeing him in a suit is daddy.

My cheeks bloom with that thought, but they were warm before. Being this close to him is making me sweat. I wipe my hands down my jeans. I wish I was dressed a little nicer than my regular mom jeans. Janelle convinced me to wear a lowcut long sleeve shirt that hugs me pretty tightly and shows off some cleavage. She tried to get me to wear a dress, but I said that was ridiculous.

Apparently, the girl across from us, still giving us the stink eye, didn't feel that way, and now I kind of wish I was as confident as her.

Especially when Ash doesn't even glance our way, instead heading in blondie's direction with a panty-wetting smile plastered on his face. Like the smile he gave me, but it's not for me this time, and to my surprise, it hurts more than I thought it would. I've full-on convinced myself we have something between us when he doesn't even know my name.

I'm so glad I couldn't eat earlier because I think I would throw it up right now.

"You look beautiful." Ash takes her hand and kisses her knuckles. Her smile is flirty, and that's when it hits me. The guy proposing to her is Ash Pearson. The guy who is amazing in bed is ... Ash Pearson. The same guy whose ring she found. Silver with a huge diamond.

Luca takes her hand next and says something in his language I can't understand.

Janelle leans toward me and hisses, "Did you know he was dating someone?"

I attempt to swallow the knot in my throat, but it doesn't budge. I shake my head.

"Shit."

She grabs my hand and tugs me away from the scene, but we don't get far.

"Hey," a deep, incredibly sexy voice calls after us. Janelle tries to keep pulling me, but that voice is so demanding and so ... sexy that I fail to keep walking. "You're the girl from the audience."

He's talking to me. For the first time, his English accent is directed at me, and the only thing I want right now is to disappear. Especially since I can feel tears burning the back of my eyes. It's ridiculous to cry over a childhood crush having a girlfriend, but the disappointment in my chest is heavy.

Somehow, I turn and face the three of them. He's moved closer, and that same heart-wrenching smile tugs on his plump lips.

"I could hear you over the entire gym."

I think that's meant to be a compliment, but I blush from embarrassment anyway.

Luca steps forward, an equally beautiful smile splitting his face, but the girl stays back, still glaring. I don't understand what her problem is, maybe because we are making her late to what she assumes is her engagement.

"I know you," Luca says. Ash raises his brows toward his teammate, confused as I feel.

"You do?" Janelle asks, thankfully, because I'm still attempting to swallow.

"Si." He nudges Ash. "She is from the video coach showed us. The high schooler with a jump serve comparative to yours."

Realization hits Ash and me at the same time, but we have different reactions. He snaps his fingers and his smile grows, where I wish the ground would swallow me whole.

I know what he's talking about, unfortunately, but I can't believe he saw that. Last year, we were having fun competitions at volleyball camp. One of them was jump serving. There were only two other girls who could jump serve and make it over. The head coach was so impressed she had a video taken and posted it on their Facebook pages along with several others. Mine was the only one to go viral and get passed around like crazy. The last I knew, it had like three million views. Apparently, one view was Ash Pearson and his entire team.

I might die on the spot.

"That's her," Janelle says proudly. "She's the best server in our entire district."

"I do not doubt it." The truth in his voice alone makes my heart thunder. Then his eyes drop down my body, and I nearly combust. It's not sexual, more admiring, but it doesn't stop my pussy from flooding my underwear. Having his eyes on me is giving me feelings I've never felt before. "What are you two doing here?"

Stalking you. *Janelle releases an awkward laugh, making me wonder if she was thinking the same.*

"Summer vacay," she tells him.

"How long are you in town for?"

She nudges me, apparently giving me the not-so-subtle signal it's my turn to talk now.

I clear my throat, but my voice is raspier than normal. "Uh, I go to school here now." I leave out the part where I only applied here because of him.

To my absolute pleasure, he perks up. "Do you? Well, in that case." He digs around in his bag while walking closer to us. With each step, my entire body vibrates, almost to the point my teeth chatter. I clamp my mouth shut, and he stops. A whiff of him floods my nose. It takes everything in me not to lean forward and take a deeper breath.

"Here." He extends a hand with what looks like a business card. His business card. What am I meant to do with this?

My hand shakes as I grab the card. I think he laughs under his breath, but blood is pumping so loud in my ears I could be making that up.

What I'm not making up is the spark I felt when my fingers brushed his. I know it was real because his stormy eyes fly to mine and narrow as we pull our hands away.

He clears his throat and lowers his hand. "Call me the next time you are free. I would love to see your serve in person and might be able to give you pointers."

I stare at the small card with his actual number on it. Holy shit.

"She's free tomorrow," Janelle blurts.

I glare at her, but Ash pulls out his phone. He has the mountains as his background; cute. He pulls up his calendar, and I've never seen a calendar so full before. Despite being full, he shoves his phone away and nods.

"Half one?" he asks. "We can meet here."

Oh my God.

I think I black out because the next thing I remember is Ash shaking my hand and telling me how excited he is to work with me.

It's not until they are gone that everything hits me. I fall against the wall, unable to support my weight any longer. Maybe it's the high level of emotions, but tears burn my eyes. I drop my head to my hands.

Janelle slides down next to me and wraps her arms around me.

"She's not even that pretty."

Who . . . oh. His soon-to-be fiancée. Right. I wasn't even thinking about that, distracted with everything else, but when I think about it, I cry harder. He might want to coach me, but he's not in love with me.

6

I THROW MY FEET over the edge of my bed and slam my hand onto the alarm, stopping the blasting of the world's most grating noise. We have open-gym today, and as much as I don't want to go, I have to because I'm the coach and I scheduled it. I considered sending Luca, but Mum convinced me it would be good for me, and I was too tired to argue.

I bump into Janelle in the hallway, and she's holding a bag and is dressed for volleyball and definitely not the freezing temperatures outside.

"Good morning." I think she attempts to whisper, but it's nearly louder than her normal talking voice. "I thought I could come. Show the newbies what's up."

I chuckle and head for the steps. "Alright, your first task can be making sure Luca is up." I made a mistake scheduling the open-gym before school, and Luca is a pain in the ass to get up.

We reach the kitchen and find Henry leaning against the counter eating an apple.

"Why are you up so early?"

"I haven't gone to bed."

Janelle brushes by me and rolls her eyes, muttering something under her breath. She's not sold on Henry yet.

Henry doesn't seem to mind her hostility, based on his smirk as he watches her dig into the fridge. I even catch his eyes falling to her ass before he forces them to me. I cock my eyebrow but say nothing. The last thing I want to do is set Janelle off by calling out Henry for checking her out. I don't know how she would handle that information, and it's too early for anything dramatic.

"I'll go get Luca up now." She throws a thumb over her shoulder as she backs out of the room.

"You have any idea how you are going to manage that? He's not an early riser."

A flirty grin spreads over her face. "I have a few ideas, yeah."

I'd rather not think about her ideas. Luca and she are a mistake, simply because I know he will never settle down, and I think Janelle would like to. She doesn't seem that pressed about getting him to commit and seems to be enjoying the casualty of it, but I just hope it stays that way.

When I turn from grabbing a water from the fridge, Henry is staring at me, eyebrows pinched and lips flattened.

I grab the apple from him and take a bite out of it. "What?"

"She hasn't fucked Luca, right? Parker was just being dramatic the other morning."

"I have no business discussing other peoples' sex lives." I attempt to pass, but Henry places a hand on my chest.

"Seriously, Ash. Have they fucked?"

Why my brother is so concerned with who Janelle has or hasn't fucked offers an uneasy feeling. He doesn't care about anyone or anything, so why does he look almost anxious to hear my answer.

"A few times."

A flash of disappointment, maybe even jealousy, passes, and that confuses me the most.

Janelle's giggles break through the awkward silence between Henry and me, and his gaze is pulled to her. Luca saunters in after her half asleep, half dressed, and wearing a sloppy grin.

Janelle stops and looks around, her hands on her hips and mischief dancing across her face. "Well, if this isn't the start of a porno, I don't know what is."

Luca barks out a laugh, Henry scowls, and I simply roll my eyes and turn to the sink.

"Only in your dreams, love."

Janelle turns and scowls after Henry as he walks past her, she narrows her eyes, but it's obviously a forced emotion. "More like my nightmares."

"You say potato." He winks and disappears out the door, leaving her to turn to me and cross her arms.

I hold up my hands, not wanting to hear it, and she grumbles.

Her parents should be home today with Thanksgiving being in two days, so I'm hoping she will head home. I would never say that, but my son isn't a fan of her being here, and apparently, neither is my brother. So, it would just be easier.

Looking out over my gym at the twenty girls lined up, my heart aches to see the only one who isn't here. There could be a million girls standing in front of me, the best players in the world, and I would still pine for that one.

"Good morning. Thank you for getting up for practice. Especially since it is not mandatory."

A few girls seem surprised it's not, but I asked Luca to state that in the email. I glance over my shoulder to him, and he grins.

"Well, since you are here." I clap. "Shall we get started?"

Early in my career if you would have told me I would be a coach one day, I would have spit in your face. That seemed like the biggest insult to the best server in the country with an ego bigger than the gymnasium. Even when my coach had mentioned the opportunity to be his assistant coach after my second year, I was offended. Now, looking out at the all the girls eager to learn from me, it feels good. My talent would be wasted if I didn't coach. They say those who can't do, teach, but I disagree, at least when it comes to a good teacher, because I have years of knowledge and experience I plan to pour into each of them. Mold them to be the best player they can be.

Last season, my focus with Payson wasn't on her playing, not fully, but this season she will be a senior. This is the big leagues when it comes to scouts and her future, which she already has interest, but I have bigger plans, and I expect them to pan out. We can fuck after, but the moment her foot touches this gym floor, I am no longer anything besides her coach.

I hope she's ready.

"Gather!"

I've always enjoyed the sounds of shoes squeaking against the floor. The girls stop in a half circle around me. One thing about this group, they look incredibly young. Most are juniors, but even Payson looked older than they do. Maybe that's just me wanting to believe she did.

"How are we feeling?"

Breathless, most of them give a thumbs-up instead of words. I'll take it, being out of season and all.

"Brilliant. You may go, unless anyone has any questions, feel free to ask now."

A brunette from the right side of the group raises her hand. Sadie, I believe her name is, the setter.

"Yes?"

"Where is Payson?"

I wasn't expecting this question. I assumed rumors had spread in the school hallways and I wouldn't be forced to answer an awkward question like this. It's a fair question, Payson is known for volleyball, and it's not like she would choose to miss a practice if the choice was given to her.

Mutters break out, most likely questions on where she is. A few people mention vacation, sick, even someone goes as far as saying she moved. Then I hear one loud and clear.

"Maybe she's back in juvie."

I narrow in on the brunette on the opposite side of the group. She's not smiling and genuinely looks like she's not being sinister, but still. I won't have anyone making shit up about my girl.

"Payson is a bit under the weather but will be back soon," Luca answers. I guess I took too long.

"Until then, you better practice, because Payson is going to come in here and make everyone one of us look bad." Janelle winks at me.

I nod a thank you before asking if there were any other questions, then dismiss them when no one has anything to ask.

Luca falls into his usual seat in the office, and the chair under him complains at the sudden weight. "That went well, yes?"

"I think so." A few girls brought me their physicals, so I take the time filing them before leaning back.

"I have a good feeling about this season," he tells me.

Fat snowflakes flutter to the ground outside the office window, and I think over his words, eventually coming to the conclusion, I don't have the same feeling. I'm confident Payson will be awake come next season, but I don't know if she will be in the state to play. It's not that I came here specifically to coach Payson, but she was a large part of it. The only reason Amanda ever reached out to me was because of Payson's obsession, so in a way, I guess Payson is the reason I'm here, and if she's not here and I'm not coaching her, why am I here at all. I enjoy coaching, but I enjoy it more when she is involved. I can't imagine coaching these girls and not one of them being Payson.

7

PARKER IS SITTING AT the counter working on schoolwork when I come down after a short nap. Before heading for the fridge, I kiss his forehead.

"How was school?"

When he doesn't answer, I turn to face him. Still occupied with whatever is in his textbook, not paying me any attention. "Parker."

Still nothing.

"Park, how was school?" My voice is firmer.

As my annoyance for being ignored lately is at its peak, I walk over and smack the counter across from him. He lifts his eyes and jumps.

He pulls the earbuds I didn't see from his ears and sighs, clutching his chest over his heart. "Papa, mi hai spaventato." *Dad, you scared me.*

"Scusa. I kissed your forehead when I entered, figlio."

He taps his chest a few more times, then runs the same hand through his hair. "This project at school has me drowning."

I hate the thought of my son stressing about schoolwork. I can admit I haven't been a great dad lately, or really since he moved in with me. Payson consumes me, and unfortunately, she is more ... difficult than Parker—but Payson isn't my daughter. She might be my girlfriend, the woman I will one day marry, and the mother to my future children, but Parker needing his father is as important.

Another thing I have failed at.

I squeeze the back of my neck, hoping to release some of the tension threatening to cause a knot. "What is it? Maybe I can help."

Parker smirks, looking so much like me. "Do you know anything about advanced biology? I have to draw all these images." He gestures to the papers scattered about.

"You have to draw these pictures? Can't you just trace them?"

"No, they have to be big, like the size of the paper."

Bloody hell.

"And it's due tomorrow. I forgot until the teacher mentioned it today. I spent most of the day working on it, but I only finished two of twelve drawings." His brows furrow as he looks over the rest of the work he has to finish, and I do the same.

"Well." I scratch at the back of my neck this time. "I suppose I could help, but you've seen my drawings, Park. I'm not an artist and can't promise you'll get a good grade."

He grins, most likely remembering the drawings I used to send him. They were nothing more than stick figures, but he used to draw me pictures, so I started doing the same for him.

"I'm desperate, anything is better than turning in nothing."

I'm meant to head to the hospital soon, but I've slacked on Parker since he's moved in with me and can't keep being a half-ass father. I was one for sixteen years, even if I only knew about him for twelve. I failed Payson in more ways than one, I refuse to fail my son. It's different, but I need to give him the attention he deserves, and if that means a night attempting to draw biology images with my so, so be it.

I step out to make a call to Jethro while Parker gets things ready for us.

"Hello?" He sounds as tired as I feel.

"It's Ash."

"I have caller ID."

Why Payson must share blood with this dick is beyond me. "How is she?"

There's a pause on his end, and my heart rate spikes.

"She's fine. The same. A few hand twitches, but that's it. I had someone come in and bathe her. Better than they do here."

Letting out a sigh, I pinch the bridge of my nose. I hate that I will not see her tonight. I also hate that someone else bathed her. God, if she would just wake up.

"Parker needs some help with his school project—"

"You don't have to be here every day," he grumbles. "Your name is on the list for them to call if something changes."

"I'm her boyfriend." I seethe. Except that's not fully true. She's wearing a big ring on her finger that says something entirely different. I'm surprised he hasn't mentioned it, actually. Not that it will change anything.

"Don't fucking go there right now."

"What is up your ass today?"

"I'll talk to you tomorrow. Will you be here tomorrow?"

Of course I fucking will be, and I tell him exactly that before I hang up and head to help Parker.

"It looks like a cock." Parker gasps between laughs.

We've been laughing at my latest drawing for three minutes at least, but every time one of us sees it, we crack up.

We got a few more recruits, as in everyone in the house, so it took us no time at all to finish. Even if Janelle had to redraw several of them. She's saved the day, and no one has yelled at each other. It's been a really good night for what it is. I just wish Payson were here. She would love being surrounded by everyone.

I slip away to call Jethro while the others try and decide on food. He doesn't pick up, and my anxiety spikes, but I dial the room number instead.

Expecting Jethro's voice, I'm thrown off when a younger male voice enters my ear instead.

"Hello?" the kid says again when I don't answer.

Who the fuck is with my girl? And where is Jethro? "Is this Payson Murphy's room?"

"It is. You are her coach, right?"

"I am." My voice is a growl. "Who is this?"

"Clay Kjelberg."

Clay. I know that name, but where—right. The guy who she told her friend she was fucking. I know the rumor was a lie, but it doesn't stop me from hating this kid. He came to a few games, and if I remember correctly, he was taking photos.

Either he is a pervert or a photographer, and neither make me like him anymore.

"Why—"

"Stop harassing the youth," Jethro bites through the phone. "He's visiting his *friend*."

Friend. The words his and friend should not be in the same sentence regarding Payson. I have no interest in telling Payson who she can and cannot be friends with, but I will if necessary.

Jethro is quick to fill me in on her being fine and hangs up before I can get another word out. I'm tempted to call him back to bitch him out but decide against it. I'll wait until I see him again so I can punch him in the bloody face.

The room has calmed when I walk back in, and Janelle and Parker are still drawing, but the adults are leaning back in their chairs chatting. It's a nice feeling, having a full house. I hope Payson wants a lot of kids because I would like a house full. The image of Payson swollen with my child causes me to lose my head. It makes me want to pump her full of my cum until a baby pops out, but I know that's not logically the best idea. I should at least let her graduate high school before I baby trap her.

"What are you pissy about?" Henry asks when I drop into my seat.

"Nothing."

Janelle looks up from her work then, studying me, and grins. "You called Payson's room and he answered, didn't he?"

How the fuck does she know?

"I told him to go up tonight. He's been asking me when he should and since you were here"—she shrugs—"I figured it was a good time."

She cannot be serious. As if she planned on a secret visit while I was distracted. I'm not that absurd. If he would have walked in while I was there, I might not be happy, but at least I know what is being said and such.

Maybe I am that absurd.

"Who is he?" Henry asks. *Nosy wanker.*

"Clay Kjelberg. Payson's *friend*."

There's that bloody word again.

Parker lifts his head from the paper now. "Clay? The blond kid?"

"You know him?" Anger bleeds through each word.

He licks his lips before answering, as if he's unsure if he should.

"Parker," Janelle warns, and I'm ready to fucking blow.

"Someone better tell me what the fuck is going on right now."

My mum scolds, but I don't register what she says with the blood rushing past my ears. Luca, Henry, and even Dad seem to be getting a kick out of this, but I certainly am not.

Parker and Janelle share a secret look, and now I know I prefer when they are ragging on each other instead of whatever this is.

"Fine." She sighs. "But it's totally not a big deal, and I swear if you tell Pay I'm the one who told you, I'll deny it and make up something about you.

"Anyway, a while back, Payson started her period at school." Yes, I remember that vividly. "She bled through her skirt and had asked Clay to walk behind her so she could go change."

A growl rumbles through my chest, and Janelle rolls her eyes.

"Will you calm down. Anyway, they tripped on the way to the lockers and fell, and somehow, he got blood on his pants. That's all."

That's *all*? Is she bloody joking right now. Sure, it might not be the biggest deal, but I have heard nothing about this. If it wasn't a big deal, then why was Payson keeping it from me?

"Yeah, I walked up just as he was pulling her into the gym." Parker nods, agreeing with Janelle.

"See, no big deal." She smiles, but the room is dead silent besides the clock ticking on the wall over her head. She must realize I don't agree with it being *no big deal*, so she elaborates, but it doesn't matter. My *fiancée's* pussy touched another guy—at least that's all I can see in my head—and now that guy is sitting with her and I'm here.

What if she wakes up and he's the first one she sees?

"Clay is harmless, Ash. Payson could strip for him, and he wouldn't bat an eye. He would probably tell her some medical fact about her body, or something. He's not into her like that, trust me."

But it's too late. I'm pushing from the table and grabbing my keys before she even gets the last word out. I refuse to not be there when she opens her eyes. She has to know I'm the one who loves her more than anything.

Payson

"You need to wake up, Jailbird. I . . . I can't do this without you anymore. Thanksgiving is in two days. Open your eyes, babygirl. Please. I'll be forever grateful."

"Also, if I hear about your period blood ever touching another man, I'm going to have to kill him, Jailbird."

8

"PAPA. DAD, I HAVE to get to school."

I peel my eyes open, confused to see the living room instead of my bedroom. I can't remember much after getting home. I know I went to the hospital, but they turned me away because visiting hours were over. The only reason I left was because Jethro came out and assured me he was the only one in the room and he let me kiss Payson and say goodnight. After that, I came home and broke out the alcohol. Not a foggy idea what happened after.

This whole thing is finally starting to catch up to me.

"Okay, yeah." I stretch my arms over my head, not enjoying the cracking, but the aching in my head makes me grumble. "Sorry, I forgot the busses weren't running today."

Parker helps me to my feet, and it takes a lot longer than it should, but eventually, I'm wobbling next to the couch, mostly upright. He heads to grab the rest of his stuff, and I stop off at the bathroom to brush my teeth and fix my mess of hair. I really should get it cut, as it's past my chin, but I can't find it in me to care.

"Heading to the car!" I shout for Parker, not caring who I wake meanwhile. He shouts to give him a minute, so I head out to get it started and warm before we need to drive. Thank God I have a garage so I don't need to clean the snow off.

I enjoy snowboarding, when my knee allows, but I loathe cleaning off cars. I hear Northern Michigan gets a bloody ton of snow; it'd be cool to see, but I don't understand how they live full-time in that. Wonder if Payson has ever been up there and if it would be something she'd like. I hear it's beyond beautiful in the summer.

I'm leaning my forehead against the steering wheel listening to the radio when the passenger door flies open and Parker drops in, followed by a thud of his bag on the floor.

"Those three shots really get to you, old man?" He smirks and I glower.

"Be nice to the old man who spent hours drawing a nucleus."

I break into a grin, unable to pretend I did anything, and we both laugh, but I wince against the throbbing in my head.

"I had fun with you last night, Park. Even if it was biology homework. It was nice for all of us to hang out."

His smile drops a hair, but he nods. "Me too, Papa."

I reach over and grab his hand, and he glances my way. "I know I've been a bloody awful dad to you for far too long, but that changes now. I will be around more. Anything you need, you let me know, okay? You come first, Parker. I'm sorry that wasn't clear since the beginning."

I love and hate the happiness spreading across his face. That shouldn't make him so happy because it should already be obvious, but it wasn't, and that is my fault.

We pull up outside the school, and he hops out. Before closing the door, he leans down. "I hope today is the day Payson wakes up."

My throat tightens, but I force a smile. "Me too, son."

He taps the top of the car and backs up. "If I fail biology, just know I'll have to live off you forever."

I snort and throw the car in drive. "Get inside and don't you dare fail. Janelle put in too much work."

Parker hurries inside, most likely wanting to get out of the cold—he hates the snow—and once he's inside, I peel away. Home is where I planned on going, but that's not where I end up. The hospital sits in front of me, taunting me by holding my fiancée hostage. I can't find it in me to open the door and get out.

I can't keep sitting here, day in and day out. I will because I love her, but it's starting to weigh on me that she's not waking up. The twitches were exciting at first, but I want more. I need more. I need her awake and to know everything is okay because the more time passes, the more I worry it won't be.

I don't know how to handle it if it's not. If I can't just command Payson to do what I want. What if she wants nothing to do with me. I can't get over her, and I don't want to. Payson Murphy is the other part of my soul. The missing part I have been searching my entire life for. We will end up together, eventually. No matter the path to get there, our happy-ever-after is waiting patiently for us.

It's Thanksgiving, and I know Mum will need help cooking, but I don't want to get out of bed. I don't want to celebrate a holiday where I'm meant to give thanks when I'm feeling the opposite of grateful. I have plenty to give thanks for, but the one thing I wanted most didn't happen. She's still lying in that bed, immune from everything happening around her. She has no idea it's Thanksgiving, or that her aunt is probably mourning the loss of her dad and sister today instead of celebrating. If my family wasn't here and I wasn't looking forward to Parker's first Thanksgiving, I would stay with her since Jethro went out of town to visit Olivia for the day. Payson's aunt is up there, so with her unaware of how important Payson is to me, it's not settling well.

Eventually, when the sun is high enough and I know Mum must be elbow deep in food, I pull myself from bed and head down. She doesn't really need help cooking Thanksgiving, Dad is American, after all, and we celebrated every year with all the traditional foods, but it would be nice to offer the help. Might be a good distraction too.

Stopping outside the kitchen, I watch as Mum and Dad converse and move around the kitchen so naturally. Like they've been doing it for years, because they have. I guess maybe my parents are the reason I put so much pressure on Payson and myself. I want what they have so bad. Payson has seen only bad examples of relationships, but I grew up watching my parents, who make the love they share beyond obvious. Dad is always touching Mum, and Mum is constantly looking out for Dad in a room when not. They are like magnets, and that's why it's difficult for me to pretend I'm not in love with Payson. Our story is different, given our ages, but it doesn't make my love for her any less. Just more complicated. I can't randomly grab her and lay a kiss on her lips—I can, and I have—but we need to be careful about where we are and who is around.

The day I can simply pull Payson into my arms without the worry of someone calling the police on me, might be my favorite day yet.

"Good morning, sweetheart. Happy Thanksgiving." Mum looks over her shoulder as if she knew I was here the whole time.

"Morning."

She wanders my way and plants a kiss to my cheek after I lean enough for her to reach.

"Happy Thanksgiving, Pops." I slap Dad's back before opening the fridge and pulling out my milk jug. Drinking from the jug started when I was a kid. I loved milk and would drink so much of it that Mum started buying me my own. When I moved out and had roommates, I always labeled mine because of it.

"Glad things never change." He kisses my cheek before continuing whatever he was working on before I walked in.

"Do you need any help?"

Without looking up, Mum tells me, "No," then adds, "You can head up to the hospital for a while. We will make sure everyone is good here."

I squeeze the back of my neck as I think about what to do. On one hand, it'd be nice to see Payson on Thanksgiving, but on the other, this is Parker's first. I don't want to miss out on it.

"Go," Dad says, laying a hand on my shoulder. "Just be back for dinner at three, okay?"

It's half to nine; that's six hours I could spend with my girl, even if I spend four, it's better than none. I need to figure out how to not make it obvious to her aunt that our relationship is more than coach and player.

Stopping off at the store, I pick up two sets of flowers. One for Payson's aunt, figuring it can't hurt to butter her up, and the other for Payson. I try and get her a new bouquet daily because I'd like her to wake up to fresh ones whenever she decides to open her eyes.

Payson's aunt seems as surprised to see me as I expected. Now standing in front of her with two sets of autumn flowers, I worry how obvious I'm making it.

She simply smiles, though.

"Happy Thanksgiving, Coach."

"Happy Thanksgiving, ma'am."

Payson looks like her dad's side of the family. Even if the only member of that side I've met so far is Jethro, it's beyond obvious they are related. I'm not sure how no one noticed before now, but I digress. She does, however, share similarities with her mum's side. Her mum had dark hair, but her Aunt Vicky's hair is light brown. Their lengths are the same though—short.

She eyes the bouquets in my hands with narrowed, questioning eyes, and I wonder—just for a moment, if she will call me out. But she doesn't, and her whole face brightens when I pass her one of the two, and I think whatever she was thinking is lost. "Oh, aren't you the sweetest. Thank you."

I replace Payson's flowers before taking a seat across from Vicky.

"How has she been today?"

Vicky regards her niece, a beat of sadness passing before she forces a sad smile. "A few hand twitches here and there. I thought I heard her say something, but I'm pretty sure I imagined that."

"What did you think you heard her say?"

"Ask. Like ask a question, but I don't know. It doesn't really make sense, but I didn't mention it to the doctor."

She's right. Payson saying *ask* wouldn't make sense. But Payson saying *Ash* would. Hope blooms low in my stomach; is it possible she's been dreaming about me? How did she say it, happy, sad, confused, excited? These are all things I want to ask but know it would be too obvious.

The moment Vicky excuses herself to the restroom, I grab Payson's hand and place a kiss on her knuckles before doing the same to her forehead, nose, and finally lips.

"I'm here, babygirl."

I wait and wait, but nothing happens. Even though I didn't hear her say my name, knowing she did is enough to let me leave the hospital with new faith. She will wake up soon, I can feel it.

Payson

"It's time, Ray-Ray."

"But I'm not ready."

Grandpa cups my cheek with rough hands, and I melt into him. "You have your whole life ahead of you."

My lip wobbles, and I'm not able to hold back the overwhelming sadness flooding through my chest and body. "I'm going to miss you so much."

"I know, but I'm always going to be here" He pokes my chest just over my heart. "When you see the sun or feel the wind, give a little hello, because that's me visiting you."

I don't know how to live in a world without my grandpa, but if he wants me to try, it's the least I can do.

9

I TAKE A DIFFERENT path into the hospital this time. There's no real reason, but something told me I should go this way, so I did. I pass several rooms, some filled, some not.

"Lost?"

I jolt at the unexpected male voice behind me. Looking back, a tall man offers me a friendly smile.

"No. I'm here more than I'm home lately." I try to smile like it's a joke, but it's not funny, and very true.

He chuckles low and deep from behind the small desk. It doesn't make sense for there to be a desk in the hallway, but he's wearing a white coat, so he obviously works here. He tugs on the coat. "I know the feeling."

"Of course. Have a good day." I back away, but his voice stops me.

"There are elevators over there." He points to the side hallway instead of the one I'm heading down.

I glance down the hallway, but I can't see anything from here.

"Get you to the fourth floor quicker."

Why am I questioning this man? If he works here and says it's quicker, then fine. I'm beat from last night, and my knee is fucked. Besides, I look run-down, still wearing my sweatsuit. He probably doesn't want me to wander the halls.

"Brilliant. Thank you."

He offers another bright smile. I'm halfway down the hallway when I hear his voice again. "You're welcome, Ashley."

"Thanks." A few steps later, it hits me that not only did he know what floor I'm going to but he called me Ashley. My heart is oddly steady, but my mind is working overtime. "How do you . . ." I pause at the empty hallway behind me. Frowning, I debate whether I should go look for the man but decide against it. I'm tired, maybe I'm imagining things.

He was right though, the elevator brought me to the fourth floor. The opposite side I usually land on but here, nonetheless.

There's an odd feeling in my chest as I head toward her room. It's not good or bad, just there. I'm passing a room when that feeling intensifies. So much so I have to look in the room to see what the hell is giving me this reaction. I try and avoid it for privacy reasons, but it's not a hospital room. It's the hospital's chapel.

My eyebrows furrow, then I lift one and look toward the ceiling. *Really?* I ask in my head, like I will get some kind of answer. I really am losing my mind.

I'm about to walk away when someone inside stands. Someone I know. I walk through the door, shocked when I don't immediately catch on fire. But I guess if Jethro Gilbert is in here not burning alive, I should be fine too.

The floor creaks, and he whips his head in my direction, rolling his eyes immediately. "What are you doing here?"

I don't fucking know. Shit, shoot. Sorry. I glance up at the Jesus statue in the front of the small room. Deep-red carpet covers the floor. Three wooden pews are on either side of a small isle, and in the front, there is a small raised stage. Each pew has the things you're meant to kneel on and pray. That's when I realize what Jethro was doing.

"You repenting for your sins?"

He scowls at my deflection of his question, but I don't know why I'm here. "Hardly."

He doesn't elaborate, but my head is pounding, so I don't push. Instead, I head to the second pew and fall into it with a thud. Jethro takes his seat next to me, and a few moments of silence pass, but they're not awkward.

"I just want her to wake up."

His words catch me so off guard I crack an eye open to make sure it's still Jethro I'm talking to. "Me too."

"Figure if Paul devoted his whole life to this shit, might be worth it during a moment of weakness. It's not like God would be doing me a favor, he'd be doing Payson one, and she's innocent enough for his love, right?"

She's innocent enough for all the good in the world. It's too bad all the good in the world isn't what she has been exposed to.

"I feel fucking ridiculous talking to myself in here, though."

I crack a smile. "Bet you look it too."

He doesn't smile but a hint of amusement crosses his face. He looks as tired as I feel.

"How was your Thanksgiving?"

"My daughter didn't show up. Apparently, I missed the memo that Black Friday shopping now starts on Thursday, so I did some work in a shitty café before turning around and coming home. Yours?"

Yikes. "Mine was actually good. Been better if Payson was there, but I think Parker enjoyed his first Thanksgiving, so what more can you ask for?"

"Not much." He shrugs.

A few silent minutes pass, and I'm able to lean my head back and close my eyes. "I have to admit, it is peaceful in here."

"I know. I've been coming here since the third day. Sometimes I . . . pray. There's a small beat of awkwardness before he says pray, but I'm not sure why. "Other times, I just sit here because this seems to be the only place I can fucking breathe."

Tell me about it.

"I just want her awake. I can't do anything if she is laying in there."

"You're a good uncle." I can say what I want about Jethro, but he has gone above and beyond for Payson after not being in her life for that long.

"Now."

I don't reply. That guilt is his to deal with, and if I'm honest, I resent a part of him that just sat back and watched as my girl suffered. He didn't truly know what was happening, but he didn't bother looking into it to find out either.

He could have saved her so much hurt. So many people, including myself, could have saved her, but if we would have, would she be my girl—fiancée? I don't know why I assume she needs to be mentally damaged to want to be with me, but it feels that way. Normal people don't date men twice their age, and normal men don't date seventeen-year-olds, rightfully so.

"Are you sleeping?"

"No."

"Then why the fuck are you snoring?"

Was I? I push myself to sit up and groan. I don't feel like I fell asleep, but maybe. I'm not young anymore, that's for bloody sure.

"Late night last night?" He eyes me curiously.

"Unfortunately, no. I'm just old."

His lips tilt ever so slightly. "You're just now figuring that out?"

"Apparently." I twist on each side, letting my back crack. It gives me a little release but not much.

"Have you looked into Blue Gate at all?"

Him mentioning that place builds any tension I just let out. "No."

He sighs as if I'm the one that's a pain in the ass. I've not looked at the place he wants to send Payson because I don't want her going. She needs to be here with me, not in California. Even if she doesn't live at my house, because I agree with Janelle, that's not what Parker needs. We are finally in a good place, and I don't want to lose that, but I want to be in the same town at least.

"Mr. Gilbert?" a small voice behind us says.

We look at the small nurse with wide eyes. "Oh, good morning, Mr. Pearson." I don't know how she knows my name but seems everyone does around here.

"Hello."

"What is it?" Jethro snaps. Good to see he's a dick to everyone, not just me.

"Payson's awake."

10

THE MOMENT I STEP inside the room that has been causing me so much agony lately, it all disappears when I'm met with the brightest pair of green eyes, and it all fades.

She's awake. Her bed is positioned to have her sitting up, and her eyes are open.

That's all I wanted, to see her eyes.

The weight of a million bricks lifts from my shoulders, and for the first time in what feels like forever, I'm able to let out a full breath.

My girl is awake.

Jethro rushes in behind me, but she doesn't even look at him.

"Ash." Her voice is rougher than ever, but I've never heard a more beautiful sound.

I rush forward and tug her into my body. She doesn't hug me back, but I once again feel her heart beating with mine, and life falls back into place. No matter what happens, this is what's important. Us, together.

"Hi, babygirl," I whisper for only her to hear. There's only a nurse and Jethro here, but still.

Finally small arms wrap around my waist. She doesn't squeeze, but I get the feeling she can't. Weak from weeks of no use.

I hold her like that for a long time, enjoying the feeling, until Jethro clears his throat for the hundredth time. Even as I pull away, I stay close to her side, and to my pleasure, she keeps a hold of my hand.

"Nice to see you awake," he tells her.

"Yeah."

Her eyes drift around the room, a line of confusion etches between her brows, but that turns to sadness to the point tears are filling her eyes. I know why she is crying right away, and any relief I was feeling, dies and is replaced with absolute dread.

I pull her into my side and shoot Jethro a look, but he doesn't understand her crying because he doesn't know her like I do. This isn't a good time for me to rub it in that next to me is where she belongs, but I really want to.

"I got you, babygirl."

I hold her as she sobs against my side. My own tears threatening to rise.

"He's really gone, isn't he?"

Fuck. This is so much harder than I could have ever imagined. How do I tell her that her grandpa died. She knows, but I don't want to be the one to confirm it.

Reading my mind, Jethro takes the chair on the other side of her and places a gentle hand on her arm. It's meant to be comforting, but it looks awkward. Like he's comforted no one a day in his life.

"He is," he tells her. I dip my head in a silent thank you, and then he dips his.

Her sobs grow, and eventually, I'm not able to stop a single tear from dripping down my cheek onto the top of her head. Jethro pretends not to notice, or maybe he doesn't because his jaw is working overtime, as if he's fighting his own emotions.

Eventually doctors and nurses come in, stealing Payson's attention from me. I keep close, not even by choice but because she's not let go of my hand once. I've caught the looks from the staff, but if holding my hand is what she needs, then that is what I will give her. Consequences be damned.

Once we're alone again, I settle on the bed next to her and let her curl into my side. She's been quiet all day during the numerous tests, aside from speaking when the doctor asked her something, and somehow, her silence is the worst part of this. If she is silent, I can't get a read on her. At least not when I don't have her focus.

"I don't know what to do." Her voice is so quiet I almost don't hear it.

"Nothing." I keep my voice gentle. "You simply need to worry about healing, the rest can be dealt with later."

"I'm scared."

Me too. I don't tell her though. "We will figure everything out."

She nods, settling in deeper. "Me and you?"

I press my lips to the top of her head and suck in a deep breath. "You and me, babygirl. Always."

11

PAYSON'S MEMORY IS BETTER than anyone could have imagined. She is passing all the "tests" with flying colors. The doctors couldn't be more thrilled. I'm happy too, but she's not mentioned her grandpa since the first day, and it's starting to worry me. She catches me watching her often, and I play it off as just not believing she's awake, which is true, but it's also because I'm waiting for her to explode.

I know Paul would say Payson's state is a miracle, but I'm not Paul, and I say it has everything to do with my girl's impressive strength and stubbornness.

There are still several things in the air, but she gets to go home tonight. As much as I wish it was my place, I now agree Jethro's is the best. I still have a house full, and that's not what Payson needs. I'd love her to meet my family, but I don't think now is the time. Mum offered to push their flight back so they could stay, but I assured them it wasn't necessary. I'm fine now that she's awake. She also made me promise I would fly Payson to England soon so they could meet officially, and I did because I'd love nothing more than to show Payson England.

Jethro agreed to take some time off work since Payson will need constant monitoring. I think that's the only reason he agreed I could come to his house to sit with her, not that he had much of a choice. Payson is attached to my side, and I'm not complaining. She has knee surgery in a week, and the doctor said we all need to sit down and discuss what happens after. Well, he didn't include me in that, but I will be there. I can't imagine how she will handle that news. Do I think it would be good for her? Essentially, yes, but she has to want it, and I'm not sure she is ready for all that just yet.

I thought Payson being awake would allow me to sleep better, but she's been up for almost an entire week and my sleep is still shit. I'm up checking my phone repeatedly a night, worried I might miss a call from her. I haven't yet, but it doesn't stop the anxiety. My family left a few days ago, and the house has been quiet, but it's nice. Luca, Parker, and I are making sure we eat dinner together as a family every night, and soon, Payson can join us. Instead of spending most of my time at the hospital, I've been at Jethro's.

Things couldn't be better between us, the same as before, and I'm ecstatic, but Jethro and I watch her like we are waiting for the other shoe to drop. Neither of us can figure out what is going on in her head. Yesterday, she was able to remove the bandages on her arms, she had me do it, and she flinched when the cuts were revealed. We didn't talk about them, but I kissed each one, then her lips, and promised her everything was okay.

I don't know what else to say, if I'm honest. I'd love to believe everything is okay, but I'm not sure I do. What are the odds Payson is just fine now? Not high. She lost her grandpa, the one person in this world—besides me—who she loves more than anything. Cutting has been a part of her for years, and I'm not convinced that part of her is just over. Maybe everything since the last time has been enough to rid her of it forever, but I'm just not convinced.

"How is Payson today?" Luca walks into the living room, taking his place in the chair across from me and eyeing the TV as he turns it on and flicks through channels. I just got home from Jethro's since Parker should be home from school soon and I needed to make dinner. Payson was napping when I left, which she's been doing a lot. The logical side of me realized she's exhausted and needs sleep. Even though she just woke up from the longest nap ever, her body doesn't feel that way and she's tired a lot. The other side of me worries she is sleeping so much because she is avoiding certain aspects of her life.

Like when Jethro mentioned taking her to her grandpa's to pick up anything she might want. Instead of breaking down, she said, "No thank you." I once called Payson out for being calm because it didn't settle with me, and we are back at this place where I don't know what to expect from her. Good days that aren't really good days at all, because she's so... calm. Or bad days when everything eventually hits her.

Payson is emotional—even if she says she's not, and seeing her emotionless doesn't settle well. The difference is, this time I know she's not cutting. Jethro is very strict about her wearing short sleeves, and he's gotten rid of or locked up anything she could use to cut herself. Plus, his house is set up like Fort Knox with bloody cameras everywhere. If she was going to be anywhere other than with me, I can't lie that Jethro's is probably a good place.

"Fine, she was napping when I left. Again."

"Ah."

The air between us is awkward. It has been ever since Payson's attempt. I don't blame him for acting the way he did and raging at me. I only wish he did it sooner. My love for Payson blinded me from what was really happening. Luca saw it the entire time, at least after he discovered I was cutting her.

Truthfully, things haven't been normal since I asked—no, demanded—he eat Payson's pussy, and I have no one to blame besides myself. I thought it would help the immense jealousy I feel anytime I see her with the opposite sex, it didn't. I didn't kill Luca on the spot, but that's not because I didn't want to. He is my best friend, so I guess it helped a small amount, but the anger I've felt for him ever since wasn't worth it. It's not a lot, because I know it's my fault, but there's annoyance deep in the shadows anytime he's around. I know he feels the same for me, but for a different reason. His is at least valid.

He turns on a football game—English football—and we settle in to watch. About halfway through the game, Luca mutes it and faces me. My body tenses, unsure what he will say. He doesn't look pissed, or annoyed, almost excited, so I relax a bit.

"What are your plans for the summer?"

"I've not thought that far ahead, why?" Luca is heading to Italy, but my plans were to just hang around here. I hope he's not about to ask to bring

Parker. I'm not ready to be away from him when we are in such a good place finally.

"You should go home." He licks his lips.

I blink, not understanding. "Last I checked, this was my home."

He doesn't smirk, laugh, or even shift. "To England."

"I haven't lived in England in years. I'd hardly consider that my home."

Luca leans forward and grabs a magazine from the table between us and slides it across to me.

Football Programs to Jumpstart Your Professional Career. In small letters just under it is something about it being held in England.

"I think it would be a good thing for Parker. He really loves football."

I know it would be. The reason we even have the bloody magazine is because I've been researching the best path for Parker. If Luca would have opened the magazine, he would see the notes and dog-eared pages from when I read it the first hundred times.

"I know this." My voice is firm. "But he just got settled here. He was uprooted from his life—twice. I am not sure he could handle a third time."

"Him or you?" His face softens for the first time since he sat down, and I see a glimpse of my best friend. "Remember when volleyball was your entire life? You would—and did—do anything you could to be your best."

He's right. It wasn't easy moving countries at such a young age. Especially when my family couldn't follow me, but it was worth it. Mostly. If Parker did this, I would move with him because there is nothing serious holding me. I love coaching, but I love my son more. I'd be lying if I didn't look up coaching positions in England either. There aren't many options, but that's not saying it's impossible. My ego would love if I made volleyball more popular over there. It'd be a lot of work but worth it.

Parker most likely wouldn't mind the move if football was involved. Maybe that's why I never mentioned it to him. I could quit my coaching position. It'd be upsetting to leave the girls because I really love watching my team flourish, but with their record last season, I bet there wouldn't be an issue finding my replacement. A process I would be a part of, I'm not leaving it to just anyone.

My house would easily sell in today's market; for more than it's worth too.

I can uproot my entire life; besides one part, and that part is the most important of them all. Next to Parker, Payson is the most significant person in my life.

The question is, am I holding my son back while waiting for her to turn eighteen? I know once she does, she will easily move with me . . . but is that the best for her? I have two futures to consider, and I'm not sure they line up. How can I make Payson, who loves volleyball, and Parker, who loves football, equally happy in one place. America has great options for football, but it is nothing to England, and the same is true for volleyball but opposite. Hence me moving here years ago.

"Just think about it."

I have been and am still lost on what is the right move. If she didn't come . . . could Payson honestly survive me leaving? Not even a breakup, because we are never breaking up—but would my absence be too much for her to handle? She doesn't do well with people exiting her life, and I don't want her to feel like I'm yet another person who walked out on her.

But Parker is my main priority, he has to be because I've failed him long enough.

I drop my head to my hands and close my eyes, trying to think but failing. A second later, a warm hand lands on my shoulder, then Luca speaks low.

"I do not envy the decisions you must make, fratello. But remember, absence can make the heart grow fonder."

I lift my head enough to meet his comforting eyes. "And if it doesn't?"

"Then it was never meant to be." He squeezes and drops his hand.

My chest aches with the thought. Payson and I are meant to be, I've known that from day one. Bloody hell, I knew that before day one. She is mine and I am hers.

"You are thinking too hard, Ashley. I do not think you are giving Payson, or your relationship, enough credit. It is stronger than you think. She is stronger than you think."

"I don't want her to have to be."

He takes a seat next to me. "Maybe it is the push she needs. She is going to Blue Gate soon. This could allow her to fully heal without worrying about missing home because you won't be here. Payson has always had a crutch—cutting and then you. Without either, maybe she will realize she doesn't need that escape and she will begin to rely on herself."

"Or without one, she will resort to the other," I deadpan.

"I do not think you give her enough credit either."

Maybe not, but I don't know if it's a risk I'm willing to take. If I'm not around, who will make sure she doesn't harm herself again? Right now, I am trusting Jethro, but even that is proving to be difficult and I'm only a few-minute drive if I speed. If I am in a different country, it's minimum an eight-hour flight. A lot can happen in that amount of time.

A life without Payson isn't something I'm willing to live ever again.

12
Payson

HAVE WE ALWAYS GOTTEN so much snow, or have I been watching it build up for too long? Out of the week I have been in Uncle Jet's house, I've watched the snow double on the edge of my outside railing.

Being here is weird. I've never been in Uncle Jet's house before. It's not like I was friends with Olivia growing up. A part of me still can't believe he is her dad, or step who raised her—whatever. At least she's not here, though. The last thing I want to deal with is her bitchiness.

Everyone has been acting weird toward me, and I'm not sure why. No, I do know why, but I wish they would stop. I'm so close to exploding, and everyone tiptoeing around me doesn't help. Thankfully, I'm tired a lot, and whenever my head gets too full and the memories or whatever get to be too much, I go to bed.

My arms itch more than they ever have—but I'm ignoring that too. That is my ticket for right now—ignore everything until I can deal with it properly. I'm not sure when that will be, but it's definitely not right now.

I have so many questions. A few I don't want the answers to, but I worry when I ask one thing, it will lead to another, so I stay quiet.

"Ready to see your room?"

I turn from the large window that overlooks a beautiful flower garden and nod. I've been staying in one of the several spare rooms for the past week, and workers have been in and out of what I guess is my room, finalizing it.

"Sure." I don't understand why he insisted on redoing an entire room for me. His spare room is nicer than anything I've had before, but I'd be lying if I said I wasn't excited.

Uncle Jet leads me through his house, or mansion, considering it's probably three normal-sized houses in one. Each room is like the last. White walls with dark-wood flooring and some of the most incredibly tall ceilings. Whoever furnished the place did an immaculate job; the heavy furniture complements well.

The house is perfect, a little too perfect if you ask me, and that gives me an odd feeling in my stomach.

The outside is actually inviting—surprisingly, considering who lives inside. Deep-gray brick with black trim, a perfect representation of Uncle Jet, classy with a hint of darkness in the depths.

"My room is just there." He points to a set of deep wooden double doors off the steps at the end of the hall. I've not been on this side of the house yet, like I said, it's massive. "This will be your room from here on out." He points to the room to the left of his.

I glance behind us at the six or so doors and back at him, lifting an eyebrow. Why must my room be right next to his when there are so many options.

"You require surveillance, Payson. Besides, this is the easiest if you need me. With you having surgery tomorrow, it's just easier." His brows bunch. "Now go look."

"Pushy," I mutter but listen because I am curious how he decorated my room. It's not like he knows much about me or what I like.

I only take a few steps before I can see inside, then I realize I don't have a door. Before I can even ask, he interrupts.

"Safety precautions."

"I need a door." I can't believe this is even a question. I'm a teenage girl living with a man I hardly know, a bedroom door should be a basic thing.

"You have an en suite with a door. You may change in there, but the main door is nonnegotiable."

I lift my eyes to his hard ones and cross my arms over my chest but drop them when his glare lowers to my arms. I know what he sees since he is forcing me to wear short sleeves. "That's a little fucked up, you know?"

"Payson," he growls. "Don't push me on this. I am not budging, and stop fucking cussing at me."

I level my stare, and he tilts his head in a cocky manner. Knowing he's more stubborn than me, I'm understanding why Olivia was a bitch if this is how he was with her too.

Turning, I step into my room—without needing to open a door. The whole door thing leaves my mind instantly. The rest of the house is perfect, a space anyone would find pleasing. This room, however, *my* room, is perfect in a different way. It's perfect for *me*. From the light-blue walls to the fuzzy rug spanning the dark floor. The bed is huge, and spread across it is a quilt. I move closer, and my eyes widen when I recognize everything on the quilt. It's made from my T-shirts, some from when I was a kid. I drag my hand over all the familiar fabrics. Even some of Grandpa's ties are sewn in, framing the shirts. I always wanted something like this. But how would he know that?

"Do you like it?"

"I can't say how much." Emotion pricks at my eyes, but I quickly brush it away. "I've never seen so many pillows on one bed."

He chuckles, for once sounding friendly.

There's so much to look at, from the white desk in the corner full of various items, to the large windows that cover the wall to the ceiling. Uncle Jet follows me over to them, and we stare out at the garden. I'm glad I can view that from my room. I don't know how long I'll be here, so I will take in every moment of this.

"Olivia always loved flowers. We planted that together a few years ago. The last thing we really did together." The heavy emotion in his voice tugs on my heart.

"Why?"

A beat of silence before he sighs. "She grew up. I stopped being who she wanted to hang out with."

Typical growing-up stuff. "I don't understand why she would choose to hang out anywhere besides here." I spin, taking in the rest of my room. "What could the outside world possibly offer that she couldn't get here?"

"Some people are never satisfied."

I guess; I just don't understand how. I know if Uncle Jet did this for me, he must have gone overboard for Olivia's room, considering she is his daughter.

"I guess if you grow up with this kind of thing, it becomes redundant."

Uncle Jet dips his chin once. "Most people aren't so appreciative of a simple bedroom." His tone isn't rude, in fact, it's a little sad. It's odd looking into his eyes and seeing a hint of guilt resting in the depth. I look away and shrug.

"It's not simple to me." My eyes land on the wall behind my bed. I didn't notice because I was so amazed by the pillows, but I smile. Moving closer, I'm able to view the several photos. They range from me and my friends as little kids, to some from this volleyball season. A couple of me and Ash make my heart beat harder. My smile grows with each one.

"Where did you get all these?"

Uncle Jet clears his throat. "Janelle was the designer of your room. You think I would have picked any of this out?"

I giggle; it does seem ridiculous when he says it like that. Makes sense why it's like someone dug around in my head. "Guess not."

"Yes, well, I will let you get acquainted. I will be in my office, which is the door across from this one."

So, his bedroom and office are right next door to my room. *Great.* Next he will tell me there is a camera in my room. I glance around but find nothing. He must realize what I'm looking for because he sighs.

"There are no cameras in here like there are in the rest of the house. There is one right outside your door, but I cannot see your bed from it."

He says that like it's a gift or something. "If you prove that you need one in your room, then there will be one, but for now the lack of door should be enough."

"You know, I sort of feel like I'm back in juvie. I only tried to kill myself, not someone else this time, you know?" I laugh despite it being a really bad joke. I expect some retaliation, but he simply turns and leaves the room. *Well, fine then.*

After an hour, I'm pretty acquainted with my room and en suite. Feels even crazy to say *my* en suite. I've always shared a bathroom with someone, and now I have my very own with a soaker tub I plan to use before I can't because of my stupid surgery tomorrow.

I fall onto my bed and relish how comfortable it is before pulling out my phone. A photo of Ash kissing my cheek stares back at me, and I smile. Pulling up my texts, I decide to text him first.

> **Me: My room at Uncle Jets is like four times the size of my one at hrandpas, going to take some getting used to for sure.**

To my surprise, he doesn't reply. Frowning, I snap a photo of me lying on my new quilt and send it to him.

> **Me: This quilt is much cooler in person :)**

Finally, after another ten minutes of me pretending to look at other apps, my phone pings with a text.

Ash: You look beautiful, babygirl. The quilt is very you, and I love it almost as much as I love you.

Me: Come over and youcan see how comfy it is for yourself ;)

Ash: We both know he is not letting me anywhere near your room. I will stop by later tonight after dinner, okay?

Me: Okay, see you soon!

Several more minutes tick by. My stomach tightens while I wait. I'm not used to having to wait for his replies.

Ash: I love you so much.

A normal and sweet text, but it doesn't make that bad feeling deep in my stomach go away.

Shaking it off, I send a few hearts, and click off. I know Parker will be home soon, and then they will have dinner and whatnot, so I'll leave him to that. It's so weird everyone else is still in school where I should be. No one has mentioned when I have to go back, but I assume it's soon. I must be so far behind. I should text Clay to see what is up with schoolwork. He was on my visitors list a few times too, so I better thank him for that.

I have a few texts from various people. Mostly the girls on my team wishing me better, and a few from Clay, several about homework and a simple, *Come back to school* text, very Clay.

Me: Be honest, how far am I behind?

To my surprise, bubbles pop up almost immediately.

Clay: Not too bad. I have been collecting your assignments. Let me know when a good time is to drop them off.

Me: You are the best! Whenever really. I'm staying at Olivia Gilberts house, it's a long story. You live near here, right?

Clay: Yes. I can drop them off later tonight, if you would like?

Me: If it's not a problem, that'd be great.

Clay: Great. See you later.

Next, I pull up Janelle's chat. She's on vacation with her mom, but we've been talking daily, basically since I woke up. She's also pissed she wasn't here when I woke up.

Me: Could my room BE anymore perfect? Seriously, Jay. You nailed it.

Unlike Ash, and like Clay, she replies immediately.

Jay: I KNOW! I'm so glad you're finally able to enjoy it. Expect a sleep over every night once I'm home!

Me: Uncle Jet is going to lose his mind LOL

Jay: Payback for having to deal with his moody ass for the last couple weeks.

Jay: How sick is that blanket? My nanny did an amazing job, right??

Me: Seriously in love. Kinda sad I don't get to wear the shirts anymore though.

Jay: Oh no, guess you will need to go shopping. Besides, your boobs are too big now stop being ridiculous.

Jay: We are nearly back to the hotel room, call you in like ten!

Me: I'll be waiting impatiently

Like she said, ten minutes later, my phone rings with her ringtone.

"Hello."

"Oh my word, it's good to hear your voice."

"We've talked like every day for a week." I laugh. "How is vacay?"

She groans loudly. "Yeah, but I'm still allowed to feel that way. Anyhow, being on vacation with my ex is *not* fun, believe it or not.

"Strangely, I think I can believe that."

After telling me about the trip, Janelle fills me in about her time in California, since even when I was present before everything, I wasn't really. She has made a few friends from class but promises I'm still her best. Apparently, she has told them all about me, but I didn't ask what she told them and she didn't say—that's fine by me. I can only imagine what she came up with. She hasn't mentioned Ronni once and neither have I. I don't know what is happening between us. After Week of Pink, I kind of thought everything between us would be better, and it was for a while, but it seems weird again. Everything in my life seems off, but what is bothering me most is that Ronni's name wasn't on my visitation sheet once, even though I know she was in town from her social media posts.

Jethro steps into my room, telling me it's almost time for dinner, like he has done it a million times, but it's only for the past week and is so weird every time. Like we are playing house, except we're not playing and this is my life now.

I shove my phone into my sweats pocket before trailing after Uncle Jet. Despite having surgery tomorrow, my knee feels *okay*. A little loose, which makes sense, considering everything, but it's just odd I'm walking today, and tomorrow I won't be due to a surgery that's meant to fix me.

"How was work?"

"Fine. How was your chat with Janelle?"

"How did you know who it was?"

He glances back and shoots me a *duh* look. "There are not many people, if any, you laugh that loudly with. I could hear you across the hall clear as day."

"Wouldn't be able to if I had a door," I volley back.

He rolls his eyes but says nothing. Because I'm right.

"Dinner will be ready in thirty."

"I had a lot of dreams while I was in there, you know?"

Ash is stroking my hair but pauses and looks from the TV to me. We are lying on the coach, just watching movies, and thankfully, Uncle Jet gave us some privacy. It's like I'm . . . a teenager, I guess. But it's comical because Ash is in his thirties and has to follow rules like he's seventeen too.

"Like what?"

"Well, I had one where you were engaged to Coach Buckingham."

His eyebrows fly up, a taunting grin splitting his face. "That right? And how did that make you feel?"

"Stabby," I joke. "It was so weird, I was at your game to meet you, despite you being so old." He frowns and I giggle. "Totally fangirling, and yeah, you were engaged to a different woman, but you agreed to coach me." I scoff.

His chuckle rumbles through his chest and against my cheek. A soothing sound and one of my favorites. "That sounds like a good dream to me."

I shoot him a murderous glare, his smile doesn't faulter.

"Because it's there in between the lines. You just have to look, babygirl. If that scenario were true, we would have still ended up together."

"What do you mean?"

"If I was younger in this scenario, which the timeline doesn't make sense I was playing for college but agreed to coach you. *But,* if that were the case, we would have started out in an affair, but the end result would have been the same."

I eye him for a passing beat. *Oh, he's serious.* "Why do you think that? I'm a good girl."

"The best," he growls and nips at my cheek. "But you are the one with my ring. I never even considered marriage to anyone before you and here you are after only months together with my nan's ring on your finger. You are the one I would choose in every timeline, Payson. The only reason anyone would have had my ring on their finger, would be because I hadn't met you yet."

He grabs my hand to hold it up, allowing both of us to admire the prettiest ring I've ever seen. It's gold with a teardrop-shaped blue sapphire surrounded by smaller diamonds. Truly is beautiful, and if I had thought about my engagement ring at all, I like to think I would have picked one like this. The fact it's his nana's makes me believe that, I don't know, we really are meant to be.

"Besides, younger Ash would have loved your obsession even more than I do now."

I elbow him, but giggle and drop my head to his chest. "I still can't believe you proposed and I didn't even get to see you on one knee."

"If it makes you feel better, I wasn't on one knee, but that can be arranged. Should I plan a proper proposal?"

My heart speeds up, but not in a good way. "Like in public, with people watching? Absolutely not. Honestly, doing it while I was unconscious was the best decision."

He leans down and brushes his nose over mine, a gentle smile tugging on his lips. "Yeah, but I didn't get to hear you say *yes*."

True. "But you know I would have anyway."

He purses his lips and leans back. "True. But it doesn't matter. You could tell me no and I would still force your hand in marriage."

There's the Ash I love. I know most women would hate their boyfriend—er, fiancé—bossing them around the way Ash does me, but I love it, and he knows I love it. "That's a little sick, you know. Grooming me, forcing my hand in marriage. Kinda gross, *Coach*."

My heart bursts when he throws his head back and barks out a loud laugh. It echoes against the tall ceiling, and I relish in the deep gravel of his laugh. It's so good not focusing on anything but us right now.

"We were never just going to be player and coach, Pay. I had you in my sights before you even walked into that gym."

"And I, you."

He drops his hand to the side of my face and drags his thumb over my bottom lip. "God, I fucking missed you."

Unexpected tears prick my eyes, mostly because I can feel how much he means that. I can't imagine how hard these past few weeks have been on him. If roles were reversed, I don't know what I would've done.

"I'm sorry." My voice is a whisper, but he shushes me anyway.

"Do not apologize to me, please."

"But—"

"Payson, please," he snaps, but it's not mean. More of a beg. "I hold too much guilt for everything, so hearing you apologize for my mistake . . ." He stares off into the distance and shakes his head. "Just, please. Do not say sorry."

Guilt? Why on earth does he have guilt? It wasn't his fault my grandpa . . . I was pushed over the edge and cut myself. "I won't apologize, but, Ash"—I stroke his cheek and beard until he turns his stormy eyes on me—"nothing is your fault. Please do not think that."

His lips flatten, then he bares his teeth. "I *cut* you, Payson." He yanks my arm—harshly and lifts it into the setting sun so the word beautiful, along with my other cuts, is highlighted. "I carved your beautiful skin and believed I was *helping*."

There is no point in arguing with him. He has let himself believe for weeks that this is all his fault, so nothing I say will help. But there may be something I can do.

I pull my arm away and push onto my knees. I know there are cameras in this room, but I also know Uncle Jet isn't sitting there watching them. He isn't a fan of our relationship, so he's definitely not going to want a front row to our interactions.

I straddle his lap and wrap my arms around his neck. "I love you." I move and press my lips to his. He kisses me back, but he's hesitant. Maybe because where we are, or because he's afraid to touch or hurt me, but I need him to. I won't have sex on my uncle's couch—that's weird—but I need more than the pecks I've been getting. And I think he does too.

"Whether you want to believe it or not, you did help me, Ash." I feel him wanting to pull away, but I don't let him. "I didn't feel beautiful before you."

He scoffs, obviously not believing me. "That is impossible."

"Is it? I have all these scars." I hold my arms out between us. "Scars that remind me of every bad moment I've ever had. Each one of them makes me feel dirty . . . besides yours. I know I should have never asked you to cut me, and maybe you should have never agreed, but at least I can look at a few of these, and this"—I point to the word beautiful—"and feel anything other than dirty. Now, not all the scars on my body are reminders of the bad times. They are reminders of how deeply we were lost in each other."

I stare into his stormy eyes, and my heart skips a beat. I hope he can feel how much I mean what I am saying. I know a lot of people would look at our relationship and the age, or the toxicity—because it's there—but I hope at least a few could see how strongly we love and care for each other. It might not always be in the right way, but I wouldn't take him any other way, and I wouldn't change a thing about our story.

"One day, we are going to just be a boring married couple, but I'll always get to remember these first moments when feelings were so fresh, so *raw*.

Maybe you'll never see what I do." I wrap my arms back around his neck. "But I think that reminder is lovely."

He cups my face and stares into my eyes before settling on my lips. I lick them, anticipating him kissing me.

"I'll never know what I did in this lifetime to deserve you."

Then he kisses me, and it's not the kind of kisses I've been getting lately. It's the kind that steal your breath but you keep kissing because it's just that good and you don't care if you pass out. I sink my hands into his long hair and pull it away from his face.

He grips my hips and growls, low and deep. "Jailbird, if you don't stop humping me, I'm going to fuck you on your uncle's couch."

Right now, that doesn't sound like the worst thing to ever happen, but then I remember who my uncle is and the fact I'm almost positive he's legit killed people. Despite the ache between my legs, I slow my movements. He pulls me back into a kiss, this one slower, less feverish but just as good.

I don't know what state I will wake up in tomorrow, because like everyone else, I'm waiting for the drop. But in this moment, on this couch, with Ash holding onto me like he needs me to breathe, I know whatever comes up, I will be okay because it will always be me and him.

13
Payson

I'M DRIFTING OFF TO sleep in Ash's arms when the doorbell rings. It's never gone off before, so I jump.

Ash grumbles. I'm guessing he was almost asleep too.

Knowing Uncle Jet is upstairs and I'm closest, I slip from the couch and head for the door. Not to my surprise, Ash follows while rubbing his eyes.

I throw open the door. "Oh, hey, Clay!"

I feel the mood shift over my shoulder without even having to look at him.

"Payson. Good to see you awake."

His eyes shift behind me to Ash, then back. His lips flatten and his eyes droop, like he's bored. "I have your work."

He holds out a stack of papers, and I grab them. "Thanks, Clay. Seriously, this is so helpful."

"I put in some of my finished work for help." Help is code for copy. Has been since freshman year.

"You are a saint, Clay Kjelberg."

A hint of a smile flashes, but it's gone just as quick. "I try. If you have any questions, you have my number."

It took longer than expected, but Ash's arm snakes around my waist, claiming what's his. Clay doesn't seem bothered by it, though. He simply blinks.

"Totally. Thanks again."

He steps back. "I live right up the road. If you are really confused, just call me, and I will come over." If I wasn't used to Ash's harsh grip, his fingers on my hip would be causing serious pain. As if Clay notices Ash's anger, the corner of his mouth tips mischievously. A look I've never seen from Clay. "Night or day, Payson."

My mouth drops, and his shoulders bounce as he heads for the G Wagon parked next to Ash's truck. *Did Clay Kjelberg just proposition me to get a rise out of my boyfriend—fiancé?*

Ash slams the door and pins me against it, ravishing my neck, chest, jaw, and any place skin is showing.

"Ash." I blow out a breath. "He was kidding."

"I fucking hate that kid."

I laugh. It's Clay we are talking about. Ash doesn't seem to share my amusement, and his kisses turn into bites. I'm sure he's leaving behind marks.

At least some things never change. I pray Ash is always that one thing.

14
Payson

UNCLE JET IS A psychopath. There is no other explanation for this man's schedule. He wakes up at three a.m. to workout, which consists of two hours of weight training, then a five-mile run minimum. He says he normally runs around town, but because I'm here, he is using a treadmill. I am all for a good workout, being an athlete and all, but that much activity before the sun even rises is absurd. I woke up the other morning from a bad dream, and heard thumping, so I went to check it out. I was definitely pleased to find him running versus what the heavy thumping sounded like.

I haven't seen a single person—let alone a woman—since I arrived almost eight days ago. I'm not interested in meeting any of his company, but surely, the man has needs. *Gross.*

"Are you ready?" Uncle Jet pops into my room and frowns. "That is what you're wearing?"

I glance down at my sweatpants and matching sweatshirt. Sure, the collar of the shirt and cuffs are ripped, but what does it matter? "I'm going in for surgery, Uncle Jet. Not a fashion show."

He sighs like he does a lot during our conversations, as if it's exhausting just speaking with me. "Why didn't you mention you needed new clothing? I will get you a card so you can buy whatever you need."

"I don't want it. I have clothes." Less now that some were used for my quilt, but enough. Besides, I don't need him spending any more money on me than he already has with my room and feeding and housing me.

"I wasn't asking."

"You should get that tattooed on your forehead for how often you say it," I mumble.

"Quit making me say it, then."

I never had a parent I argued with in this way. It's almost refreshing, but damn, is he infuriating.

"Good morning, Payson. Ready to be cut open?"

"Er, as ready as you can be, I guess."

Dr. Nick laughs before engaging Uncle Jet in conversation about all the boring shit, like my aftercare and healing time. The same stuff he mentioned last week when we set up the surgery.

Eventually, Ash wanders in with two coffees and passes one to Jethro. "Morning," he grumbles before taking a seat next to me. When the doctor leaves, he leans over and kisses my forehead. "Good morning, babygirl."

"Hi." I smile. He returns one, but it doesn't meet his tired eyes. "Not sleeping well?"

He shakes his head, but Jethro sits on the opposite side of me and grumbles, interrupting anything else he might have to say.

"You have to knock that shit off in front of me."

Ash's jaw locks but again, he stays silent. Very unlike Ash.

After a few minutes of them discussing my aftercare, Luca wanders in also carrying a coffee. Unlike the two broody assholes, his smile is as bright as ever, and it so nice to see his friendly face. I haven't seen him since . . . well, I can't remember, but I know it's been a long time.

"Good morning. How are we today?"

Grumbles come from either side of me, but I smile despite their grumpiness. Luca makes it impossible to be upset. His personality is so lighthearted, you'd never know the loss he has endured. It's rather encouraging seeing how positive and happy he is after losing the love of his life.

"Good. You?"

"Fantastico, thank you, Payson." If he feels the tension between these two, you'd never know with the amusement resting in the depths of his hazel eyes.

"I've missed you."

He flashes his bright teeth, but my head is quickly turned and a different set of lips mash into mine. Ash nips at my bottom lip and pulls away—or is shoved away by my uncle.

The warning coming from Ash does the opposite of scare me like I think he is going for. I want him to act like a caveman. I like when he is all jealous and possessive. Toxic, maybe, but hot, nonetheless.

Jethro and Ash continue their asshole-stare off while Luca makes himself comfortable and tells me about how he plans on heading to Italy for the summer to spend a few weeks with his family.

"I would love to visit there someday," I tell him. I've never thought much about travel, but Italy is one place you hear all about. Besides, I love Italian food.

"You do have family in Italy," Jethro says.

We look at him, and Ash asks him to explain.

"You are a quarter Italian. You never wondered about your appearance?"

I never thought about it. "How?"

Uncle Jet leans back in his chair and crosses his arms over his chest. "It's complicated, but my grandfather is full Italian and still lives there today. Your grandmother's dad."

Wow. I have a great grandpa in Italy. Cool. I would like to learn more about my dad's side of the family, eventually. Now that I've lost most of my mother's side.

I try and not think about all I've lost, it's easy for the most part. Being at Uncle Jet's, I can pretend *he* is waiting at home for me. Except we've gone a long time without speaking now, and that's not normal.

The heaviness of knowing I lost something claws at my chest, moving up my neck until it cuts off my breathing all together.

He's gone. He's really gone and not coming back. I'll never see him again. He won't be here when I wake up. I can't call him. I won't ever sit in church and listen to his sermon. I'll never feel his hugs or hear him tell me he loves me after I say to have a good day.

I never told him I loved him. Did he know? He had to have known, but even if he knew, wouldn't it have been nice if I'd told him?

Every feeling I felt that day in the little old house on the hill floods me like a dam burst open.

Over the last week, I've wondered how I could ever get to the point of wanting to die, but right now, in this bed, with three sets of eyes staring at me and not one of them the gentle eyes of my grandpa, I know how I got to that point. The fact I have to live the rest of my life knowing my grandpa isn't on earth with me any longer is like nothing I've felt before.

How am I meant to live in a world where my grandpa isn't?

I don't think I can.

15

TEARS FILL HER EYES the moment everything hits her. Her lips wobble and her eyes bounce from each of us, panic, worry, and hurt growing with each glance.

Her chest heaves as she gasps for air.

Everything inside me screams to grab her, pull her into my body, and save her from these thoughts. But I can't. I can't stop her from grieving. We knew this moment was coming, but fuck, if this couldn't be a worse time.

I can't save her from her mind, but I can comfort her. I pull her against my body and bury my head into her neck. "I'm so sorry, babygirl."

Her sobs are loud. "I c-can't live w-w-without him, Ash."

My own emotions come to be too much, and I squeeze my eyes closed. It's been weeks since we lost Paul, but seeing and hearing Payson struggling is bringing everything back up—and more.

When I pull away, her face is red and blotchy, tears pour from her eyes, and she shakes her head.

I shoot a look at Jethro, but his eyes are firm on her and his jaw set, obviously pushing any emotion he is having far from the surface. Exactly what

I do whenever Payson isn't involved, but seeing her having a breakdown, is tearing my insides a part.

"I'm so sorry," I murmur repeatedly. What else do you say? This is a situation I can't make better. Anything I do or say can't bring him back. That's the only thing that would make everything better, and it's impossible. Knowing there is nothing I can do, bloody kills me.

She clings to me like her life depends on it, and I wonder if it might.

Eventually Jethro steps out, and a few minutes later, the anesthesiologist and doctor follow him back in. They give her the medication to put her to sleep, and despite her trying to fight it, she fades.

Jethro explains the situation, and they offer their condolences. Before they wheel her to the operating room, I lean down and press my lips to her forehead and say a silent prayer. It's not something I do a lot, and I haven't since she woke from the coma, but if anyone can help my girl right now, I hope it's Him.

The doctor comes back sometime later to tell us Payson is halfway through and doing amazing. Luca headed out to get us food, and Jethro and I sit in her room in silence.

"What happens now?"

Jethro runs a tattooed hand down his face, and sighs. "She's going to be a mess. I saw that look in her eye."

So did I.

"I can help."

But he shakes his head. "No. Payson is going to need professional care, Ashley." His jaw tics. "I understand you want to be the one to heal her, but Payson's healing is not up to us, it is her responsibility."

My molars cry out with pressure from grinding them. "She can't do it alone."

"No one can do it for her."

This is such a bloody predicament to be in. The selfish part of me wants to demand I can handle it. The other part, the smaller but better part, wonders if a professional might be a better answer.

I wish I knew the right answer, but I don't. I can only hope—and pray—that whatever happens is the best option for her.

"So, where do we go from here?" Jethro's brows raise. "Don't give me that fucking look. You can think whatever you want about me, but I love her more than my selfish side."

A beat passes, and then he dips his chin. "I have looked at several places that specialize in the type of care Payson requires. Including the one that is near Janelle, so I reached out to her family since they are out that way seeing if they would check it out for me. It has amazing ratings, and she toured the place. Says it's more like a"—he raises both hands making air quotes—"'Hella fancy hotel than a care center.'"

"She thinks it would be good for Pay?"

He nods.

If Janelle thinks it would, then it must be *okay*. She would never have Payson sent somewhere she didn't think would be good. The only issue is looks can be deceiving.

"I want to fly out and see it for myself. I was going to go in a few weeks when she is back in school, but considering she is going to need it sooner than later, I'd like to go soon."

"She can stay with me."

His lips flatten with disapproval, but he bites back whatever he is thinking, and it's a good thing because I'm a fucking thirty-three-year-old man; he has no authority over me. I don't care if his niece is his responsibility, she's mine.

"I'm trusting you to care for her. That means sometimes being a dick."

"She doesn't call me Ash-hole for no reason."

He half snorts. "Fine. I will get a flight for tomorrow. Gone a day, two max."

"Fucking move there for all I care. Payson is my *fiancée*, and one day will be my wife, stop treating her like a child and me like a horny teenage boy."

"She *is* a child."

My voice comes out a growl. "She hasn't been a child in a long time, and you bloody know it."

There is no denying Payson was forced to grow up before she should have. No one goes through the shit she did and stays innocent and child-like. As much as I wish she grew up having a normal childhood, she didn't, and I can't change it now. Maybe there is still a part of Jethro that blames himself, and I'd be lying if there wasn't a part in me that felt the same. Since walking into her life, he has looked out for her, and that's all I can ask.

"My main priority is seeing Payson thrive. She is too brilliant for anything else," I say.

"All I've ever wanted was to see her come out on top. I failed Jason, and even if she isn't biologically my daughter, I've always looked at her more of an estranged daughter than a niece."

I level my stare with him. "So, we are in agreement. Payson's healing is our number one priority."

"Yes."

I stand and hold my hand out, he takes it in his, and a silent truce is formed.

16
Payson

My room at Uncle Jet's is amazing, but waking up to Ash breathing against my neck is better. He's so peaceful when he sleeps. Since my surgery yesterday he's been over-the-top helicopter. Constantly checking on me even if I told him a single minute before I was fine.

I appreciate it, though, and it feels amazing for things to be somewhat normal between us. I know before surgery I had a breakdown, but I've been fine since. Maybe it's the medication they have me taking. Ash is meticulous with it, only giving me a single pill when necessary, and he double-checks my mouth to ensure I swallowed. He mentioned something about me storing them or something absurd, but I don't argue.

If I'm being honest with myself, the weight Ash carries is enough to make me want to kill myself, for real this time. Knowing I have caused him so much . . . *chaos*, is deafening. I love him more than I've ever loved anything, but look what I am doing to him. Look what I do to everything and everyone around me. If only everyone else understood how much better their life would be if I wasn't here to weigh them down with my issues.

I lightly drag my finger over that deep crease between his thick eyebrows and frown. I love the way it shows his age, and I love the scowl that causes it, and knowing the reason for the scowl has the pit in my stomach opening wider, threatening to swallow me whole.

"Good morning, Jailbird."

Ash's morning voice is even sexier than normal, and his accent is the thickest when he is tired or drinking.

"Hi."

Thick arms wrap around my center. He doesn't pull me against him, most likely because my leg and the stupid brace they have me in, but I relish in the comfort of him anyway.

The surgery went well, as far as I know. Ash said it was quick. It hurts more now than it ever did but the doctor said that is normal and once I'm healed, I will be as good as new. Ash mentioned I will probably need to wear a brace for a while, though. I guess that's fine, as long as it doesn't affect my playing.

"What do you want for breakfast?"

It's totally inappropriate for me to be horny with everything going on, but holy shit, his morning voice is panty wetting. With my leg, I'm unable to roll to my side, but I attempt to push my ass into his groin, happy to already feel him hard. I know it's from it being morning, but I don't care. It's been too damn long since I've felt his erection. My hand slips between us and I wrap it around his shaft. He tenses and pulls me tighter against him, trapping my hand between us.

"We can't," he growls into my ear, but it's weak.

With my hand trapped, I grind my hip into him instead, and he groans my name. A sound I *love* to hear.

"Please," I whisper.

"Payson." The distress in his voice almost makes me feel bad for pushing him. *Almost.* He nuzzles his head into me and breathes. "You are going to be the death of both of us, babygirl, and there is not a single better way I'd rather go."

My stomach aches knowing he is probably right. Especially with what I know now, but I push that to the back of my head where it belongs and focus on the now.

"Please, Ash."

He tsks and nips at my ear, not enough to hurt but as a warning. "What do you call me?"

"Daddy," I breathe, and when he moans low and steady into my ear, my entire body pricks with goose bumps.

He releases my arm enough I'm able to stroke him.

"You have no idea how bloody good that feels, Jailbird."

I squeeze him tighter than I should, and he grunts. I scowl when he peeks an eye open at me. "If I'm going to call you daddy, then you're definitely not going to call me that."

"You can't deny you love when I call you jailbird anymore, *Jailbird.*" Ash presses a wet kiss to the side of my face and licks. "Not when that's the name you reacted to when you were in your coma."

Damn my subconscious. "Fine. But it's babygirl when you are about to fuck me."

His laugh is deep and rich, like a really good chocolate sauce. "Deal—*babygirl.*"

I continue my slow stroking, and his hand ventures around my body. He rolls my nipple between his thumb and finger, and my back arches. The movement tugs on my knee, and I grunt, but the pleasure outweighs the pain. Ash pushes my back down with the other hand.

"If we are going to do this, you are going to tell me when it hurts, Payson. No more pain."

If his voice wasn't clue enough he isn't kidding, using my full name is. "Okay," I say, although I'm not sure how to survive without pain; as long as I can remember, it's been a part of me.

His hand on my stomach slides down my front onto my good thigh and lifts it enough to wrap around his hip, exposing me completely. I tried to go to bed naked, but he demanded I wear a shirt after I refused to put on an entire outfit. I guess he thought the thin fabric would keep us from doing this.

I impatiently wait for him to touch me *there*, but he teases me everywhere else instead, so by the time he does, I'm nearly falling apart.

"You're soaked."

"It's been a while," I pant.

He grins against my cheek, then presses his lips to me. "I know, babygirl." He grabs his dick from me and slips it between my legs, dragging the head up and down carelessly. "I said no more pain, but this might hurt for a small moment."

The tip slips in easily, but when it comes to the rest, he has to cover my mouth to mute my gasps until he is seated inside me and I've calmed down. It wasn't painful, but definitely not as easy as I remember.

"Is it going to be like that any time we go a while without sex?"

"Yes." He kisses below my ear. "Let's not go a while ever again."

I gasp when he pulls out and slips inside again. "Okay."

Ash and I have fucked in a lot of places, in a lot of positions, but this one is different. A good different. Maybe it's because it's been a while. Maybe it's because he is holding onto me like he is worried I'll fade away. Or maybe it's because he is fucking me so slow, I'm able to feel every vein in his dick and it's driving me crazy.

"I love you, Payson Murphy."

"I love you, Ashley Pearson."

I sink my hand into his long hair and pull his face back to mine before placing a deep kiss on his lips.

He turns my head and moves his lips to my throat. It wouldn't be Ash if he didn't sink his teeth into me any chance he got. He's being gentler than he has before, and I wonder if it's killing him not being able to throw me around, or if he is enjoying this as much as me. I love any sex with Ash, but this is different. There has always been some power play when we fuck, but right now, I can't feel it, and it's odd that I don't miss it. Knowing Ash can take anything from me at any moment is one of my favorite things, but the slow thrusting and the way he is being so loving makes me feel like . . . well, like we're real partners. Like everything between us isn't just a kink.

He must be feeling it too because he whispers, "Marry me."

"I already said I would. April fourth, remember?"

"Like I would forget." He cups my pussy and presses two fingers against my clit. My hips roll, causing tugging on my knee, and I hiss. Ash's movements slow while I shift to a comfortable position. "April fourth is less than four months away, babygirl. You better start dress shopping soon."

"The following year."

Ash removes his hand from between my legs, slides it up my body, and wraps it around my throat but not enough to cut off any air. "If I have to wait a year, you're going to owe me something big, Jailbird."

"Like what?"

"I'll think about it."

I can't imagine what something big means to Ash. Like getting married at eighteen isn't big enough. A baby comes to mind, and my stomach sinks. I know nothing for sure, besides what that doctor said a few years ago about it being difficult if not impossible for me to have kids, but we can cross that bridge whenever it happens. Besides, there are other ways to have kids.

Ash doubles down, and we come at the same time. We lie that way for a long time, his dick—now soft—inside me and his hand still between my legs until the throbbing stops. He rolls to his back, and I position onto mine.

"How does your leg feel?"

Now that he mentions it, it is sore, but I didn't feel it during sex. I don't want him to hold off on me any longer, so I lie. "Good."

"Wrong answer." Ash reaches over and grabs my meds from his side of the bed along with the water bottle and passes them to me after opening the bottle.

I take the meds because I know it's best to take them before the pain than after it picks up, and he grabs the bottle from me, returning it to its spot on the table. Then he looks down at me like he is waiting for something.

"What?" He flattens his lips, causing a frown to turn down my lips. "Stop looking at me like that.

"I'm debating how awful of a person I am for fucking you two days post-surgery."

"I don't think you're an awful person at all, if that makes you feel better." I giggle.

The faintest smirk crosses his face, and he sighs. "You look like an angel, but damn it all if you aren't going to send me to Hell."

"Even the deepest of sinners have a shot at Heaven."

Ignoring me, he slips from the bed and stretches his back. I watch in awe at his naked body and all his muscles shifting under his tanned skin. "Do you tan naked?"

"Sometimes. Why?"

"You don't have any tan lines."

He chuckles as he wanders to the bathroom. A moment later, the steady stream of the shower sounds. I haven't showered since my surgery, and now thinking about it, I'm self-conscious that I let him fuck me when I haven't bathed. He didn't seem to mind, nor did it stop him from ravishing my neck, no doubt leaving behind hickeys I'll need to attempt to cover before Uncle Jet gets home tonight. Ash mentioned they called some sort of truce: Jethro won't bother him about dating me if Ash somewhat keeps it in his pants, at least in front of him. I think it's sweet they agreed to that for me, but if Ash continuously leaves behind hickeys, I'm not sure how long it will last.

"Can I join you?" I shout, hoping he can hear me over the water.

Ash steps into the doorway a moment later, still naked. Still sexy. "As if I would ever say no." He grins, and my stomach fills with butterflies. Even though his hair is long and the gray is more prominent when it's long, right now he looks like a teenage boy about to do something he knows will get him in trouble.

And I kind of love it.

17

I WONDER IF THINGS with Payson will always be complicated. If there will always be two sides of our relationship, or if over time, they will become one. I battle between caring for her how a boyfriend would care for his girlfriend and how a father would care for his daughter. It's bloody confusing.

"Your hair is getting long." I run my fingers through her hair—nearly to her ass now, making sure all the soap is out.

She hums an answer. I've wondered if she would fall asleep on me in here a few times, but she says it feels that good. I didn't think someone else washing your hair was that enjoyable, but I guess she finds it as pleasant as I find washing her tits.

"I'm going to miss you when I go back to Uncle Jet's."

Fuck. I forgot he was coming back today. "Stay here."

"I can't and you know that." She could. He would just be a wanker about it. "Besides, you have Parker to care for. Uncle Jet has no one."

I can't argue there. I've done what I feel like is a good job balancing between them the last two days, but that could be because Payson slept on the couch most the time, so I was able to help Parker with any homework he had. We ate dinner together and it was enjoyable, then after, Parker let Payson pick a movie and she picked *50 First Dates*. We watched that together brilliantly, at least until she started snoring next to me. Balance is possible, but soon, Payson will need more help, and I promised Parker I would help him practice football since the season is starting soon.

"I will stop by every day, and you can call me if you want me when I'm not there. When we live together, expect to never leave my side, though."

"I'm so glad you still want to live with me."

I tilt her head up, and her eyes flutter open. "What do you mean still?"

She shrugs. "I wasn't sure if after . . . everything, you would still want me."

I crouch down so we are eye level, with her sitting on the shower bench, and take her face between my hands. "I still want you. I will always want you. Every day, every moment—every bloody lifetime, Jailbird. You and me, remember?"

Her lip wobbles but she nods. "Always?"

"Forever."

While Payson naps on the couch, I head to the kitchen to prepare a late lunch. After the shower, I changed the sheets on my bed, then we crawled back inside and just talked. It was nice not having to think and to just enjoy moments with my girl. We're avoiding discussing her grandpa and what happened after, and I know eventually those things will need to be discussed, especially after Jethro gets back. For now, I'm fine with not mentioning either topic until she is ready. I think the medication is helping her keep the emotions at bay, and while I'm not giving her the full dose and I was skeptical to even give her what I am, I'm glad it's able to provide her with enough ease to allow her to relax. The last thing she needs is to break down while trying to heal from surgery. It's best to focus on healing one issue at a time, and right now, her knee is the focus.

I just get our plates made up with the chicken salad I whipped up when my phone rings. Seeing Jethro's name fills my body with dread. He is probably calling to let me know he is home and she can head there now.

"Hello?"

"Are you around Payson?"

"She's on the couch sleeping, why?"

"I need to talk to you, but I do not want her hearing."

Assuming it's about the care center, I glance into the living room to ensure she is still asleep. When I hear the familiar soft snores, I truck back to the kitchen and lean on the counter. "Okay. How was it?"

"We will discuss that later. I called to let you know I need to stay here for a few extra days."

"Yeah?" I wonder if he notices my voice perk up.

"Don't act so happy." He did. "My guys caught onto Fred's trail. They think he is somewhere in California."

Whatever happiness I was feeling for Payson staying a few extra days is gone and replaced with the anger hearing his name brings. "Where?"

"I don't know, but he was a Marine back in the day, and there is a base here, so we are going to ask around."

"Seems obvious."

"I agree, but maybe that's just it."

"He's hiding in plain sight," I mutter.

"We've been assuming he left the country after not finding a trace of him anywhere, so if he is here, people are going to lose their jobs. We underestimated him, most would hide out, change their name, and flee the country after murdering someone, but he stuck around."

"Either he has balls or assumes no one will come for him."

"Or he doesn't care if we do. He knows there is no real proof besides his disappearance after and absence from the funeral. They don't look great, but they are circumstantial. Payson's word and trial will mean something, but he probably doesn't think she will talk."

"Do you?"

A long pause answers for him. "I don't need her to talk because when I find him, I'm killing him on the spot."

After everything he's done to my girl, to her family, and probably more, I feel nothing when he says that. "Make it hurt."

Jethro fills me in on the care center and how Janelle said she would call Payson and chat up California, then slip the center into the conversation. I'm not exactly on board for the sneaking around, but if it will get her help, I'll leave it alone. Jet and I agreed we are not sending Payson to California unless we know Fred is not there.

We hang up, and I drop my head between my shoulders and sigh. What a fucking headache this is. The only good thing about Fred possibly being in California is that is a long way from here, meaning he probably isn't coming after Payson like I have spent nights awake worrying about. Whether he comes after Payson or not, it doesn't matter because there's not a chance in hell I'm letting him get anywhere near her.

18
Payson

"WE NEED TO DISCUSS your schooling."

Ash slides a plate of eggs and toast, no beans, across the island to me.

"It's eight a.m., can't it wait?"

He shakes his head and shoves a bite of his toast—with beans, into his mouth. "No, I just dropped Parker off, and I was thinking about how much time you've missed. Have any of your teachers been in touch?"

I stare at him in disbelief. "No. Clay brought me my work, remember?"

"You should get it done and turned in."

I blink and blink again, not understanding what his deal is and why this is important to discuss first thing this morning.

"Why are you hounding me during breakfast about schoolwork? Who cares if I miss a few assignments? I'll make them up when I go back." I don't know when that is exactly, but the cuts on my arms are healed and I'm getting around better on crutches. I probably could have gone today, but he didn't mention it, and neither have I. Not like I'm in a rush to sit in class for eight hours a day again.

"You graduate next year, Payson. If you aren't caught up, you will not graduate."

"Obviously, but I have over a year to worry about it. If I'm too behind this year, which I know I'm not because I've been ahead of schedule my entire school career, a few weeks of missing work won't matter, but if I am, then I can also take summer classes."

He drags a heavy hand down his face. "Just please email them about it."

I hate that he is treating me like a child. So maybe the first thing I did after waking up from a freaking coma wasn't email the school about missing assignments, but like I said, I have never been behind or even gotten less than a B minus in any class, ever. I have never needed anyone on my back about finishing my work, and I don't need it now.

"I'm not Parker. Like, you know I'm not actually your child, right? I'm your *fiancée*. I don't need you checking in on my schoolwork like you're my dad, because you're not."

Heat radiates between us, but not the kind I'm used to. It's been a while since we've argued, especially like this.

"Don't act like a child and I won't treat you like one."

My eyes widen. "Act like a child? Please. I can't remember the last time I got to act like a child. I'm sorry I didn't get ahold of my school, but you have no right to get after me about it." I shove my plate away and reach for my crutches. "There are ways to talk to people, especially the ones you *love*, and that's not it. Come find me when you've removed the stick from your ass, *Dad*."

An argument like that is one I would expect from Jethro, not Ash. In fact, it sounds so much like Uncle Jet that I pull out my phone once I get to the couch and fire off a text to him.

Me: Dod you tell Ash ot bitch at me about schoolwork?

Uncle Jet: Excuse me?

Uncle Jet: But no, should I have?

Uncle Jet: Stop fucking cussing.

Me: I'm pissed and my fingers aren't working dast enough. It's eight am and he just got afterme about ducking homework. Felt like I was having a conversation with younso thought I'd ask.

Me: I can't decide which of you is the bigger asshole sometimes.

Uncle Jet: Good morning to you too. How is your knee?

Me: Yeah, fine, tha ks. When are you coming home?

Uncle Jet: You're that mad at him that you'd rather stay with me?

Me: No. Just curious.

Uncle Jet: You really need to work on your texting abilities.

Me: Yeah yeah I've been tokd.

Uncle Jet: But soon. What I was here for turned out to be a dead end. End of the week at most.

Me: Great. Stay safe.

Uncle Jet: You too.

Uncle Jet: And do your homework.

Me: You're the worst ever. Bye.

I don't see Ash for a lot longer than I expected, and then when I do, he is shirtless and wet. Dickhead. He knows I can't stay mad at him when he looks the way he does. I will certainly try though.

"Hi." His breath is heavier than normal, which tells me it's not water dripping down his chest, it's sweat. You'd think that would be a turn off—it's not.

I ignore him by slowly flipping through a random magazine I grabbed as I heard him on the steps.

"I didn't know you could read Italian."

Focusing on the page, I frown when I *can* read the words because they aren't Italian. I shoot him a glare.

He slaps the small towel in his hands over his shoulder and chuckles. When he takes his seat at the end of the couch opposite of me, I battle with being disappointed he's not closer and happy he's not. "I'm sorry for getting after you this morning, baby."

"Why did you?" I hate that my voice sounds so small.

His gray eyes flick away, and his eyebrows bunch. "I have a lot on my mind, but none of that is your fault, babygirl, so I am sorry I took it out on you."

It's like I'm looking at Ash for the first time without a filter. He looks run-down and like he's barely holding it together. His body is as immaculate as always but he's thinner than he used to be. Deep bags rest under his eyes, and I wonder what he is doing all night while I sleep because he's obviously not. His hair is long, which isn't a bad thing, but all of it together is a flashing red light I didn't notice before. Has he been like this since I . . . Guilt rips through me like a hot blade. I caused the great Ash Pearson to crumble. The last time I noticed he was slipping, he hate-fucked me. I don't think that will happen this time. One, I can't physically handle it, and two, I'm not sure he could either.

The thought of Ash being weak never occurred to me. I've always counted on him to hold and protect me, but what has been happening to him while he was busy protecting me? I've been so blinded by my own pain I never considered what it was doing to Ash.

"I love you," I whisper because I don't know what else there is to say.

His dull eyes brighten for a moment with a gentle smile that only hurts more. "I love you too. Always."

Forever.

19

I OPEN THE DOOR to a snowy Payson smiling up to me. My heart calms, and I pull her into my arms. She's not healed from her surgery, but she's off crutches and can walk. Physical therapy starts after the first of the year.

"Merry Christmas, babygirl."

Her voice is muffled against my chest as she replies.

Janelle bounds up the steps, carrying a handful of presents, and a big smile on her face. "Merry Christmas, Coach." She stops just inside the door and passes me a small box. "This one is from me."

I glance at Payson, but she shrugs.

"Well, thank you, Janelle. Your gift is under the tree."

"Sweet!" She bounds off like a child on . . . well, on Christmas Day. Behind her, her mum, stepdad, and ex walk through the door. They each look at how my arm is wrapped around Payson but say nothing. Janelle must have given them a rundown. Still, her mum's smile is tight and uncomfortable. Which is fair.

Finally, Jet trails up the steps, taking his sweet time.

"I prefer not heating the outside."

He rolls his eyes. "Merry Christmas, Scrooge."

"Yeah, back at you, Grinch."

I shut the door, and Payson turns in my arms to look up at me with doe-like eyes. "I bet one day, you two are going to be best friends."

It's Christmas, so I'll let her believe whatever fairytales she wants, but I can promise that is never going to happen.

Payson

I never cared for Christmas growing up. *He* always dragged us to his mother's house, and it was never enjoyable for anyone involved. Being around so many people I actually like is nice, though.

Ash's tree is modest, not overly decorated and could definitely use more tinsel, but I wasn't able to help decorate this year. Next year for sure.

He served an amazing dinner that kept me wondering if there was anything he was bad at. I doubt it. Now sitting around the tree with so many loved ones, my heart settles. I lean back against Ash's chest. It's a little weird with Janelle's family and Uncle Jet here, but it's Christmas, and I think we are all looking to have a drama-free evening.

We're mostly done with presents when Ash kisses my head and scoots out from behind me, saying there is one he forgot about.

When he returns, he's not carrying anything, he's holding a leash. My heart stops, and when the cutest yellow lab I've ever seen trails into the room, my heart bursts.

There's no way. But he walks up to me, passes me the leash, and grins, but I can't move.

He got me a dog. He actually got me a dog. I've always wanted a dog! But how did he . . . the interviews Amanda had us fill out.

The dog jumps forward, coming to kiss me. Unable to help myself, I let it sniff me before I throw my arms around it. I don't squeeze it hard, but I don't think it would mind anyway since it falls on my lap and shows me *his* belly.

"Please tell me that he is mine and I get to keep him."

"He's yours, babygirl. Are you surprised?"

I shoot a *duh* look up to him. "Surprised?" I wipe away the stray tears that have fallen. "I've never been more surprised in my life. What's his name?"

Ash's mouth falls open, but he's not the one that answers. "His name is Todd, how cute!" Janelle squeals.

I hold Todd's face, he licks my nose, and I giggle. "I love him so much."

Ash once again settles behind me and then pets *our* new dog.

"I can't believe you got me a dog."

"Me either," Uncle Jet growls.

I giggle into my hand. Todd looks to be an older pup, so at least he should be potty trained.

"You said you always wanted a dog." He kisses my temple. "You deserve to have everything you ever wanted."

I couldn't love him more if I tried.

"He's a service dog." Janelle falls onto the ground next to me, to get her turn to pet Todd's belly when he turns over for her. "Like an emotional support dog, so he is trained and can go in places where most dogs aren't allowed."

"What's he trained to do?"

She shrugs. "Comfort, I guess."

He's already doing that. I've watched so many shows and movies where they have dogs, and I've been jealous every time, and now I have a dog. I have my very own dog. I cannot believe I'm so lucky.

"He's also trained to help with panic attacks," Ash mutters, only for me to hear. "I already checked with Blue Gate and sent in his paperwork; he is allowed to go with you."

Ever since Blue Gate was mentioned a couple weeks ago, we've tried to not talk about it. We agreed after the holidays I would go, and that was it. It took some convincing, but after my last panic attack over my grandpa, I know it's what I need. I don't know what it will be like, or what they will have me do, or do to me, but Uncle Jet, Ash, and Janelle all say it is a nice place. I have the option to leave whenever I want, so it's not like I'm stuck there, and that's nice to know, I guess.

The other big change isn't so nice. I glance over at the luggage near the front door but still out of the way, and swallow hard. Ash must follow my eyes because his grip tightens and his breathing stutters.

"I'm simply a phone call away."

I nod, knowing if I open my mouth, I'll cry.

"One single flight and I can be here, okay? Ready to pick you and Todd up."

I nod again, and he kisses the side of my head, hard.

"You and me until the end of time, remember? We will get our forever, babygirl. Just a bit down the road."

I know he's right, and I know I need this. *We* need this. Ash hasn't gotten any better; he's lost even more weight. Even Parker pulled me aside last week to demand to know what is going on with his dad. That's when I finally accepted everything. Ash isn't just my fiancé, he's a dad, a brother, a friend, and a son. But even if he wasn't those things, he's still the love of my life and I'm hurting him. Even if it's unintentional, which of course it is, the effects are still visible. I know going to Blue Gate and him moving to England are the best options, but it doesn't mean I have to like it.

I wish it was easy for us, but I've not lost hope that one day it might be. It's just not today.

20
Payson

"ARE YOU ALL PACKED?"

"You're like a ninja." I turn from the window to greet Uncle Jet leaning against my doorframe with his arms crossed over his chest. "But yes. Nearly. Just need to grab my toothbrush and straightener in the morning."

He kicks off and heads inside the room. "How are you feeling about everything?"

"Honestly?"

"Would I ever want anything else?"

Touché. "I'm scared. I'm scared what it's going to be like. I'm scared what they are going to do to me. I'm scared it's not going to work." I twist my lips, praying I don't cry. I've done my best to keep my feelings inside lately, so I just need to do it for a little bit longer. Todd trots over, sits at my feet, and nudges at my hands. He's definitely helping a lot. An emotional support dog sounds fake, like an excuse someone would use to get their dog in places they aren't allowed, but the short time I have had with Todd has been so nice, his company alone is comforting. "And I'm scared about what being away from Ash will do to me."

Uncle Jet stalks forward and wraps his big arms around me. He's not as built as Ash, but he's definitely as hard.

"You have no reason to be scared, Payson." He cups my shoulders and sits on the edge of my bed so we are eye level. "I did three background checks on the building and everyone that has ever stepped foot inside, and I checked it out for myself in person. If I didn't believe it was a safe place for you, you wouldn't be going. You will have the option to keep your phone or not, it's entirely up to you and if you want the outside distractions. If you don't, there are still phones in every room and I had them program my number into your speed-dial one." He pauses, then mumbles, "And Ash is number two, per his request."

"Thank you." I bury myself back into him for a tight hug. "For everything."

"Anytime, kid." He pulls away and stands. "Now, get some sleep."

Oddly enough, I will miss him bossing me around.

I've been sleeping good with Todd curled up next to me—despite Uncle Jet complaining about the dog being on the bed—but not last night. Last night I slept like shit. A dreamless sleep, which is the norm lately, but I tossed and turned the entire night, as much as my knee allowed. I can't wait to start physical therapy to get all functions back.

Looking in the mirror, I take in my appearance. My hair has gotten long, nearly to my ass, and I'm due for a trim, at least, but I'll leave it for a little while longer. My skin is milky because I haven't been in the sun in a while. I guess California might help with that.

Overall, I look older, but it's not in a good way. I look run-down. I guess how you feel on the inside is reflected on the outside. It's been a while since I've really looked at myself. I rarely think about my appearance despite Ash constantly complimenting me.

How did we not notice how the other was looking? I would find Ash sexy no matter what, and I assume the same about him for me, but this isn't normal aging.

I look away and grab my toothbrush. There is no point in focusing on it. When we come together again, we will be a powerhouse, I can feel it.

There's a heavy knock on the door, and then his voice is muffled through it. "I'm taking our bags out to the car."

"Okay. I'm almost done."

I'm winding up my straightener and not paying attention when I lose my balance. I reach for something to grab onto but the towel slips from my hands and I slam against the shower door. The glass splits, then shatters before I feel it.

Everything in my body aches as I sit on the bathroom floor, covered in my own blood. Panic sets in because I don't know where I'm bleeding from, but it's everywhere. Reluctantly I flip my arms over and I'm hit with that same feeling from the day I tried ending it all. I can feel Ash behind me, holding me and begging me to stay awake. That was the moment I regretted my decision, but by then, it was too late. I had accepted my fate and was okay with it.

"Payson!"

I snap my head up to Jethro breathing hard and glaring at me, and behind him is Todd trotting around, obviously stressed but unable to get to me.

"I-I fell." I shake my head quickly. "I wasn't, I mean—I didn't." Words fail to come, but I need him to know I wasn't cutting myself.

He rushes forward and clears the glass from around me. "Are you okay? What the fuck happened?"

"I-I lost my balance a-and fell." Before I can stop them, tears burst from my eyes. With shaky hands, I reach for Uncle Jet, just wanting some comfort. He is hesitant, but I cling onto him. "I swear I wasn't cutting. I fell. I promise I fell."

I've never felt so disgusted with the idea of cutting.

He shushes me and rubs my back. "I need to check you over for glass stuck anywhere. Where does it hurt?"

"Everywhere." A sob rips through me at the same time the memory of saying goodbye to my grandpa fills my head.

"Easy, Payson. You don't want to cut yourself anymore."

He's right. I don't. I'd be lying if I said the thought hadn't occurred over the last couple weeks, but in this moment of Uncle Jet's sighs and Todd's whimpers, I wish I never would have picked up a blade a day in my life.

But that's the thing, you can't go back in time and change things. Every decision you make is forever.

And that really blows.

21
Payson

THE DRIVE TO THE airport is quiet. I'm pretty sure Uncle Jet believes me about not cutting, but I'm still embarrassed I had a full-on mental breakdown. Probably the first of many. Plus, he had to look me over to make sure I had no glass in my skin anywhere; it was awkward.

"Are you sure you can miss more work? I mean, Janelle is there. She can help me get settled."

He side-eyes me. "I own the fucking business, Payson. I can miss as much work as I please. What are they going to do, fire me?"

True, but it doesn't make me feel any less weird that he has probably missed more work in the last few months than he ever has, and it's all because of me.

"Stop worrying. I can see the wheels in your head spinning. I am fine, and I can work from my phone or laptop if I please."

"Okay, but when you are unemployed and broke, don't come begging at my doorstep."

The corner of his lips flick up in a cocky way. "Deal. But it would take me a while to lose billions."

Billions? Geesh. I assumed it was a lot, but *billions?* "Well, okay then."

The last time I was at this airport, I was coming home from Week of Pink. I'd like to say that was a happier time, but it wasn't. I was just delusional enough to believe it was. The only thing I wish was the same was that Ash was here with me. We agreed it would be best if he didn't come. I know it took everything inside of him to not demand he does, but I can't grow in an environment where he insists on coddling me. I don't need excuses, I need progress, and I think I finally got through to him the last time we talked. He's still not happy about me being here, but I'm hoping I can go home a better human. I want to rise to Ash's level instead of drag him down to mine.

I twirl the ring on my finger and think over the same three little words he's been telling me since the beginning.

You and me.

I've tried to think what that really means several times, and each time, I come up with something new. I don't know if there is one single definition, and it never occurred to me that sometimes *you and me* would mean you and me have to be apart for a while.

I didn't even consider I would get to fly first class with Uncle Jet. Ash complained about having to fly economy for Week of Pink, but he couldn't buy me a first-class ticket and not the rest.

I can't imagine trying to fly economy with no leg room and this brace. Not even sure that would be possible with Todd. Where would he sit?

"Have you always been rich? Like, did you grow up like this?"

"In a way, yes, we were more well off than most." He takes a sip from the drink he was given. They gave me champagne, but Uncle Jet took it from me—not that I argued.

"I remember when I was little and my parents used to complain about money. If my dad was rich, why did they have issues?"

Jethro hates when I mention his brother, and this time is no different. His face hardens. "Our parents were well off. That money wasn't ours. Everything I have now is because of me. Hunter didn't work as hard as me."

I guess that makes sense. "How did you get into . . . whatever it is you actually do. Stalk people?"

He rolls his eyes, but even if that's not what he thinks he does, it is. I'm pretty sure what he does isn't even legal most of the time, so yeah, it's stalking. "Long story. Let's just say my business is a branch off of an old family business."

I narrow my eyes. "That's the worst explanation ever."

"Well, that's all you're getting, kid."

I settle into my seat with a huff. "Have you heard from my brother? You know, your son?"

Again, he glares at me. "Yes. Last I knew, he and Amanda were packing for their move."

Moving? Shows how much I know about my own brother. Not like he has tried to keep in touch either. I get an odd text here and there. We had a quick call on Christmas, but he never mentioned moving. I know he is dealing with shit in his own life too, so I don't take it personally.

"Moving where?"

"North Carolina. Amanda got a high school coaching position there."

Wow. Good for her. "What is Jason doing?"

Based on Jethro's harsh tone when he replies, "Nothing." I'm guessing Jason is still dealing with his drinking problem.

"We are preparing for takeoff. Please switch all electronic devices to Airplane Mode."

Before I turn on Airplane Mode, I pull up my texts.

Me: Taking off. I love you so much.

I snap a quick photo of Todd at my feet and send it along with the text.

"Ma'am it's time to place your phone on Airplane Mode."

I nod at the flight attendant until she walks away and then read through my texts.

Ash: Cute. I love you so bloody much, Jailbird. Call me when you can, okay?

Me: I will.

Ash: Anytime you miss me, look down at that ring on your finger and feel my love. That ring is a promise, babygirl. You and me, always.

Me: Forever.

"Ma'am."

I exit out of my texts and press the button for her to see, then set my phone down on my lap and turn my attention out the window.

"Ash?" Uncle Jet asks after a minute.

I nod, not trusting my voice to stay steady.

"It'll be okay." He taps my thigh once. I think he meant it to comfort me, it doesn't, but it's nice he's trying. I've probably pushed him out of his comfort zone more than anyone has. I can't see Olivia needing comforting all that much.

I never used to either, and now I require a dog to keep me afloat. Maybe one day I'll be able to do it myself. Who knows, maybe Blue Gate is the answer to all my problems. I doubt it but maybe.

22
Payson

CALIFORNIA IS HOT. WHAT the hell business does it have being eighty degrees on January sixth? I'll tell you, none. I can't remember what the weather was like for Week of Pink, which I should, that was only months ago, but it must have been hot as well.

Janelle's squeals could be heard across the entire airport. She takes off running toward me, but before she can reach me, Uncle Jet steps in front of me.

"Jet." I groan like a bratty teenager.

He looks at me over his shoulder. "You have already fallen once today."

Janelle shoves around him and throws her arms around me. "I wouldn't have pushed her. I know she's fragile right now." She pulls away and grins before dropping to her knees and greeting Todd.

After grabbing our bags, which Janelle insists on taking from me, we head for the car Uncle Jet had Janelle brought here in, because he said he wasn't risking his life by getting in a car she was driving. I can't even argue with that.

"I called Blue Gate, and they said you can have visitors every weekend and I can even stay over! How fun will it been to have sleepovers every weekend!"

Jethro groans like that's the worst thing he's ever heard, but that actually sounds like heaven to me.

"I can't wait."

There is one thing I remember about California, the noise. Cars honking, sirens blaring, the constant sound of footsteps hitting the sidewalks. There is always activity. I know they say New York is the city that never sleeps, but I'm thinking the same might be true here as well.

The buildings are so tall. I bet they have amazing views from their top floors. Especially the buildings on top of the hills.

We have lakes in Michigan—a lot of them—but being this close to the ocean and able to smell the salt water is something else. I snap a few photos with my phone and send them off to Ash with a small message.

I turn my attention to my best friend as she digs through the bucket of snacks between her and Uncle Jet.

"So, any cute boys in California."

Janelle perks up before snatching up a bag of Teddy Grahams and turning as much as the chair will allow. "Yes, and no. Yes, they are hot, and no, I've not gotten with anyone because my daaaad is up my ass twenty-four seven." Janelle has always had this thing where she sings random words in her sentences. I usually hardly notice it, but I guess it's been a while since we have been together.

Jethro couldn't look more out of place than he does right now. He's typing away on his phone, but he's brooding and seems unimpressed by our conversation.

"I'm beginning to think you are smart for going older." She drags her eyes over to Jethro. "Are you single?"

I slap a hand to my mouth, but it does nothing to mute the gasp. For the first time ever, Jet's mouth drops open and his ears turn a deep pink, then he snaps it shut and scoffs.

"Yes, and old enough to nearly be your grandfather. Now stop looking at me like that."

Dad, yes, but not grandfather. He's exaggerating. Janelle must know it too because she rolls her eyes in an overly dramatic way. Not that he is paying us any attention anymore.

"Maybe if my mom was like four when she had me you could be my grandpa, but fine, I get it. You can't handle someone so young and full of life." His eyebrows quirk, but he still doesn't look up. "My bubbliness would ruin your whole broodiness persona anyway."

I've missed Janelle and the lightness she brings to any situation. "What happened with Luca?"

"He's a free bird." She shrugs. "Not interested in commitment."

"You had a relationship with Luca?" Jethro stops pretending to be on his phone and engages in the conversation, but he still doesn't look happy about it.

"No," Janelle says, and he sighs, relieved.

"Yeah, they just had sex a few times. No relationship, though."

Sharp eyes dart between us, like he's trying to figure out if we are lying. Eventually, he shakes his head in defeat. "What the fuck is wrong with your coaches?" It's not a question I thankfully have to answer. "Glad I sent Olivia away."

Janelle and I exchange glances because we are too. I wonder how this season would have gone if she had been on the team. Maybe Alyssa would have minded her business and stayed out of mine. Maybe I wouldn't be in a brace healing from surgery. Or I could be worse off because Olivia is nastier than Alyssa. I won't tell him that. Janelle might, though.

"Olivia is a bitch. She will be lucky to find anyone that wants to deal with all that." She shoves a mouthful of popcorn into her mouth, a blank look on her face. "No offense, though."

I've made it a point to not discuss Olivia, because even though he probably knows how she is, that's still the little girl he cared for like his own for the last eighteen years.

"None taken." His voice is tight, and eyes narrowed.

With enough begging, Janelle and I got Uncle Jet to take us to Janelle's favorite coffee shop to get a light snack before we get to Blue Gate. A pleasant surprise greets us when we pull up and the word *bakery* rests next to *coffee shop*.

The smell of sugar is potent when we step inside, and I suck in a big breath because there is nothing better than the smell of freshly baked desserts. The décor is rustic but in a hip way with rough edge wood throughout and mint-green walls. I see why Janelle likes coming here, very her.

Janelle wanders up to the counter and starts chatting to the woman behind it like they are longtime friends, and for all I know, they could be, or she could have just met her. Janelle is way more sociable than me. I hang back with Jethro, trying to decide what I want from the several options of cupcakes.

"Know what you're getting?"

"Nothing."

"Come onnn, Uncle Jet," I singsong, channeling my inner Janelle. "Sweets are good for you; they might sweeten you up a little." I nudge him, trying to lighten the mood.

His usual scowl doesn't budge, but he caves after I give him my best puppy-dog eyes. "Ash is in for a long future," he murmurs on the way to the counter.

"What can I do for you?" The plump woman behind the counter greets us with a bright smile. Her eyes dart to Todd sitting at my feet, but she says nothing, and her smile doesn't dwindle the slightest.

"Hi! I would like two vanilla bean cupcakes, please."

"Of course, anything to drink?"

"I'll just take a lemonade, and . . ." I look to Jethro, wondering what drink he would want, since he is being unusually quiet. "Black coffee, please."

"You know your dad well." She beams. I don't bother correcting her, and neither does he. Honestly, I like that people might think he is my dad. I never had that sort of thing before, and he's the closest thing I've ever had to a dad, besides my grandpa. "Anything for the puppy?"

I glance down at Todd still sitting so well, but his tail is wagging. "Do you have anything for dogs?"

"Of course we do!" She claps, obviously excited by this. I can't help but to match her grin.

"Then, yes, please."

She busies herself with getting our orders, and I step back from the counter, allowing others to look. This place is busy for being one p.m. on a Wednesday.

"You didn't correct her," Jethro states.

"Neither did you," I throw back, giving him the same side-eye he is giving me. Looking back, I have no idea how I didn't make a connection of us being family. The woman is right, we look very similar. Especially with my hair slicked back in two boxer braids and his slicked back. Same bone structure, same eye shape. My features are feminine, but it's uncanny. I look more like him than his own son; Jason favors our mom's looks.

"Good job on the order, by the way."

I smile with pride. Not like it was that hard, who doesn't like a vanilla cupcake? And Jethro is a traditional man, so a black coffee seemed the most logical.

"Here you two are," the woman says as she slides a small tray over with our order. Her face stretches with a friendly smile. "I hope you enjoy, and you come back now, alright?"

"I love cupcakes, so you can count on it." I laugh.

Uncle Jet grabs the tray since I'm in a brace and have Todd, and we make our way across the semibusy building to Janelle sitting in a booth. Her brownie is gone but she's still working on her drink.

"This place is fantastic, right?"

I slip into the booth next to her, and Todd takes his usual spot under my feet, enjoying the puppy cake Jethro placed down for him. I can't believe I went so long without a dog. He is the best company, distraction, friend. He's simply the best. Ash mentioned he considered getting me a puppy but figured that could wait until we live together. I agreed, a puppy might be too much responsibility right now. It feels like Todd is often taking care of me instead of vice versa.

"So cute. I can't wait to eat my cupcake."

The pink cupcake wrapper is as cute as the rest of the place. I almost hate to throw it away. I bring the cupcake to my mouth but first suck in a deep breath to smell the sweetness. The flavors explode in my mouth. You wouldn't think a vanilla cupcake could be all that good, but they can. I've had many flavors of cupcakes over the years, but vanilla is always the best. Especially when it's made with real vanilla like I know these are.

I swallow my first bite and look up to ask Jethro how his is, but it's gone. He chews as if he ate the entire thing in one bite. My eyes widen.

"That good?" Janelle snorts. I bite back my laughter, but his face deepens in color. He takes a swig of his coffee and dabs his face with a napkin.

"Are you always a pain in the ass?"

Janelle slaps her chest, really putting on a show for him. "I am an angel."

"A fallen one, maybe." He huffs before flicking his eyes my way. "You couldn't have picked better friends?"

I shrug. "Nope. Small school."

"I beg your pardon!" She gasps. A few people glance our way, but she pays no attention and neither do I. I'm used to people looking at us when we are in public because neither of us care to not act like ourselves for the sake of others' judgement. Jethro, however, seems mortified from the attention. I secretly enjoy his mortification, to see such a hard-ass man who wears suits and is covered in ink get embarrassed from two teenage girls, is comical.

After I finish my cupcake, Jethro takes care of our garbage, and when he walks back to the table, he doesn't sit down. It hits me that we aren't just here for a visit. It slipped my mind why I'm here when Janelle came around. She makes me forget a lot of the bad things, because it's nearly impossible to be in a bad mood when she's around.

"Ready?"

Emotion pricks at the back of my throat. Like Jethro can see it, he offers a hand, and when I take it, he helps me up and lowers his voice. "You can change your mind at anytime, kid."

I could. I could say no and that I wanted to go home, or I could stay for a vacation and visit with Janelle, but what will get solved? My issues haven't gone away on their own yet, and I don't think they will magically go away without any outside assistance. Right now, I seem okay, but what about when my bad days and moments happen? Will I still crave a blade when I'm thirty? Is Ash always going to need to keep an eye on me because I'm unstable? No, I refuse to live a life like that.

I don't want to be broken anymore.

Standing up straight, I lay a hand on Todd and pet him, knowing I can't be the best owner I can be if I don't heal.

"Putting off the inevitable doesn't stop it from coming."

He dips his chin, but I sense the hint of pride when he says, "I support whatever your choices may be."

"Just not my choice to date my coach," I joke, trying to lighten the mood.

"No." He huffs. "Besides that."

He can say whatever he wants, but I think deep down he actually likes Ash, and I could see them eventually becoming friends. Way, *way* deep down.

Blue Gate is huge. At least triple the size of Bayshore High. You wouldn't think this is where suicidal people, like myself, come to get help. I didn't do a ton of research on the place, but enough to know it's very discreet with everything. Extensive therapy and addiction rehab are just two of the several services offered.

White spackle walls, arched doorways and windows, and red terracotta roofing tiles give it the feel of a vacation destination. The grass around it is the greenest I've seen since we got here, and the landscaping is immaculate. I can't imagine what price Jethro is paying to have me stay here.

A large Blue Gate Help Center sign greets us in the middle of the half-circle driveway. The driver pulls up right in front.

My stomach has been in knots since we left the bakery, and it tightens when the driver pulls my door open. The hot California air is a harsh contrast to the cool of the AC, but it doesn't stop my shivers.

Janelle wraps her thin arm around my center and presses a kiss to my cheek. "It'll be good, Pay. I can feel it."

Glad she can, because the only thing I can feel right now is my cupcake threatening to come back up.

Jethro steps in front of me and levels his stare. I straighten and answer his unasked question with a nod. Gently he helps me from the car and steadies me.

"It's not too late to turn around," he mutters, but I simply shake my head.

I'm not just doing this for me. I'm doing this for everyone I love. I've not been the best version of myself, well, ever, and it's time I am.

23
Payson

THE BEAUTY FROM OUTSIDE doesn't stop when you walk in the doors. It's as light and breezy in here as it is out there. I half expected it to be like a prison on the inside—they invite you in with the landscaping and boom, bars on windows inside. Sorta like juvie, but it's not. Long open hallways with windows on each side allowing a nice breeze to fill the room around us. It even smells good, like lemons. A large front desk greets us with two smiley workers sitting behind it.

"You must be the Gilberts," the woman says as we walk forward.

I look up to Jethro, letting him take the lead.

"Yes, Payson Gilbert." He shoots me a look like he's waiting for a reaction, but I don't give it. Using his last name keeps my business even more private because Payson Gilbert doesn't actually exist. Fine by me.

"Thought so," she says before typing on her computer. "You already filled out the forms, so we don't need to do anything there. If you give me one second, I will call someone down to show you around."

"Thank you."

We step away to give her space to do her job, and Janelle hooks her arm in mine and leans close. "Isn't this place gorgeous?"

"Yeah, you'd never know it's a place for people with issues."

Jethro grunts. "Sometimes people just need a break in life, that is what this place is for. A break and a new start."

A new start sounds pretty good, but how achievable is it? How realistic is it to relearn how you think? My way of thinking is when anything bad happens, you slice your body open, will that go away? It's been muted since waking up, but surely, at some point it would come back full force.

That's how I deal. That's how I've *always* dealt with things. I'm sure without people breathing down my neck, and my newest pup keeping my emotions at bay, I'd probably have a few more cuts.

It's not that I don't want to think differently, more along the lines of everyone else around me, it's just hard to believe it's achievable.

But if I want any chance of a normal life with Ash, I need to do this. He deserves a wife who doesn't require a suicide watch.

Another worker in the same crisp white uniform steps off the elevators. He looks around and smiles when he sees us. It must be in their contract that they have to smile, or these really are the happiest people on earth. Even the guy who came out to pick up Todd's *bathroom break* when we got here had a smile, and I know for a fact that's not a smiley job. He's pushing a wheelchair I assume is for me, and normally, I might groan about having to ride in it, but I'm sore. Without any kind of medication, a wheelchair ride sounds good right about now.

"Hi, I'm Freddy."

I freeze hearing his name. The smile I was forcing falls, and a thin coat of sweat covers my body. Todd nudges my hands with his head until I pet him.

Janelle squeezes my free hand.

"You got a middle name?" Jethro barks.

The worker, seemingly unfazed, nods. "Alan."

Jethro shoves a hand out, and the guys takes it and shakes. "Nice to meet you, *Alan*." He emphasizes his name. "I'm Jet."

My stomach bottoms out, but this time in a good way. He called himself Jet. He's never done that before.

"Nice to meet you."

Uncle Jet drops his hand and places it on my shoulder. "This is Payson and her friend Janelle."

Alan shakes our hands before offering me the wheelchair. He helps get my leg positioned up and then starts the tour. He mentioned a pool, so I asked to see that first.

What's better than having a pool? Two pools. One outside and one inside for on the rare occasions it storms—according to Alan. Not only are there two pools, but they are massive. Easily the biggest pools I have ever seen in real life. A few people are swimming laps, others are sitting on the edge or in the chairs surrounding it. Reading or chatting, they look so . . . casual.

Alan continues the tour, showing us everything from the cafeteria where I get the option of eating in my room or in the courtyard, to the fitness center. I say fitness center because it's not a simple gym. It's an entirely separate building behind the main building and about half the size but still huge and equipped with a weight room, a sauna, a wellness center where I will have my physical therapy, a gym, and a full basketball court. When

I asked if they had volleyball nets, he typed a code into the panel on the wall and the floor opened and a code-regulated net appeared. Ash would probably get a boner from the setup they have here.

"Payson's room number is 202 and is located on the second floor, facing the courtyard and pool, per your request."

I didn't request anything on my form, so must have been Jethro. *Sweet.*

We get on the elevator and Alan presses the number 4 instead of the 2 like I expected. When the doors open, my eyes widen. It's not another floor, it's the roof. He wheels me forward, and I'm able to see everything. Three of the four edges are boarded with flowers and shrubs, obviously used as some friendly barrier, as if to say *please don't jump off.* The fourth side has no barrier, but there are two guard-looking men on each side and one in the middle, obviously to stop any attempts. It overlooks the outdoor pool and is a beautiful view. People are hanging about, and they glance at us but go back to their own thing without a care. I've seen every kind of person here and every age as well. It's nice. I guess Jethro was right about everyone needing a break at some point. I narrow in on the three easels along the edge and the girl around my age painting on one of them. I can't see what she's painting, but she seems as lost in her painting as I get in sports.

"Shall I take you to your room now?"

"Um, yeah. That would be nice, thank you."

"Of course. And you are allowed up here at any time. In your room, you will find the codes to get in anywhere, including the volleyball net code."

Sweet. It'll be a minute before I can utilize it, but it's good to have anyway.

Alan fills us in on the schedule around here as we make our way to the second floor. Breakfast is at seven, there is a snack at ten, and lunch at noon. Another snack at one and dinner at five. There is also an optional snack at ten p.m. if we choose, and a twenty-four-seven a la carte, so I definitely won't be going hungry.

"There is a shift change at three a.m. and three p.m., but you will deal with the same nurses weekly, and the weekend staff is pretty regular as well. Give it a few weeks and you will be familiar with all the faces."

That's nice. I'll be able to get used to people. "What about my physical therapist? Will they be the same?"

"Yes. Dr. Stephan is our full-time physical therapist. He has a select few nurses that work under him but all the same daily."

We are walking past yet another sitting area when my eyes snag on two photos of probably the prettiest people I've ever seen.

"Who are they?"

Alan pauses and regards the images. "Ah, that is Mrs. and Mr. Ludgate. Crew and Penelope. They own Blue Gate and several help centers around the United States."

Wow. They could almost be siblings for how much they look alike, but they definitely make the hottest couple ever. I wonder if I'll get to meet them at any point.

"Hot and successful. Nice," Janelle comments. Thankfully, Alan chuckles under his breath and isn't offended as he continues forward.

Alan pulls up outside room 202, puts on the brakes for the chair, and walks in front of us with his back to the door. "We usually leave the patient and their family to get acquainted with the room, but if you would like assistance, I am happy to help."

"We can handle it," Jethro tells him.

"In that case, it was very nice to meet you, Payson. Family." He crouches to give Todd a treat from his pocket. I don't know where he picked that up or if they all just carry treats, but Todd enjoys it, nonetheless. "I will give it an hour before sending up the night nurse who will be looking after you your entire stay."

After another thank you, I scramble from the wheelchair and Alan takes it and makes his way back down the hall. Janelle is the one who pushes open the door, but they wait for me to enter first.

I take a deep breath, hoping to calm my nerves and step inside. The room is much larger than I expected, but everything else has been too, so I'm not sure why I'm surprised.

White marble floors are complemented by light-blue walls. There are two windows that overlook the pool and courtyard, like he said. To the left, is an all-white bed I assume must be mine, because the other bed across the room has a tie-dye comforter laying across it and the walls over the bed are covered in various drawings.

"I didn't know you were going to have a roommate," Janelle comments.

"Me either." I look at Jethro, and based on the furrowed brows, he didn't know either.

"I will go speak to the front desk." He turns but I stop him.

"It's fine. It might be nice to not be alone."

He pauses.

"Just let me see if she's nice at least."

He strides across the room and critiques the paintings. As if that will tell him anything about my future roommate. "Fine, but if you want your own room, you let them know immediately, and it will be done."

I leave him to whatever he is looking for in those paintings and head to my side. Janelle has made herself at home on my bed. Lying on her side with her hand propping up her head. "What are you thinking? Pretty fab, yeah?"

"Seems more like a vacation." I blow out an easy laugh. "That court will be nice to use once I'm back on my feet, right?"

"Totally. Figure out whoever plays so we can crush them."

I snort. "Deal."

"Oh, here." She twists around and grabs a blue gift bag from behind her. "This was on the bed."

"What is it?"

She shrugs and passes me the bag. I let go of Todd, that's his signal he's off the job and can function like a normal dog, and he trots over to Jethro. Despite Jethro being grumpy about having a dog in his home, Todd has taken quite the liking to him.

Flipping the bag around in my hand, I shrug. "Must be something they give to new patients." I twist the tag to see if anything is written on it, and there is.

Jailbird.

My throat tightens but relief floods throughout my body at the same time. He couldn't be here, yet he always finds a way to be there. I don't know what I ever did to deserve him, but I'm so damn lucky. I don't even know what could be inside the small bag, but I also don't think I want to open it with people around. Janelle is one thing, but knowing Uncle Jet is hovering over my shoulder and this is a gift from Ash, I'm not sure I want to risk it. I place it on the table, and Janelle's mouth drops.

"I know you're not about to make me wait to hear what lover boy got you."

I shush her, Uncle Jet is still looking at the painting and I'd prefer if he didn't see the gift at all. "I will call you as soon as I open it." I nod, drawing her attention behind me.

"Ahhh, okay. Fine." She's not satisfied with that answer, but it'll have to do. I'm dying to open it as well, but I'd like to be alone.

Forcing my attention away from the bag, I check out the rest of the room. At the foot of each bed is a large cabinet meant to be a closet. Across the room is the bathroom, it's closer to the other girl's bed, but that's fine. The marble continues in the bathroom, but the walls are tiled the same instead of the blue. There are two shower stalls, each with a privacy wall so you can get undressed and dressed in private. The toilet is in its own little room, and there are two sinks with equally large storage and counter space. The girl has various bathroom items on one of the sinks and in one of the showers, so I'll just use the other, no big deal. It's so nice we don't have to share sinks or showers.

I hear the click of the door, assuming it's the nurse with my bags Jethro said he was having someone bring up. I walk over only to be greeted with neither of those.

The girl I saw painting on the roof stands in the doorway, covered in paint, and wide, nervous eyes darting from each of us.

"Uh, hi. I'm Payson. I'm guessing you are the owner of that bed." I flick my hand in that direction.

She takes a moment to answer but eventually nods. "Yes, sorry. I haven't had a roommate yet and forgot they had mentioned someone would be moving in today. I would have cleaned." Her dark cheeks bloom a deep red as she glances around the room. I follow her lead and look around, even though I don't need to. There's not a single thing out of place. "I'm Abby, by the way."

"Nice to meet you."

Jethro's shoes click as he walks behind me. His arm stretches out next to my face, offering his hand. "Jet, Payson's dad."

Janelle jumps up from the bed and hurries over. "Janelle, Payson's sister."

Jethro groans and I giggle, but the girl simply stares at us. After a minute, Jethro lowers his hand when she doesn't take it, and the room grows awkward.

It didn't occur where we are, and like me, Abby probably has some . . . issues and maybe being greeted with new faces is overwhelming for her. I guess Uncle Jet got the same idea because he pushes me toward my bed, allowing her to have her own space.

She doesn't look much older than me, maybe a few years. She's pretty, and obviously talented. I can't help but be curious what landed her in here. I suppose since we are roommates, that stuff will eventually come out.

In public, people walk around with all kinds of stories and nobody wonders about them, but in here . . . it's safe to assume everyone has a traumatic background. I know Uncle Jet said this could be a place people come for a break, and while that might be true, there has to be a reason they chose this place. Other than the stunning facility, there are several amazing opportunities for proper care.

While we chat amongst ourselves, I notice Jethro looking over my shoulder quite often. I can hear her moving around, but I don't know why he is watching her. There is a look I don't recognize in his eye, almost like confusion, but it doesn't make sense. He never pays attention to anyone that's not important to him. I suppose he is studying her, getting a read on her with his weird stalker vibes to see if she will be a good roommate or not.

My bags get delivered, and Janelle and Jethro assist in unpacking for me. Janelle takes the clothes area, and Jethro makes my bed with my new quilt. A small part of home. I also packed a few photos from my wall that he lays on my table, promising he will get me frames.

When done, they shove my bags into the bottom of the closet and we take a step back to appreciate my small space. It might be small, but it's comforting.

That's all I could ask for.

Dinner time rolls around, so we head down to eat. I'm not overly hungry; my stomach is still in knots. I don't get bad vibes from this place, but it's new, and me and new don't exactly get along all that often. Todd has hardly gotten to relax all day because I'm so anxious—poor pup. Alan mentioned there is a dog area where they can just run and play. I guess Todd isn't the first service animal to accompany a patient.

There are way more people here than I expected, even for the size of the building. The entire time we were walking around, we only saw a couple handfuls, but there are at least a hundred people who aren't in scrubs, so I know they are patients or family of patients.

"Holy shit," Janelle comments after seeing everyone. "I wonder if there are any hot guys here."

"Janelle," I hiss. "These people aren't here to be hit on." At least I'm not.

"You never know. This could be the best meet-cute. Like a rom-com."

"Or a dateline story," Uncle Jet mutters.

Janelle giggles. "Maybe. If you would just date me, then I wouldn't have to risk it."

He rolls his eyes. "Let's get in line before she gets kicked out and I suggest not letting her visit on the weekends."

Janelle and I fall into an easy laughter as we head for the line. It moves quickly, even with all the people, so we are in and out within ten minutes—that's nice.

It's only gotten hotter outside, but the umbrella on the tables creates a nice shade so it's not terrible. We could have eaten inside but chose to eat out here.

"This might be the best hospital food I've ever had," Janelle says with a mouthful of her chicken sandwich.

"I don't think I'd even class it as hospital food." My salad is nice and crispy, and the chicken is actually hot. The sauce tastes homemade as well, but I'm just not overly hungry. There were like ten options on the board we ordered from, and walking by the other tables, I saw most of them, and they looked equally amazing. "Todd seems to be enjoying his too."

The workers provided me with a dog-friendly dinner and assured me they would be happy to make his meals every day. This place is almost too good to be true. I wonder what drove the Ludgates to open a place like this. Several places, according to Alan.

After Janelle and Jethro finish their food, we clean our space, and instead of heading to my room, we go for a walk down the walking path to let Todd get some exercise. Alan mentioned it leads around the property and would be a good place for walks with Todd. I can't do anything strenuous just yet, so this will do for now. It's even shaded to keep it cool on his paws. I'm not avoiding going to my room, but I'm not ready to be alone yet, and I know they will leave once we go back. Jethro has to get checked into his hotel, and Janelle has class tomorrow.

"This would be a nice running path, if I could run."

"You'll be able to soon." He rests a heavy hand on my shoulder. "Until then, walks are good. It will be good for you and Todd to get fresh air."

In other words, don't stay locked in your room. I wouldn't have, anyway; this place is too beautiful not to fully experience it. I'm eager to get onto the court, but for now, the pool will be nice. I've never had a pool, but

Janelle does, and we used to spend most of our summers there when we weren't at their cabin. Her mom used to tell us we would turn into fish if we spent any more time in the water.

"Have you spoke to Ronni at all?"

I shake my head. "No, she texted me when I woke up, but I haven't heard from her since."

Janelle blows out an annoyed breath and mutters something I don't understand.

"Have you?"

"Nope."

"At all?"

Hurt flashes across her face and she shrugs. "Nope. I've only seen her a handful of time since I moved."

She doesn't mention the fact Ronni was in Bayshore during my days in a coma, and neither do I.

When Janelle mentioned moving here, I looked up the distance from her to Ronni and it's not far. The fact they haven't hung out is surprising, and I'm understanding why Janelle is hurt. It's obvious it wasn't her stopping them from meeting up. "Maybe she's been busy."

"Yeah, busy partying." She shoots me a regretful look. "Forget I said anything."

My eyebrows bunch because that doesn't sound like Ronni. "Is Ronni partying a lot?"

Janelle is hesitant but nods. "Like all the time. Don't you follow her spam on Instagram?"

"No." I shake my head. "I don't get on there that often anyway."

"Right, well, yeah. She posts constantly with a drink in her hand, and last weekend there was a photo of her snorting something."

Jethro stops abruptly and shoots a harsh look at Janelle. "Veronica is doing drugs?"

I can hear Janelle thinking *oh shit* from here, but I'm not worried about Jethro. Of all the things Janelle has said to him today, this is what she is worried about?

"I don't know, I don't hang out with her anymore. I'm just telling you what I saw."

He drags a hand down his face. "Christ, life was a lot easier when you guys were small."

"Tell me about it," Janelle and I reply.

"I will be back in the morning. They approved me to stop by until I fly out in three days."

Emotion clogs my throat, and I know if I open my mouth, I might cry. Funny to think about, considering just a few months ago nothing could make me cry, and now it seems like that's all I can do.

"And I'll be back this weekend for our first sleepover." At least that is something exciting to look forward to. Janelle peeks over her shoulder, then leans in close to my bed where I'm sitting. "Try and make friends with Abby, she seems cool."

"That's the plan," I whisper. Abby has been doodling on a sketchpad with headphones in since we got back to my room, but still, I don't want her hearing us. Not that saying I'll try and make friends with her is bad, but it's weird.

Janelle squeezes me tightly and kisses the side of my head before pulling away, then holds my arms, and her bright eyes fill with tears. "I'm so happy you're here, Pay."

Me too. I have a good feeling about this.

She steps aside, and Uncle Jet takes a seat on the edge of my bed. "Are you comfortable?"

That is the hundredth time he has asked me, and like last time, I say, "Yes."

His harsh eyes soften a touch. "Okay. Call me at any hour and I can be here."

"I'm fine, Uncle Jet, I'm not a little girl."

"Everyone needs someone sometimes, no matter the age."

"In that case, you can call me at any hour too, just in case you need someone."

A look of annoyance crosses his face, and I giggle to myself.

He leans toward me, and my eyes widen. He presses a fatherly kiss to my temple. Gripping my shoulders, he levels our stares. "Heal, Payson. Not for me, or Ash, or even your grandpa. Heal for yourself. You deserve that much."

Heal for me? I guess I can try.

Once they are gone and the dampness on my cheeks has dried, I prop myself on my bed and reach for the bag I shoved under it so Uncle Jet wouldn't ask about it. I don't know why but this feels like a private thing.

Which is why I waited until Abby picked up her shower stuff and a change of clothes and headed for the bathroom.

Taking a deep breath, I reach inside and pull out the first thing I feel.

It's a note.

I unfold it and begin reading.

My dearest Payson,

The moment you quite literally stumbled into my life, you flipped it upside down. What I expected to be a lustful obsession, turned out to be so much more.

There is not a moment of our time together that I regret, and I hope you can say the same. Although half my age, there are many things you have taught me. One of them being patience.

Which I know will come in handy during our time apart. Don't worry about me or anything back home. I just want you to heal.

But once you do, babygirl, you are to never walk away from me again.

Letters are a bit outdated, but I wrote this in hopes you can read it whenever you are missing me. Just know when you are missing me, I am missing you so much more. Give Todd extra cuddles for me and show him my picture often so he doesn't forget his dad.

You are my entire world, babygirl, and one day we will get our happy ending. It's not today, or tomorrow, but one day this will all be in the past. We will wake up together, eat breakfast together, just simply be together like we both so desperately deserve.

Look at your ring, that is a promise—my promise to you. I promise you forever, babygirl. Promise me the same.

All my love forever, Ash.

Don't give up on us, baby, we are just getting started.

My heart booms in my ears. With a shaky hand, I reach into the bag and pull out a small box. I attempt to swallow the lump in my throat, but it's impossible.

There's a large black jewelry box. It can't be a ring; I've already gotten that. I open it and tears spring to my eyes.

Inside in the most beautiful bracelet I've ever seen. It's gold, like my rings, and several charms fill the chain. Some reminding me of Ash, others of Janelle and everyone else I love, but it's the small cross and what I recognize as one of Grandpa's cuff links made into a charm that makes my throat tighten to an uncomfortable degree.

I recognize this one because it's the same one he wore to my nana's funeral. How does Ash know that?

I pull it out and hold it into the light. My eye snags on something behind the foam, and I pull out the small card. Confused, I open it.

Ray-Ray,

A sob rips through me seeing my grandpa's very familiar scratchy writing staring back at me. It takes a long time before my vision is clear enough for me to read the card.

Ray-Ray,

Look for me in the sun, in the wind and rain, because I am there. You might not be able to see me anymore, but I am always there.

The moment you were born, you brought so much love and joy into the world. Over the years, your joy dwindled, but I never lost hope that you would one day find it again.

Recently, I've seen glimpses of it. I have my theories, but they are simply theories. Whatever the reason for it, I hope you hold onto that.

Life is too short to not be happy. Whatever decisions you make in life, do them to be happy.

My only wish for you is to find even a small part of that little girl with bright eyes who wasn't afraid of love.

Don't be afraid, Payson. Love is God's best gift.

Love hard, be happy, and thrive, sweetheart. I know loss hurts, but forget the hurt and remember the love.

Look for me in the sun. I'm there, Ray-Ray.

Grandpa

24
Payson

June

THERE COMES A POINT in every vacation, no matter how nice the vacation is, that you get homesick. I'm at that point. It's beyond nice here, and I've come to love several people, but I miss Bayshore.

More importantly, I miss Ash.

Our letters aren't cutting it for me anymore, and I know a phone call won't satisfy my need either. I need him. I need to see him—feel him. My time here has helped me with all my bad habits . . . besides one. Not that I wanted it to help with that one. The one visit on what will be our future wedding anniversary was months ago and I'm itching for more. But something longer than a weekend.

There's a sudden knock on my door. I set the shirt I was folding down and head over, but it flies open before I can. Janelle is the first person I see, but she's not alone. Monica and Mika stand smiling behind her. My eyes widen, my confusion shifting slowly to excitement at seeing familiar faces Janelle has been here weekly like she promised, but I haven't seen the other two for what feels like forever.

"What are you doing here?!" I throw my arms out, and they surround me in the best group hug ever.

"To check out the sick pool Janelle keeps posting about." Monica laughs.

"And the cutest puppy ever!" Mika squeals before dropping to her knees and greeting Todd, who wastes no time rolling onto his back and flashing his tummy, awaiting pets, which are delivered immediately.

We pull away, and I tilt my head, questioning Janelle because I know I haven't posted any photos; I've not even had my phone.

"I told you to check Instagram." She rolls her eyes, but I know she's not really annoyed.

We move out of the way to let Mark, another employee I see around often, bring in their luggage. They have plenty of it; the poor guy has at least five bags on his cart. They can only stay the weekend and it's already Saturday morning, so I don't know why they need that much luggage for one night, but I digress.

"Anything else I can do for you ladies?" He turns in the doorway before leaving.

"No, thank you," we reply.

"Very well." He dips his chin. "Enjoy your visit. And someone will be up with two more cots."

"Thanks, Mark!" I shout after him.

Spinning around, I bite back a smile because I already know what is about to come out of someone's mouth if not all of them. Seeing their dreamy faces, I know I'm right.

"Mark is fine."

"He's so cute!"

"What's his shoe size?"

The last one is Janelle, to no one's surprise.

I drop onto my bed, shaking my head. "Mark is cute, and so is basically everyone else here, so you guys are going to have to keep it in your pants and not embarrass me, okay?"

That's asking a lot from them, but they agree.

"And the whole shoe thing is false anyway." Monica shoves at Janelle on the other bed across the room. Mika sits by me.

"Is not," Janelle argues.

"Yeah, I don't know. Ash's feet are pretty big, but his dick is massive."

Monica squeals. "How is it going with coach lover anyhow?"

Janelle meets my eyes across the room. She's nearly bursting at the seams to share the news.

"Well . . ." I dig into my shirt and tug on my necklace. Holding it up, two out of three mouths drop open and the other sports a huge smile. She's seen the ring numerous times, but it doesn't stop her from joining in when Monica rushes forward. Mika and she take time looking at the ring, each with their own comments on how pretty it is.

"It's so you." Mika smiles.

"You know the craziest part is, it was his nan's. He didn't even pick it out specifically for me."

"That's fate if I've ever heard it." Monica lowers it back to my chest. I put it on a necklace since I've been doing so many ring-unfriendly things. Ash wasn't thrilled when I told him, but I promised I put it on properly most of the time, which I do, but I just got out of the shower after taking Todd on a run.

"We get to come to the wedding, right?"

That's when Janelle decides to butt in. "Yes." She narrows her eyes at me, attempting to be intimidating, but failing. She's been trying to bully me into a wedding since the moment I said I didn't want one.

"No." I sigh. "I'm not doing a wedding without my grandpa."

She knows she can't argue with me there, it's basically my trump card. Although, I really do feel that way, it's an easy way to get her off my back.

An awkward beat passes but Monica interrupts it.

"Coach is never going to let you skip out on a wedding."

And there is the bigger trump card. Ash's stubbornness. He is so adamant about seeing me in a white dress walking down an aisle, but I don't care about the wedding, I just want the marriage. Marriage might not be important to anyone else, and honestly, I'm not sure why it is to me, because look at the examples I've had, but to have that tie to Ash is something I've dreamed about before I even knew what it meant.

I want to call him my husband and me his wife. Without the big show of it.

I'm sure there is something I can come up with to convince him to drop the need for a proper wedding. Maybe anal. Or a baby. I've not healed that much that I think I'm ready for a baby, but it might be the one thing Ash wants more than a wedding.

I did, however, think he would fly here and force my hand in marriage when our future anniversary came and passed, but he didn't. He came here and we spent a lovely weekend together, but there was no marriage, and he once again threatened that because I was making him wait an entire year, I would owe him something big.

The best part about Blue Gate is showing off any scar I want and not feeling embarrassed because I'm not the only one with them. Not everyone has a name scarred into their abdomen, or the word beautiful etched onto their arm, but I have seen others with carvings. I was nervous about showing my body when I first got here, but the first time Janelle and I came to the pool, I saw two other people with self-harm scars on various parts of their bodies. The next time, I came down in a bikini, and haven't looked back. It's nice feeling comfortable in your own skin for once. Even with my extra weight. Over the last several months, I've eaten better than I ever have, and it's showing. I'm finally able to start running again, and I've seen some of it melt away, though.

"Is that his name?" Mika yelps after I remove my shirt. I forgot they hadn't seen it.

"*Carved* into your skin?" Monica leans closer.

I swallow hard and force any embarrassment or shame down. One thing Dr. Herringbone has been working on with me is not being ashamed of my past but accepting it for what it is and moving forward. It's harder when it's people you know seeing it for the first time, though.

"Isn't it so romantic? In like a Romeo and Juliet way." Janelle offers with a supportive smile.

I burst out laughing and drop my shirt onto the chair next to me. "Yeah. A tattoo wasn't good enough for him, apparently."

Unlike his mark. I smile thinking about his tattoo of my name. He mentioned in a letter another tattoo that has something to do with me, and I can't wait to see what he did. That pit I've had in my stomach the entire time we've been apart grows, but I shove it away and do my best to focus on my friends. I still can't believe they came all this way to visit me.

We relax in the chairs, enjoying another hot, sunny day. Since becoming summertime, or presummertime, the heat is wild. Nothing like Michigan at all but has been great for my tan. Todd, however, doesn't enjoy the heat as much, so I often let him stay inside with the front desk employees. They feed him lots of treats, and he's able to greet anyone that walks in the door. He loves it.

Various people swim but it's still peaceful. I don't know if the peacefulness will follow me home, but I hope so. I've cried, hurt, and accepted things here more than I ever had but accepting things from afar is different from being close to the pain.

Like when I have to go to my grandpa's to get my stuff and he's not there. I've shared so many memories of my grandpa with my therapist and cried while doing it, but there is a part of me that refuses to believe he's actually gone.

I'm living in a world where he's not, and I refuse to accept it. Dr. Herringbone suggested I visit his grave once I get back to Bayshore, but I don't know if I can do that yet.

My heart is still so broken over it. I've accepted my mom's death, but that wasn't nearly as hard. I wish she went out a different way, I wish we would have had a different relationship than we did, but they are all choices she made, and I can't change them now. She didn't choose to be brutally murdered, but she chose to stay with him despite all the warning signs. I know it can be difficult to get yourself out of a situation like that, but I'll never understand why Jason and I weren't enough for her to do it.

One day, Fred will be caught and he will pay for everything he has done. Or maybe he already has, I'm not sure. I don't ask Uncle Jet about him, and he doesn't bring him up. Ignorance is bliss when it comes to Fred. As long as he is nowhere near me, he can stay in whatever cave he crawled into and hopefully die. A long, slow, and painful death, preferably.

When the sun becomes too hot, I sit up and nudge Janelle. She's on her stomach and sits up groggy like she was about to fall asleep. "I'm going to swim."

"Okay." She yawns, maybe she was asleep. "I'll be there in a sec; I have to piss."

Thank God we don't pee in pools anymore.

"I'll come!" Mika cheers. Poor girl is the fairest of us all and has had to reapply sunscreen three times and moved under the umbrella next to us.

"Mon?"

Monica pulls her sunglasses down and shoots me a *duh* look before jumping up and removing her large hat and glasses.

There is something about swimming that brings out the child inside. Especially when there is a waterslide involved.

"Come on, Mika!" Monica and I cheer.

Like a little mouse, she squeaks. Janelle encourages her from behind, and they decide to go down together. Janelle slips behind her, and they're off and splashing into the water a second later.

The pool has cleared out some, so we can swim around where we please until lunchtime.

Every time I get out of the pool, my leg is stiff but it's crazy the progress I've made the last few months. I actually forget all about it sometimes. Other days, it's stiff and aches, but after some stretching, it's usually better. It feels the best when in the pool though.

We grab our stuff and head for the female shower rooms to get ready for lunch. I don't know about them, but I've worked up an appetite. Weekends are cool too because they do huge buffets so you can get whatever you want.

"How do you think this season will go with us gone?" Monica takes a seat across from me at the round table and pries her drink open.

We didn't take long in the showers because our stomachs were growling.

"I haven't really thought about it, honestly. I hope good, though. I'd love to get a state title my senior year."

"You haven't been thinking about volleyball?" She presses the back of her hand to my forehead. "Are you sick?"

I laugh and shove it away. "No, just focusing on other things. But don't worry. I've not lost any skill."

"Oh, right! How did surgery go?" Mika covers her mouth with her napkin to ask the question. The most polite out of the bunch.

"Really good. I feel mostly normal now. I have to wear a brace for the near future, but the doctors and my physical therapist are all surprised with my progress." Pride blooms in my chest. I've worked hard to be where I am, and the days when I didn't want to get out of bed, because those days definitely happened, I still forced myself to do what I needed to so my knee would heal. And it has, so I guess it paid off. It helps to have a dog nudging you to get out of bed because he has to potty or wants to play. Todd was the best decision Ash has ever made.

"I still can't believe she did that." Monica shakes her head.

It takes me a second to realize what she means, but Janelle scoffs and then I know.

"Really? I can. She's a bitch. The bitchiest of bitches."

She's still not over Collins and Alyssa, which I don't blame her. I've not thought much about the whole Alyssa and Ash situation because I don't know everything, and I'm not going to get all worked up over something I don't have all the information for. Yay for growth. One day, Ash and I will need to discuss everything, and I dread that day. Not because I am worried about anything, but because I'm ready to move past Alyssa and her drama. It seems like ancient history now.

"Has she been causing chaos in Bayshore?" I'm half joking, half not. It occurred to me she was in town alone with Ash for a short time before he went to England. I don't know if she was aware of that, but it wouldn't surprise me if when she found out, she pulled her same hysterics.

"No," Monica and Mika reply, but Monica lets Mika go first with whatever she was wanting to say. "No one has seen her. I was at a party a few weeks ago."

"A party?" Now it's my and Janelle's turn to be surprised.

Mika's pale face turns a bright red, and not just from her sunburn. "A graduation party. Anyway, someone asked about her and—"

"No one had seen her since graduation." Monica bursts out like she couldn't hold it in any longer. Mika nods.

Haven't seen her? That's not like Alyssa Burton. She loves to be seen. "Like she's missing?"

"Hopefully," Janelle grumbles.

"No." Mika shakes her head. "Like she left town."

Weird. Where could she have gone? I don't know her college plans, but maybe she left early for them. It's odd she up and left and no one knows where she is, though.

"She's not been posting on social media?"

"That's the strangest bit, she has on her spam account but it's random stuff that doesn't give anything away. Like she posted a table full of drinks the other day, but it was a table that could be anywhere, you know?"

"That makes no sense. Alyssa loves attention."

They all shrug. "We know."

"Maybe this is how she's getting her attention now. Making everyone wonder where she is, like she's mysterious now and not in your face." Leave it to Alyssa to find new ways to still be the center of attention. Still the talk of the town without being in the town. Typical. Whatever, if she's not in Bayshore, it means she will be far away from Ash when he comes back, so she can stay wherever the hell she is for all I care.

"Hopefully she stays away," Janelle grumbles. I giggle to myself.

Great minds and all that.

It's not until the sun rises that I realize we've been awake all night. After dinner, we headed to the theater and watched whatever movie they were playing. Truthfully, I can't even tell you what it was because we were too busy whispering in the back. Something with Tom Cruise, I think. Then Monica got the bright idea to take a midnight swim, which you are allowed to do. I didn't think the pool was open, but it turns out there is a lifeguard there at all hours. According to the lifeguard, Mr. Ludgate thinks it's important to give the patients the freedom they have at home but still instill the safety precautions, such as a lifeguard on duty. We've been sitting in chairs next to the pool since we got out, letting Todd dry before we head to my room. The lifeguard switched at some point because the one walking up to us now isn't the one from last night. Last night's was a young, blond boy-next-door type. This guy, however, is not. Tall, dark, and like he was molded from God Himself. Wow.

I think each of us notices him at the same time because the chatting abruptly stops. Unless my ears are tuning it out, but when I take a quick look at my friends, I notice they are all wearing similar expressions to mine.

He stops a few feet from us and places his hands on his hips. "Morning swim, ladies?"

Crickets.

That's what answers him because it's definitely not us. I finally snap my mouth shut, but it's dry.

Mika squeaks a weird laugh, but Janelle is the one to speak. It's not an answer she gives him though.

"Holy cannoli. Are you single?"

I don't know how old the guy is, old enough to laugh at her comment and not seem affected by it. Thankfully.

"I'm not, but my husband will be very flattered."

Ahh. Makes sense why he looks so well groomed. Not my type, I prefer a little ruggedness, like Ash, but this man looks like melted chocolate was poured into the perfect man mold, and here he is. I've definitely never seen him before, but I don't go swimming at what I assume is five a.m. often either.

We let out a collective sigh which makes his deep chuckle turn into a full-on belly laugh. "You have made my day and it's not even six a.m."

"Glad I could be of service." Janelle does a little curtsy. If I could have one thing from Janelle, it would be her confidence.

The guy tells us to have a good day, then saunters away the way he came and takes his seat in the lifeguard chair.

She watches him walk the entire way and puffs her lips out. "Why are all the good ones gay?"

I snort an ugly laugh. "Let's get breakfast."

Monica and Mika were feeling dead after breakfast, so we split off and they headed for my room, then Janelle and I went to check my mail. I'm due for a new letter and am getting anxious for it. We've kept up with the letter writing since I decided to put my phone away and live in the moment. We still call a few times a week using my room phone. It's a lot easier now that Abby went home. I don't have to worry about waking her up when Ash accidentally calls me at four a.m., not remembering the time difference, simply because he wants to hear my voice.

There's this small voice in the back of my head constantly making me worry that one day a letter won't be there. That when I go home, Ash will demand I give him the ring back or worse, it'll be like the reoccurring dream I keep having where he doesn't even know who I am.

I shiver at the thought. I don't know how, but that's way worse than him rejecting me. Both would suck, and probably kill me—for real this time, but if he didn't know me, then . . . then I made everything up and I really would be crazy.

"Here you go, Payson." Freddie drops my mail onto the counter the moment we step into the small mail room.

"Thanks, Freddie." I smile and pick up my stack. There are a few letters this time, and it looks like there are two from Ash. My heart skips a beat just like every time I get a new letter. That small voice will be quiet for a little while now.

I can't get the first letter open quick enough. I shout a goodbye without looking up. He tells us to have a good day, and Janelle replies for us so I can start reading.

Jailbird,

No one could be happier for you that you are finally feeling human than me, but fuck, I bloody miss you. I think about you as soon as I open my eyes and before they close at night. I'm busy during the day and you still pop in. I see you in everything.

I think it's time for another visit. We will have to kick Janelle out for the weekend, but I have to see you. Hold you in my arms because I'm beginning to wonder if you were real. I stare at your photos more than I'll ever admit. You've turned me into a proper sap. Henry says I'm whipped, and I think he might be right.

You'll have to find a new nickname for me because I don't think Ash-hole fits when all I want to do is kneel at your feet and kiss the fucking ground you walk on.

And lick your pussy too. Fuck, I miss tasting you.

You better be ready to spend a fucking week in bed, babygirl. I'm not letting you up until you're so full of my cum you'll never be dry of it.

Now I'm fucking horny.

Heal, but come back to me soon.

Yours, always and forever, Ash.

I love you.

I cry at every letter, and this one is no different, but while my cheeks dampen, my smile is huge. He's such a dork. He'd have my throat if he heard me call him that, but his brother is right. He's whipped, and I couldn't love it any more than I do.

I tuck the letter away, planning on ripping open the other one when I feel eyes on me. Looking up, Janelle's eyes are on me and wide, like she's studying me.

"What?"

"Why are you still here?"

"What do you mean?" I choke on an awkward laugh at the question.

Her eyebrows bunch with confusion and maybe a bit of sadness. "You called him Freddie, Pay. Fred-ie. A couple months ago, you froze in fear at that name, and I just heard it come from your mouth like it's no big deal."

A nervous sweat begins to creep up my spine. I don't like feeling interrogated, so I turn for the elevators. "It's not a big deal."

Janelle steps in front of the buttons before I can press one. I let out a frustrated sigh. "Don't you want to get a few hours of sleep?"

"No," she snaps, but it's not mean. More urgent than anything. "I want to know why my best friend is hiding out here."

"I'm not hiding. I've been in the same place for months."

"Pay." Her lips twist down, and my blood pressure spikes. "What's going on, for real? I've never seen you happier, like legit happy. It's been years, if ever I've seen you so . . . relaxed, yet there is one thing holding you back from being truly satisfied. Why don't you want to go home to Ash?"

The walls around me slowly crumble until I'm attempting to dig my way out but failing. And I burst into tears. Slapping my hands over my face, I try to conceal it, but her arms are around me before I can. Todd nudges his way between us and licks my leg.

"Talk to me, Pay." Her voice is soft.

I've talked more about my feelings during my time here than ever, but these aren't ones I have mentioned to anyone. It's silly, and yet it doesn't stop me from having them. Janelle lets me calm down enough before she pulls away. I wipe my eyes and step back to catch my breath. Turning so I face the large glass windows, I look out over the front of the property so I don't have to look at her.

"I'm scared."

"Of wha—"

"I'm scared that I'm going to go back to Bayshore and fall into my old habits. I haven't had a new cut in months, Jay. I've never gone that long before."

She steps up beside me, but I keep my eyes trained on the lush landscaping surrounding the property. "I haven't been able to say that since I started cutting years ago. I'm scared that being home will cause me to lose myself in the sadness of my grandpa." She grabs my hand. My lip wobbles, but I hold it in. "I've still not accepted his . . . death, Jay. I can't. I can't survive in a world where he's not."

"You have, Pay. You've been doing it for months."

Maybe, but I've been distracted by other things. "I don't want to." I admit softly. "I don't want to die. I'm not suicidal." *Anymore.* "But I don't want to live someplace he's not."

She's silent, and I don't blame her. I wouldn't know what to say either.

"But the thing I'm most scared about, the most selfish thing, is Ash not wanting me like he did. Like I'm too *normal* for him now. Ash likes projects, he likes caring for me, and what if I don't need him for that anymore?" I turn us so we are face-to-face. "What if I don't need him like I once did?"

It has occurred once or twice that Ash and I are trauma bonded. If I don't have that burden to carry around anymore . . . what if we don't fit like we think we do? I can't stand the thought, but it's one that pops into my head sometimes and is difficult to shake.

Janelle twists her lips, probably attempting to keep her own emotions at bay. "First off, you are so much stronger than you give yourself credit for. Grief is hard, might feel impossible somedays, but I know you, and when those days it hits you the hardest, you will still get out of bed and make life your bitch because you are Payson fucking Murphy hyphen Pearson, one day." A laugh bubbles out of me, and she smiles.

"Second, your grandpa is looking down at you and smiling, Pay, and he will be with you wherever you go, so you need to live your life to the fullest *for* him. And third"—she rips my letters from my hands and waves them in the air above her head—"this proves that you and Ash Pearson are soulmates. What man is writing fucking letters and without the possibility of pussy? I'll tell you—*none.* That shit is only in movies and horny books and yet here you are with a whole stack of them, his nanny's ring around your neck and you're still doubting his feelings? Baby"—she squeezes my hand tightly—"I don't know what else that man can do to prove his love to you. He has your name tattooed onto him, Pay. That's a bitch to cover up, so, you know, he must be serious."

God, I love my best friend. I throw myself at her, and we squeeze each other so tight breathing is difficult.

"You've hardly been living for years, P. It's time you live your life to the fullest and"—she pushes me to arm's length—"I know the perfect start."

"Oh yeah, what's that?"

Her face splits with a huge grin, and my own grows to match because it's contagious. She leans forward, crowding my space again, then shouts way louder than she needs to that I'm tempted to cover my ears.

"London, baby!"

25
Payson

"ARE WE REALLY DOING this?" I've never been a nervous flyer, but I've also never flown over an ocean before. I grip onto my backpack straps as we head down the hall to get onto our plane.

"Hell yes we are!" Janelle cheers.

I cannot believe we are actually flying to the UK. I've never even been to Canada, and that's only a few hours away, and now I'm flying to a whole new continent to surprise my fiancé. I wanted to tell him, and it was extremely difficult not to immediately call him when I got my phone back, but Janelle made me promise I wouldn't. She's really living her rom-com fantasy through me. I tried telling her Ash isn't the surprise type, but she only hears what she wants, and what she wanted to hear was "*London, baby!*" and nothing else, so here we are. Thanks very kindly to her dad for using his miles so we could get first-class seats for not even the price of economy. I don't have the money for either, but Janelle insisted on paying—with her parents' money. I'll pay them back as soon as I get my inheritance.

That will be the next thing I do, ask Uncle Jet if I can dip into my saving, but he doesn't know about this trip. I'm sure he will by the time I step off the plane because I'm pretty sure he has people follow me around, but there's not much he can do once I'm there . . . I *hope*. I really shouldn't push it because he might even be there waiting for me when we get off, ready to rip me a new one. He visits me monthly, sometimes more, but he doesn't stay in the room with me. I'm not sure he would even fit on their cots. When Ash stayed, it proved to be wildly difficult for us to sleep on my bed, especially when Todd tried to get up with us as well.

We step onto the plane, and my ears tune into classical music playing over the speakers. "Oh my word." I stifle a giggle.

Janelle squeals before spinning to face me. "It's so British, isn't it? Oh sorry, *innit*?"

This will be a very long trip. "I've never once heard Ash say *innit*."

"He's not the only British person in the world, I bet we will hear it before we head back home."

I hope we do, for her sake.

Finding our seat is easy enough, but the plane is massive. First class is small enough, though. Probably because the price is crazy, and normal people can't pay it. I swallow hard, thinking just how much Janelle's parents paid for this. I wonder if I'll ever be rich enough that spending money isn't always such a big deal. I guess when I marry Ash, but that's not my money, that's his. He will argue and say it's the same, but I want to make my own money somehow.

Janelle's seat is diagonal from mine but still close, and we are facing each other. There is the option to block off the seats, but we leave our divider down.

"What time will it be when we get there?"

"Like ten. That's why we took such a late flight so Ash's mom wouldn't have to pick us up at such an ungodly time." Not that she minded. Thankfully, Ash gave me her number and address in a letter, so I looked back and called her when we made this last-minute decision. I had to make sure she didn't let Ash know it was me, so I texted her first. She nearly cried when I told her our plan. I've never met her face-to-face, but I feel like I've known her for years.

Janelle whips out her neck rest and tears open the fuzzy blue blanket provided for each seat. I do the same. It's a long flight, but with it being so late in the night, I'm hoping I am able to sleep most of it.

First class is nearly full now, and the chatter around us is filled with accents. Mostly British but a few Irish, I think. I've never seen Janelle look so excited, and her head keeps whipping in whatever direction the voice is the clearest.

Some lady in the seat across the aisle from me has been on the phone since we boarded, and we've been not-so-subtly ease dropping. Not just because of her accent either, but because she's been yapping at someone about how she doesn't know why she's heading to her ex's funeral when she wishes she was the one to off him. Bold statement, especially on a plane, but maybe her ex is a pos.

I look down at my pajamas and then to her matching pantsuit. She looks ready for first class, unlike Janelle and I who are dressed for comfort. Bedtime is more like it. Her nails are long, and she's in full glam with her hair pulled into a sliced back pony. She looks rich, like, *rich* rich.

She flips her wrist. "We land at half ten."

"Well, it's only a ten-minute tube ride, *innit*?"

The moment that word leaves her mouth, I shoot a look at Janelle. She's nearly bouncing in her seat with joy, and I laugh.

"I'm going to love it here," she whispers loudly.

"Maybe you need to get you an English boy, after all." I pump my eyebrows and look around the cabin. First class is where everyone should find a man, that way you know they are rich enough to afford trips.

"Any of them besides the one I'll be forced to stay with."

She means Henry, Ash's brother. I don't actually know why she hates him, but if he's anything like Ash, I get it. If I didn't love Ash, I might hate him and his arrogance too.

The captain comes over the loudspeaker, and this time I join in with Janelle and her celebration. Not only is his voice amazing but I'm finally relaxing enough that I'm excited.

Just one little flight and I'll get to feel my man's arms around me again.

I can't wait.

26

It's too bloody hot to be working in the garden, but Mum insists on having a fountain installed *today*, the hottest day in June yet. It's not like the queen is coming round the house, so I don't know what the hurry is, but Dad has never told her no and he's not going to start now. Even if it is twenty-eight outside.

I hope Parker is doing okay at football camp this week. I'm sure the coaches know how to deal with the heat, but I might make a call when we are done here to check. I don't need him having a heat stroke.

He's loving it here, though. A little more than I wanted, but I can't blame him. Football is huge here and it excites most everyone, where in America there are so many popular sports, and football—our kind—isn't one of the tops. Good players still come from there, but I know how good it feels when the people around you are excited about the sport you play. That's why I moved from here.

Plus, I think he likes being around his grandparents, and I know they love having him around. I've seen a different side to him, a happier side. He hasn't been in a bad mood, and we've not argued once. Our time here has been my favorite thing, but there is a knot in the back of my mind that gets bigger every time I think about going back to America. Obviously, I will need to. That's where my house is, my job, and my girl. I can't simply move here, but if I think about Parker's happiness, I wonder if I can. Maybe even work at the firm for my parents for a while, but that would be a last resort. I never wanted to join the family business; I left that up to my brother.

But then there is Payson. She's not in Bayshore, but she will be. And then what? She has an entire year of school left and then college. That's why I was so persistent on her working on her missing schoolwork. I can't have her being held back another year, because I don't even know how I'm going to get through this one. We haven't discussed what will happen when she goes to college, and I can't ask her to do online classes and follow me around like a lost puppy. I can't ask because I know she would. I'm trying not to demand things from Payson and let her live her life how she chooses, but fucking hell, is it hard. If she followed me, I'm not even sure I would be one hundred percent happy with that outcome either. She's basically been in a prison her entire life, maybe not literally, but I don't want to make her feel like she missed out on anything. After missing out on a proper childhood, she deserves a proper university life. *Without all the hooking up.*

The therapist I've been seeing—per Mum's request—tells me I have excessive control mannerisms, who knew. It's what makes me a good coach but can make me a difficult person to have relationships with, is what he said. Especially in my relationship with Payson where there is already an excessive power imbalance.

I don't listen to everything he says, but I believe him to be pretty on the head with that fact. Therapy wasn't on my radar, but Mum guilt tripped me by saying if Payson is bettering herself, I should do the same. This is why I will need my own place right away if I do move here. Mum is a thorn in my ass. She means well, and she's been right so far—which you will never hear me admit out loud, but I am no longer a child who needs bossing around. And according to my therapist, I do not enjoy being told what I can and cannot do. Like I said, he's been right a few times. Doesn't take a bloke with a degree on the wall to tell me I can be pigheaded.

"I'm running into the city." Mum steps out of the house, already eyeing our progress and judging it. We are almost done, and she seems pleased.

"That time already?" Dad glances at his watch, then curses.

"William," Mum scolds and a sloppy grin stretches his old skin.

"Sorry, love."

"Mhm. Just make sure you boys are cleaned up for tea. We are having guests." Mum and Dad swap an odd look I don't quite understand, but they basically talk in their own language most of the time. Comes from years of being together, apparently. I hope one day that is Payson and me.

"Who?" Henry asks, obviously not in the loop like myself.

"You'll see. Finish up and clean up."

Dad jogs forward and says his goodbyes, then opens her car door for her. Henry lifts an eyebrow, and I just shrug. Mum is constantly having people over for small get-togethers, she's an entertainer by default. I just hope whoever is coming is someone I will enjoy being around. The couple she had over last week were wankers. Bragging about this and that and all the things their money could buy. Whatever they were bragging about isn't even a lick in the pot of what my parents hold, but we aren't braggers. The truly wealthy people aren't. Growing up, I was surrounded by fake rich people with flashy jewelry and cars. That's never been us even though my parents own and run the biggest firm in the country.

There has been chatter about spreading over to America, but that's not been done yet. Dad wants to find someone he trusts to run a branch since he is retired now. They asked me years ago, but I turned the opportunity down. Suits have never been my thing. Henry seems like the obvious choice, but it's not surprising why Dad doesn't trust him. He's been a loose cannon ever since losing Bridget. Now that I have Payson and have been in the position where I thought I would lose her, I understand more than I used to. It used to drive me batty getting calls from my mum because Henry was off fucking around, passing out in parks and shit, but if he loved her like I love Payson . . . I can't even imagine how I would have been if she didn't wake up. I look at my brother in a new light, and even though he grates on me like no one else, I see how much pain he is in, and I've done my best to be easier on him than I used to be.

Dad returns with a new pep in his step after sending Mum off. We ask about it, but he shrugs us off saying we will understand in a while. I don't bloody understand why my parents are acting so strange, but I don't particularly care either. It's almost time for Payson to call me, and we need to get done so I can talk with her.

We make haste working on the fountain, and two hours later, it's completed. The natural stone fits in well with the large house. Really brings the form of the place together. I guess that was Mum's vision.

Dad passes me a beer, and the three of us clink cans.

"Good work, boys."

"Not bad, aye. Mum should be happy," Henry replies before tipping his can back and chugging.

Dad chuckles. "Yes, she will want one by the pool now. She's mentioned it a time or two, and I think this will be the push she needs."

Brilliant. I can't complain about the work, it's hot, but it's been nice working with my family like we used to. The house Mum, Dad, and Henry live in wasn't always marble floors and delicate crown molding. When we first moved in, after the firm kicked off, it was a shithole. Took years of blood, sweat, and tears to make it the place it is now, but that's when I fell in love with fixing up things. Dad saw the potential in the run-down place with missing floorboards and a giant hole in the roof, and I'm pleased to say I see the same possibilities now. That's why I didn't mind that my place in America was run-down. I bought it, not only for the location, but because I saw what it could be.

My therapist has compared Payson to a project, but I shut that down quickly. Payson is not a broken-down house that needed to be restored. If anything, she is a diamond in the rough that needed the right environment and care to shine.

It's hours later, I'm pissed because Payson never called, so when Mum pulls in, I groan internally. I am in no mood to entertain. I haven't showered yet because I've been distracted and enjoying the weather, trying to not just stare at my phone all afternoon. Mum's going to be miffed at me, but we have over an hour before it's even remotely close to teatime, so it's not like I won't be ready.

Dad steps out of the house and throws a towel over his shoulder. He must have been doing the dishes because the front of his shirt is wet. He places his hands on his hips, but the huge smile on his face gets me. It could be because Mum is home but seems odd he's that happy when she's only been gone a few hours. I don't know anyone that loves each other as much as they do, but still. He's nearly vibrating with excitement.

Two other doors besides Mum's open, and I narrow my eyes. "Did she pick up the tea guests or something?"

"Or something," Dad singsongs.

What the fuck is happening? But the moment a tanned leg steps out of Mum's Beemer, my entire body stills and my heart fucking stops. The world moves in slow motion as I scramble to my feet and move to the edge of the steps. A blond dog jumps out and bounds right for me, barking happily.

Like a kid on Christmas who got a gift they weren't expecting, I look to my dad for answers.

His eyes sparkle with moisture. "Go get your girl, son."

Payson

Ash's mom, or *mum* as he says, is as sweet as I would expect from the few phone conversations we have had.

She squeezes me like I'm a long-lost friend, or like a mom would squeeze a daughter after going a long time without seeing her. It feels amazing being hugged with so much love. I try and not let the emotion build, but when she pulls away and I see her tears falling freely, my dam breaks and a tear drops down my cheek.

"I'm sorry." I laugh, feeling awkward, and try to wipe them as quick as I can, but her dainty hands beat me too it.

"Nonsense. Look at the state of me." We suck in a breath, blow it back out, and smile. "Even more beautiful than I remember. And your eyes, goodness me."

She's so much more British than Ash.

Her eyes flick behind me, and she beams. "You must be Nelly."

That nickname is so cute and sounds even cuter with her accent.

I let go of her, and she embraces Janelle the same way she did me. To no surprise, Janelle was already crying. Various people around baggage claim pretend not to look at the scene we are causing.

Ash doesn't look like his mom, but there are definitely similarities. Not height, though, that's for sure. She's somewhere between my and Janelle's height, and I know Ash is similar to his dad, but you can tell she is his mom for sure. Maybe because she's ridiculously pretty. Ash said his parents are probably older than I would think, but I can't image her being over fifty. I suppose with having a daughter who is thirty-six—or around there—she probably is, but she's hardly sporting any wrinkles, her blonde hair is thick, shiny, and similar in color to Janelle's. Deep-brown eyes, so warm and inviting, and now glossy with moisture, flick between me and Janelle.

"You girls are going to flip London upside down."

I'm not sure what she means by that, but it makes Janelle grin.

"Well, I am hoping to fall in love while we're here, so, here's hoping!"

Ash's mom lets out the daintiest laugh that could compare to a violin, I think. "I will keep my fingers crossed for you."

The bags take forever to arrive, but I hardly notice since Beverly—she told us to call her that or mum, but I'm not ready for that just yet—has kept us entertained with various stories of her kids growing up. It started with her telling us how on the first flight after all the kids were born Ash peed himself on the plane and had to walk around the airport half naked because they had to check their bags due to lack of room. It's comical to imagine a young Ash, she said he was around five, walking around pants-less in the airport. Now, he would have women flocking to him after seeing what is hidden behind his pants, and that thought makes me stabby, but a little Ash is hilarious, and I can't wait to tease him. She also told us about a time when Henry fell asleep by their pool with a bowl of cereal and, according to her, had the tan line of the bowl for the rest of summer, so he refused to walk around shirtless. That was just two summers ago though, which I thought was the funniest part. I've not met Ash's brother, but he sounds like a less broody Ash.

His sister, Grace, sounds lovely, and Beverly shared no embarrassing stories about her. She did say how she was born to be a mom and was always following her around and caring for her little brothers. I guess it makes sense why she has three kids now. I think I remember Ash saying that anyway.

The UK is like a different world compared to the US, at least Bayshore. I wasn't aware London has more people than New York, but apparently so, and once we step off the *tube*, as Beverly called it, I see just how true that is. Janelle and I attempt to follow her through the crowd of people, shoving our way through the same way they are shoving, to hopefully catch the subway.

The tunnels are dingy, but the people crowding them look dressed for a gala of some kind. Suits of all shades, dresses, and skirts. Women in heels, which I have no clue how they are managing all this in heels, but go them. I guess if it's something you do every day, you get used to it. And since their faces are shoved in phones and not paying any attention to where they are heading, unlike me and Janelle who are scanning around like prairie dogs looking for danger, I'd say they have done this a time or two. Todd, on the other hand, seems to thrive in this environment. He slept most of the flight, and you can tell because his tail hasn't stopped moving—his way of telling me he's ready to play.

Ash's mom is speedy. I don't know how she is moving so fast, but I'm nearly running to keep up with her walking, not to mention my bag is about as big as me and I have a dog. I feel awful for Janelle lugging two bags as big as mine, yet she's still ahead of me. I could blame my leg size, but I'm going to blame the surgery on this one. My knee is tweaking, but it's not painful, more of a pulling. Maybe I should have put my brace on before we left the airport.

After scanning our tickets, I see the light at the end of the tunnel, literally. We break out of the tunnels and the various scents of cologne and perfume, also sweat, but that could be me, disperse, and in its place is . . . coffee, I think? Mixed with air pollution. Like most cities.

There are so many things to look at, but my eyes can't find one thing to land on.

"Do either of you drink coffee or tea? We have a minute before our train."

"Do as the British do," Janelle says, hooking my arm, she's also breathing as hard as I'm trying not to. "Let's get some *tea*."

Tea is gross. I don't know how this entire country is obsessed with it. I choked mine down because I didn't want to risk insulting Beverly, not that she made it, but ew.

"The train is much less stuffy than the tubes. At least during the week. If this was the weekend, we might be standing instead of sitting right now." Beverly sits in the seat next to me. She was kind enough to offer Janelle and I each a window seat so we could see the city on our way out.

"I don't know how people would manage that daily."

"I think I could do it," Janelle says.

I definitely could not. Not only was it like running a marathon, but the amount of people is huge no thank you for me. Bayshore isn't a super small town, and I could maybe go a little bigger, but I can't imagine living in the heart of London even if I only saw a sliver of it. I would definitely like to visit for a long weekend, though. I hope I can get Ash to come during our time here.

"So much like my Ashley." Beverly laughs breathlessly. "And you sound exactly like my Henry. He works and lives in the city."

Janelle loses her smile when he is mentioned, but Beverly doesn't seem offended that Janelle isn't a fan of her son.

"Ah. Yes. I forgot about your short time spent together. Emotions were high, hopefully you can find a middle ground while you're here."

"Hopefully." Janelle's smile is fake as the day is long, but I don't think Beverly notices.

The nice voice over the intercom tells us it's time to go and says something else I'm not able to catch because it was said in a thick English accent. Janelle and I share an equally thrilled look. "I just love it here."

"Would you ever consider moving here? After school of course," Beverly asks.

Janelle ponders the thought for a moment, looking out the window as London passes by. "I think I might. I've always wanted to live in a city. New York is the obvious choice, so why not make it London?"

This surprises me. Of course, I've thought about moving here, Ash is from here—it wouldn't surprise me if eventually he wants to move back—and I don't have any family holding me back. Jethro and Jason, but I never see Jason and we live in the same country, and Jethro, something tells me he would visit me wherever I lived. I guess Janelle probably assumes the same about her parents; they can obviously afford it.

"I am not sure if Ashley has told either of you what we do." She drops her voice, I guess not wanting people around us to hear. "But we own a law firm. Helms and Pearson and we are always looking for employees. I'm not sure what you are going to college for, but if you wanted to work for us, it wouldn't need to be your forever career. It would be a good steppingstone, though."

Janelle's and my eyes are equally wide. I guess surprised that she offered her a job after knowing her for less than an hour, but I'm more surprised they own a law firm. Ash did not mention that. I'm pretty sure that's a big deal and the same kind of thing Uncle Jet owns, so they are probably close to billionaires if he is. I wish I was interested in law, geesh.

"You'd hire me just like that?"

Beverly nods like it's no big deal. "I trust my instincts, and I trust my son who has said marvelous things about both of you."

"Wow, I . . . truthfully, I don't know what to say. I'm only eighteen, so I have few years before I'll be ready for a full-time job but if you're serious, that is totally something I'd be interested in."

"Brilliant." Beverly beams. "I'm sure we could find something for you to do during the summers, office work most likely, but we would pay well."

"Absolutely. Holy—wow." *Nice save.* "This day just got so much better."

"For me as well." Beverly's smile is as bright and blinding as Ash's. She reaches for my hand on my lap and squeezes. "I am ever so glad you are here, Payson."

Something about the way she says that and the distant sorrow in her eyes makes me think she doesn't just mean here on the train with her, and I wonder how the distance has been for Ash. His letters give little away, just that he misses me, but I'm sure it's not been as easy as he's made it seem.

Emotions crowd my throat, making it impossible to reply. I force a smile and nod, but she seems to understand.

I wonder just how much she knows. I know she visited while I was in the hospital, so probably a lot, and oddly enough, that doesn't make me feel any way. Before, I would have been mortified, but like Dr. Herringbone taught me, my scars are a part of me, like everything that led to them. I wore long sleeves today, more for Beverly and his family than myself. I think I might need to change when we get to his parents' house, though, it's beyond hot here. Not at all what I thought England would be like. Where's all the rain?

I relax into the seat, watching London pass by and the skyscrapers turn to fields. A gentle ease fills my insides. I think it might have something to do with the calm that Beverly brings, but I know it's also because I'm meeting with Ash in less than thirty minutes. For the first time, I don't feel the heaviness of the baggage. I hope he notices a difference because I can sure feel it.

We still have a long way to go, but I'm ready for my happily ever after now.

27
Payson

BEVERLY TURNS INTO A driveway, leans out her window, and punches in a code into a box that causes the gates in front of us to open. I turn just enough to exchange a look with Janelle.

Fancy, she mouths.

"I promise we are not as poncy as the gate makes us seem. Over the years, as our firm has gained popularity, we've had a few opposing clients who have left with . . . disgruntled feelings. So, William had it installed for safety. Mostly mine when he's not here. Which isn't a lot." Despite what she just told us, she laughs lightheartedly.

A short drive later, a brick house comes into view. I have to stop my mouth from falling open when I see it. It's huge. We were passing similar homes on the short drive from the train station but seeing it up close is a whole other thing. All the houses were brick, but this one seems brighter, cleaner maybe. Considering Ash's mom smells delightful—and expensive, it doesn't surprise me her house is well maintained also. The lawn is perfectly green, and right in the middle is a beautiful fountain. Nice. The driveway is brick and leads right to the attached three-car garage. She doesn't pull in but stops in front of it. I was too focused on the house to notice who was out front. Not until he steps to the edge of the patio.

Someone, I assume Janelle, grabs my shoulder but I hardly feel it. Everything in my body beats for him. Lightning zaps inside me like its own personal storm.

"Let's not make him wait. I worry he might rip the door off the hinges once he realizes," Beverly encourages while pushing her door open.

"Ready?" Janelle asks.

More than anything. I lift my hand and lay it over the small lump of the ring that rests on my collarbone. *This is a promise.*

I grab the handle with a shaky hand and push it open, and Todd darts out like he knows that's his dad waiting for him, maybe he does. My first steps are wary, unsure because he hasn't moved from his spot more than to give Todd a few good pets. His features are sharp as ever, thick eyebrows angled down as he stares at me in disbelief.

God, he's beautiful.

He's gotten a haircut since the last time I saw him, and he shaved his beard to a close stubble. I loved the beard and his hair, but this is the Ash I fell in love with. I can almost see the twenty-something-year old from years ago. Except his body is different. He's not as slim as he was, instead of sleek lines, his body is hard—rigid and so. Fucking. Sexy. From years of heavy lifting. And much to my happiness, he looks healthy and strong.

Strong enough to hold me.

The moment he steps onto the ground, I take off as fast as my knee will allow until I'm crashing into him.

His arms wrap around my waist, and he pulls me tight against his body.

He sucks in a deep breath and holds it. "Jailbird." His voice is a whisper but enough to calm the storm inside me, replacing it with the serenity only he can bring. It's been months since I've felt this calm, maybe it's been forever. I've heard various forms of his accent, but nothing compares to the deep and gravel of his voice in this very moment.

I hug him just as tightly, bury my face into the crook of his neck, and cry. I'm not sure why I'm crying, but I'm full of so many emotions I guess they are coming out as tears.

"Babygirl." He sounds as if he might be fighting the tears as well. "Tell me I'm not dreaming. That you're actually here."

The giddiest laugh rips from my lips. "I'm here."

"Thank. God." Two simple words, but they mean more than he could know. I think I was more worried about our relationship status than I even knew. But the fact he is so relieved to see me and holding me as tight as he can without crushing my ribs, I know I have nothing to worry about.

My breathing steadies and a strong smell filters into my nose, not exactly *bad* but not great. I push away just enough to see his face.

"You stink."

His plump lips stretch into a cocky grin. "You like it."

"Ashley James Pearson. I told you to be showered and ready for tea."

Tea? Like a tea party?

"Oh, I will be." His seductive tone shoots straight south, offering flutters I haven't felt in a while. His eyes darken as he takes in my body. We changed after the flight in the bathroom before Beverly got there, so I'm no longer in pajamas but a simple white Henley and jean shorts. I wonder what he thinks about my few added pounds. It's not a lot that I would think he would notice looking at me, but maybe carrying me like he is. He's not struggling in the slightest, so I guess that's good.

Remembering his family is around, I lightly smack the back of his head.

"Stop it." My voice is hushed but his dad laughs anyway, obviously hearing me.

Secretly, I couldn't be more thrilled to hear a sex joke, but not in front of his parents.

"William, why don't we go inside and discuss Janelle's future employment at Helms and Pearson, let these two get reacquainted."

"I know the first thing I'm getting reacquainted with," Ash growls into my ear, and my skin erupts in goose bumps. He places a wet kiss below my ear, and my thighs automatically clamp around his waist.

"Enjoooooy," Janelle singsongs on her way past. "Come on, Todd. Leave your parents to their greeting."

The door closes and Ash wastes no time diving for my neck. I can basically see the hickey already. I should tell him to stop, but it feels so good, and I'm not sure he would listen even if I did.

"You can't fuck me on the front porch." He starts moving, and I drag his lips to mine. I grip his hair as he eats my mouth. The planets align the moment our lips meet and promise to never fall out again. I forget anything else exists. I hear chatting that sounds like his parents and Janelle, but it fades before I can focus on what is being said.

"Going to shower!" Ash shouts without letting our lips part.

I guess I'll have to get a tour later. I hold on tight as he carries me up steps and through a door.

He jolts and it slams behind us.

He tosses me, but he's on me a second later, mashing his mouth onto mine again. His big body fits perfectly with mine, like a missing puzzle piece, when he lowers himself on me.

"I need to fuck you. We can do nice later."

"Nice later," I agree, panting.

He climbs off, and I shove my clothes off. I don't know how far we are from anyone to know how quiet I have to be or anything. All I know is if I don't feel him inside me soon, I will implode.

He's only wearing shorts but still takes more time getting undressed than me, and seeing me naked doesn't make him move any faster.

"Bloody fucking hell." He groans, his eyes deepen another shade.

"I've gained a little weight—" He grabs my ankles and pulls me to the edge of the bed.

"Shut up. You are here, in front of me, legs spread, pussy bare and fucking soaked for me. You think I give a shit about any weight you may or may not have gained?"

I've missed this, holy hell have I missed his mouth.

"I love you." I breathe. "But I need you to fuck me, now."

His eyes roll back, and he drops onto his knees, now eye level with my pussy. He blows out a sharp breath, and the warm air blowing on my throbbing center sends my hips into the air. A smack sounds around us when he connects with my pussy, but I love the feeling.

I jolt again when he pushes two fingers inside me without warning. I'm biting on my lip but it's hardly muting my gasps. It's a tight fit, and his dick is much bigger than his fingers.

It will hurt and I can't wait.

28

TASTING PAYSON'S PUSSY AFTER so long has to be what it's like for a drug addict taking a hit of the good stuff after rehab. It's addicting in the best way, and with my tongue deep inside her and the beautiful sounds she's failing to mute, I wonder how I went this long without it.

Her walls flutter around my tongue, but a small orgasm isn't enough right now. My dick aches in my shorts, begging to sink inside her tight body and find it's home again, but she needs stretching. Even if she was masturbating to my photos like she mentioned in a letter, her fingers are nothing compared to the size of my dick.

I drag my nose across her clit, and she gasps.

Pussies aren't usually sweet, but I swear hers is. Fuck, it's like the best candy in the bloody world.

My tongue slips out, and she whimpers but my fingers push inside, filling her in the way she wants, and I suction onto her clit. I flick the small nub several times, and her mouth drops open, such a beautiful fucking sight seeing her come for me.

She moans my name repeatedly, a sound I've craved for so fucking long. Cum drips down my shaft—going to waste not being deep inside her.

I let her breathing steady before I place one last kiss to her pussy, an apology for how I'm about to treat her, and stand to my full height.

Payson's eyes at half-mast are such a sensual sight. She watches me push my shorts down, and when I grip my dick, she weakly pushes onto her elbows.

"You miss my dick, babygirl?"

"About as much as I missed coming like that."

There's my girl.

I prowl forward and she scoots backward, giving me room to climb up and settle between her gorgeous thighs. While gliding up her smooth legs, my eyes catch on something new. Her scars. I grab her calf and twist gently, just enough to see all six clearly.

"Do they hurt?"

Her hair tumbles off her shoulders when she shakes her head. "I've been massaging them nightly, hardly notice them anymore."

"Good. And your knee?"

"Better than before."

I slide my hand up and around her thigh and push. "So, if I do this?"

I watch her reactions closely, but her playful smile tells me before she does that it doesn't hurt, so I push more until her thigh is resting against her stomach.

"How's this feel?"

She wiggles, and I realize she's trying to get my dick inside, and chuckle. "That eager?"

"Please."

My willpower caves hearing her raspy beg. I used to be a hard-ass and make her beg until she was nearly in tears. Now I'm the one ready to tear the world apart because I can't get into her fast enough. Tables have turned, and I'm not upset by it.

Her body is at the perfect angle, and I'm able to slip my head in with ease. Eating her out was a great choice, and she's still soaked from it, but fuck, is she tight. Even using my hand to help guide it's a struggle to get inside her. When she tenses, I pull out, and when I push back in, I'm able to get farther. I do that until my hips are flush with her body, then I drop her thigh and guide her leg to wrap around my waist where it belongs.

"Feels like the first time all over again." Her voice is tight.

"Maybe." I lean down and drop my forehead to hers and kiss her nose. "But you'll be good and stretched for my dick in no time, ready to take everything I want to give you, because I'm not letting you out of my sight ever again."

The sparkle in her eye is enough to make me fucking bust. There were days over the last several months I worried what might become of our relationship, if Payson would heal so much she realizes I'm not a good fit for her. But right now, hips flush and heavy breathing filling the air, I know we are exactly where we are meant to be.

Together.

A lot has changed between Payson and me, but the way our bodies connect and move together isn't one of them.

I move slow, kissing my way up and down her body. Paying extra attention to her healed arms. Not smooth—they will never be smooth, but *no fresh cuts.*

The best stories have bumps, twists, and turns. And Payson's story is my favorite one.

"Feels different, huh?"

I swallow hard and open my eyes, allowing her to see everything I'm feeling. "I'm so proud of you."

The air between us thickens, and her eyes dampen. "I couldn't have done it without you."

"You did do it without me." She's so strong and still doesn't see it.

But she shakes her head. She moves her hands from my body toward her neck. I hadn't noticed the gold chain before now. She reaches over her shoulder and grabs the necklace with her ring and plays with it until the chain is gone. Then she slips the ring onto her finger and holds it up for both of us to appreciate.

"You were always there. This ring means so much more than a promise, Ash. It means everything. The days when it was hard to even breathe, I would sit there and hold this, and I swear I could feel you. Hear your heart through this thin metal. It's impossible, I know, but it was so real to me. No one has ever promised so much to me, yet here you are." Her lips tremble. I've stopped thrusting because, if I'm being honest, I'm having a hard time focusing on anything but her words. Not in my ear over a phone, here, right in front of me. I can see her lips move, watch her facial reactions to each word, and it's fucking beautiful. "Not only promising a future I never thought I would have. But your heart."

"My heart will always be yours, babygirl." I kiss her as deeply as I can, yet it's not enough; I wonder if it will ever be enough with Payson. It's hard to think straight. She's so easy to get lost in, and I want to get lost forever.

Payson wraps her arms around my neck and pulls me flush with her body. Her full breasts push into my chest, reminding me I've not given her tits any attention yet.

"I love you."

She smiles against my lips. "You have no idea how good that feels to hear in person again."

I do. "Your turn."

"I love you."

Three little words. Simple, yet so much meaning.

Still inside of her, I flip us over so she's on top. She wobbles from the sudden movement but wastes no time rolling her hips.

Fuuuck me.

Payson is beautiful all the time, but sitting on top of me, rolling her hips with her head thrown back, not thinking about anything besides chasing her orgasm is when she looks the best. So raw, so real, and so bloody perfect.

Her breasts sit heavy in my hands, and she whimpers when I take her nipples between my fingers and twist. I might not want to ever scar her again, but it doesn't mean I can't push her limits in other ways.

"I'm gonna come," she says, breathless from working her hips.

I twist her nipple, and her back arches. Her moans are louder, and I wonder for a second if anyone will be able to hear her, but she gasps my name and I forget anyone exists outside of this room.

Like a prayer, she chants my name as she chases her orgasm, and when I know she's coming, I quickly dive off that cliff with her. I've been ready to come since she stepped out of that bloody car.

My balls draw up, and my back tingles. I come harder than I have in a long ass time, until my balls are empty and my cum is deep inside her, right where it belongs.

She falls onto my chest and kisses me there. "Holy shit, I've missed this."

My chest rumbles with a laugh, and I drape my arms over her body and cup her ass. "Me too, babygirl. More than you could ever know."

We stay that way for so long I wonder if she drifted to sleep, but eventually, she sits up and smiles at me. It's lazy, so I know she was at least close.

She spears her fingers through my chest hair and sighs, a happy sound. "I can't believe I'm engaged at seventeen."

"To a thirty-three-year-old, no less," I add, in case she forgot.

"I know." She bites her lip and drops her excited eyes to me. "So dirty."

"And yet, you just came all over this dirty old man." I smack her ass with a loud crack, and she yelps.

"That's because dirty old men are good at sex." She giggles, and it's the best sound I've ever heard.

"Don't forget it, baby."

She bites her lip and rolls off me but lays her head across my torso and twirls her fingers in my chest hair. God, I've fucking missed this.

"Like you would ever let me."

She's right about that. Now that she's back in my life, I might never let her see anything outside of these four bed posts.

We lie in my bed for a long time, filling each other in on our time apart and enjoying each other's company, so long I don't know if hours have passed or days. I've noticed a huge difference simply in the way she speaks and carries herself. She's more confident, and I bloody love it. She seems older, wiser, and it's a beautiful sight seeing Payson come into herself the way she was always meant to.

I'm tickling her shoulder when she grips my arm with a tight hand and holds it up, a silent gasp falling from her lips. She shoots up and I follow, allowing her a better angle to see my newest tattoo.

"You didn't."

I push back her hair with my free hand to see her face. "I did."

"Ash." Her voice shakes. She holds up her arm with the same marking. Only, mine is a tattoo, not a carving.

"It seemed only fair that I scar my body with the same thing I scarred yours."

My skin burns as she trails her finger over the words *you're beautiful*.

"That's my handwriting." Her eyes are wet when they lift to mine. "How did you do that?"

"It wasn't easy. We had to piece together several of your letters to spell out those words specifically, but it was worth it."

She falls against me but doesn't let me lower my arm so she can admire it. "We are matching. But why did you add this?"

She points to the *you're*.

"As a reminder for you. If I happen to forget to tell you that day, you can look to my arm and know it's true."

There's a long pause, then she giggles. "That is the cheesiest thing I've ever heard. But I love it, thank you."

I've gotten soft, even the tattoo artist looked at me like I was off my rocker. I don't care, I'd do anything for Payson.

She curls into me, and I wrap my arms around her. "And I love you."

29

IF I THOUGHT MY brother was annoying when Payson was asleep, it's nothing compared to how he is when she's awake.

Maybe it's because anytime he says anything idiotic, she laughs. I tell myself it's out of pity because Henry is not funny, so that's the only explanation, but it doesn't stop me from wanting to bend her over my knee and spank her right here at the dining table with everyone around.

The only thing saving her ass from a red mark in the shape of my hand, is the fact her hand has not left my thigh the length of dinner for more than the time it takes her to move her napkin to her lap.

Also, the fact her skin is still flushed from sex even though it's been over an hour since our second round.

She's mentioned a few things during dinner I hadn't heard before. Like the fact the owner she had mentioned in one of the letters is only twenty-something. When she talked about him, I assumed he was an old fat bastard with a balding head, but according to Janelle, he was a *smokeshow*. Payson didn't agree, but she refused to look at me after Janelle said that.

Her appearance has changed slightly, not only is she carrying herself different, but she looks older as well. More grown and matured. Most importantly, she looks happy.

There is nothing I wanted more than to see Payson happy, truly happy. And watching her interact with my family so causally and carefree—besides Henry—is maybe my favorite thing yet.

But it doesn't stop the nagging in the back of my mind that I might not know everything about her anymore.

Then I see the fresh torn skin on her thumb, and it calms me, mostly. She is still my Payson, but she's also the Payson she should have always been. Her skin might even be tanner than mine now, and her hair is lighter, so she must have spent an exceptional amount of time by the pool. Judging by the definite tan lines I saw, I'm not sure how thrilled I am about the small percentage of her body they cover, but I'm trying to reel that side of me in.

It's difficult, and my therapist will get an earful during my next appointment.

30
Payson

ASH'S FAMILY IS . . . fantastic. They are everything I ever wanted in a family, everything anyone has probably ever wanted. Two parents very obviously deep in love. Well-rounded kids, each with a different attitude and personality—that get along, for the most part. I notice Ash's daggers toward his brother anytime I laugh at his "jokes," which aren't even that funny, but I'm trying to make a good impression. It seems to work on everyone except his sister. I get the feeling she is less than thrilled about my presence since I've caught her glaring at me a time or two. I've gone over the options in my head on what her issue could be, she's upset because her mom likes me. She's mad because she's weirdly in love with her brother like those horror stories you read online. Janelle, Ronni, and I went through a stage where we would get on *Reddit* and pick out the wildest stories we could find and read them out loud, and after, we would vote on whose was the craziest. Or she's mad because of the age gap. If I could, I'd chose the latter over either of the others.

I help Ash's mom clean up dinner, even though she told me several times not to worry about it. They all keep mentioning jet lag, but I feel fine. Janelle, however, was passed out on the couch the last I checked. I slept on the plane, though, and that probably helped keep me mostly on schedule. I wonder if she didn't.

Walking from the massive kitchen, I bump into Ash's nephew in the hallway. Ash chases after him with his hands up like claws. He winks at me.

"I'm going to eat you," he tells his nephew in a goofy voice.

The little boy, who is cute as a button with little glasses and blond comb-over, runs right into my legs. "Save me! Save me!" he begs while tugging on my dress. I'm not a dress girl, but glad I wore one for dinner since all the other girls are.

I scoop the little boy up, surprised at how heavy he is, and he clings to my body like his life depends on it. Ash trucks forward, still in dinosaur form, and I back away. A dark expression passes over his face. He throws his head back and lets out what I think is meant to be a roar.

"Hurry! Run, run!" Nelson cries, so I do.

I run through the hallway and into the kitchen since I don't know where anything else is on this side of the house. Ash still hasn't given me a proper tour.

"This way!" Beverly holds open the kitchen door that leads outside, and it's so cute how she is playing along. I sprint out as fast as I can, which isn't very fast because it's been a long day on my knee. Thankfully, Nelson doesn't seem to mind.

Beverly slams the door and pretends to struggle to hold Ash off.

A real laugh tears through me, but I'm breathing hard, so I cough it out as I run into the yard. Past the pool, there's little landscaping besides a few fruit trees, but the grass is soft and so beautiful. It's still warm out, but not bad in my dress.

"Which way?" I ask Nelson.

He points back toward the house, and since it's getting dark and I don't know this property at all, I think that's a great idea. "Where's the dinosaur?" I ask. Beverly is gone from the door, and the only other people out here are William, Ash's dad, and William, Ash's brother-in-law, or Will as I was instructed to call him, sitting on the back porch smoking from a pipe.

"Dada! Where's Uncle Dinoash?"

Dinoash, I like that.

"I don't know but you better hurry and get inside before he finds you!" his dad says. I'm taking that as a hint that Ash is somewhere out here where I can't see him and he's going to jump out at us.

"Hurry, Aunt Payson!"

My feet faulter hearing that title, not in a bad way. In fact, I quite like having the aunt title. Not only does it make me feel special but like Ash and I are seen as a real couple. I really like that. I guess if Nelson is calling me aunt, his mom can't hate me that much.

Famous last words.

I'm hurrying by the pool when Ash jumps out of nowhere . . . Okay, maybe a bush, but it scares not only me, but Nelson to the point he screams, and then I scream because he's screaming, and before I know it, I'm screaming because I'm falling backward, right into the pool.

The last thing I hear is Ash cuss before cold water rushes around me. I do my best to keep Nelson above the water by holding him up, but it's a deep pool, so I can't be sure I succeeded until I break from the surface and see that his hair is dry.

Score me.

His eyes are wide behind his glasses. "Wow" is all he says.

"Wow is right." I force a laugh because laughing is the last thing I feel like doing. I move us to the side of the pool, and Will grabs Nelson from my arms and pulls him into a thick towel right away. Ash reaches for me, and I splash him.

"You're going to regret that, babygirl."

I reach up, and he tugs me out as easily as Will lifted Nelson. He wraps a big towel around me and tucks me into his chest the same way too.

"Balance hasn't returned fully, I see."

"You're such a—" I don't finish that sentence and huff instead. "You know."

Ash's laugh is deep and from his belly, and I elbow him, cutting it off.

Grace blows through the back doors and throws her hands in the air. "What the hell is happening out here? I'm upstairs feeding Charles when I hear my son scream and a large splash."

"Calm down, Grace." Ash rolls his eyes, obviously not caring how pissed his sister is. Or how she is now glaring at me after seeing Nelson and me in towels.

"What happened?"

"They were just playing, love. It was an accident, and he is fine." Will attempts to calm his wife, but I can see from here it did nothing to help. She practically has smoke rolling from her ears.

"I'm sorry. I didn't realize how close the pool was."

"Did it move or something?" she snaps.

"Grace," Ash's dad scolds.

Ash tenses behind me. "Watch how you speak to her."

"Then what about you? She's a *child*, Ashley. She's probably never held a child before, yet you let her run around with mine in her arms?"

Ouch. I don't know which is worse, her yelling at me or her yelling about me like I'm not even here.

"I was out here too. So was your father. She was doing just fine but tripped, it was an accident." Will standing up for me definitely doesn't help my situation. She shoots him a glare before turning on me again.

"Then it's all your faults. Come, Nelson. Let's go home."

"I thought you were staying the night." Beverly frowns.

"Plans change," she snaps and turns. "Nelson."

Nelson turns in his grandpa's arms to look up at me. "I had fun playing with you."

I hate being yelled at, and I hate the situation I'm in, but it's not Nelson's fault, so I force the best smile I can and pray my voice comes out semiregular. "I had fun too."

His dad scoops him from William's arms and offers me a regretful look. He mutters something to Ash, who only gives him a tight nod in return.

"Bye, Uncle Dinoash. Bye, Aunt Payson and Papa."

I offer a wave but freeze when I see Grace glaring at me in the background. She apparently wasn't the one to tell him to call me that. *Stupid Ash.* Thankfully, she says nothing, but the look on her face says enough.

Beverly follows out after her daughter.

The air around me is thick and difficult to breathe, and not just because of the humidity.

William seems unsure what to say when he sighs and lifts his hands in a shrug. "Grace can be a bit. . ."

"Cunty," Ash growls.

"Ashley," William scolds, but seeing how angry his son is, he sighs. "I will let you two talk. Ashley, put Payson's clothes in with the dry cleaning. It goes out tomorrow."

Dry cleaning . . . of course.

Before he walks inside, he tells us good night, but I'm the only one that replies. He closes the door, and Ash still doesn't move.

I walk over and drop next to the pool, letting my feet dangle in the water. It's not as cold as I thought when we fell in, I think it was just a shock because I wasn't expecting it.

The water ripples with each kick, and then Ash eventually drops behind me and places his feet in the water on either side of mine.

"I'm sorry my sister is such a cunt. I will speak with her tomorrow because I'm afraid if I were to do it tonight, I might strangle her."

He might not be joking, but if I don't laugh, I'll cry. I lean back against him, and he wraps an arm around my body, holding me to him and not caring I'm wet.

"It's fine. Don't argue with your family over me."

His heart speeds up and thumps against my back. "I'll argue with anyone when it comes you. The only reason I didn't let her have it is because Nelson was there. Unlike her, I don't want him to see me angry."

That makes me love him even more. "I appreciate that."

"But she has it coming. No one speaks about you that way, family or not, I do not care. *No one.*"

And that makes me love him even more than that.

"I love you."

He blows out a long breath and lowers his scratchy chin into my neck. "Not nearly as much as I love you."

I don't know about that, but it's probably close.

31

Darkness is heavy around me. Thunder booms in the distance, and rain is like needles on my face. Looking around, I see nothing.

"Hello?" I shout. The storm would clue me into being outside, but the lack of lighting is throwing me off. I can't see a foot in front of me, it's so dark.

"Help me."

Who is that? I spin around but come up empty-handed. With the rain and the thunder, I can't tell which direction it came from.

"Hello?"

"Help me, Daddy."

. . . Payson? It doesn't sound like Payson but she's the only person who has ever called me that.

"I can't see you."

"Help me, Daddy."

I pick a direction and take off. The ground, although I can't see it, is mush, and my feet stick with every step. The little girl cries again, and I run for I don't know how long until eventually I break into a familiar field. It's still dark, but I can see the broken-down swing set in the background and a light post.

And Payson.

I think.

I can only just see the outline of her. She's yards away, and by the time I get closer, the storm rages harder. "What the hell are you doing out here?"

But she doesn't acknowledge me. Now that I'm closer and the lightning is lighting up the dark sky, I see her back is to me.

"Pay." I touch her shoulder, and her head turns.

I jump back and my stomach lurches. She's covered in blood. More than I've ever seen. Head-to-toe thick blood coats her body.

"You couldn't save me."

"Help me, Daddy!"

I shoot a look at the small voice.

"But save our daughter, Ash."

Our daughter? Payson smiles, and my blood runs cold. I didn't notice, or they weren't like that before, but her eyes are solid black and . . . soulless.

"Save her, Ash. Save her like you couldn't save me. Don't be late . . . this time."

"Daddy! Help me!" The little girl's, I guess my . . . daughter's voice is so scared. I can't see her, but wherever she is, I know she's terrified.

No matter how far I run, I can't see her. The moment I get close to the voice, it changes direction and is yards away again.

My body is exhausted and eventually my feet give out and I fall to my knees. A scream builds in my chest, and I tilt my head back and let it out.

Deafness falls on my ears. The storm still rages, but I can't hear it. I can't hear anything. I scream again, testing it, and sure enough, there is nothing.

Panicked, I look around. For what, I don't know. For once, it's not Payson I want to see right now.

What the fuck is happening?

Something touches my back, and I whip around and fall to my ass, as a small girl stands in front of me, out of reach.

"You didn't save me, Daddy." The little girl's lips wobble, and she drags her tiny arm under her green eyes. Green eyes, like Payson. She is similar to my baby photos, but Payson shines through in her features. She is the perfect mix of us, and it's fucking terrifying how beautiful she is.

"I tried." My voice is as mute as the storm around me. The only thing I can hear is this little girl's sniffles.

Payson fades from nothingness, now looking normal.

"It's okay, baby. He failed me too." She holds her arms open, and my eyes drop to the long slices on them and the blood that just barely trickles out.

I reach out for the girl, but my hand goes right through. "Wait," I say, but I can't hear it.

"Come on, princess. We don't belong here anymore."

The little girl's face twists with disappointment, and her frown might be the saddest thing I've ever seen in my life. Like someone kicked me, I fall to my ass, and the little girl walks into Payson's arms. Payson looks beautiful as a mother.

But I don't like this, I don't like it at all. I saved her that night, I know I did.

And what about the little girl, what happened to her? She looks perfect.

That changes as soon as I think it, and slowly a thick red line appears across her throat. Her eyes turn the same black as Payson's from earlier.

"No!" My voice booms and it startles me. I climb to my feet, but no matter how much I run, I can't catch them, and eventually, they fade from view.

A black figure appears in front of me, yards away so I can't make out if it's Payson. I walk toward it this time, hopefully walking actually gets me somewhere, and to my surprise, it does. I'm nearly ten feet away when I come to a halt. The black figure I saw is a man, but I can't see his face because he's wearing a black hood.

Not that I care about him when in his arms is a lifeless Payson.

Another scream builds inside me, but it doesn't come out.

I can't do anything.

I gasp awake. Peaceful early morning sun shines through the windows I forgot to close last night. I slip from bed and walk over to the window. With the wet wood beneath my feet, I know it rained. I stand in the window, breathing in the fresh air, trying to calm my beating heart.

What the fuck kind of dream was that?

That's the third night in a row I have had a similar dream, but tonight I got close to the man holding Payson. I shudder at the thought.

Glancing over my shoulder, a relieved breath escapes me seeing the mess of Payson's hair fanned across my pillow and Todd resting at her feet. I tried to keep him off the bed, but it was useless when Payson turned on her charm.

Today will be her fourth day here, I still can't believe it. Waking up to next to her is the best bloody feeling. If only the dreams would stop.

I press a kiss to her forehead and tuck the blankets around her so she will hopefully sleep in. We are heading into the city for a few days and it's going to be exhausting.

Parker comes home in three days, and if I'm being honest, I'm nervous how he will be once he sees Payson. We haven't spoken much about her since we came to England, being busy with other things and it's a subject we don't see eye to eye on, so there is no point in discussing it just for us both to get upset. I don't fully understand his issue with our relationship, but I understand enough. She's closer to his age than mine, and when she is around, I have difficulties focusing on anything else. That was before when she required more attention, when I worried about her slipping through my fingers. The fear is still there, but the past few days have been better than I could ever imagine days with her being. It's hard to remember a few months ago I was holding her lifeless body in my arms. Difficult until I fall asleep apparently.

The other great thing about Payson being here is my showers are much shorter—when she's not involved—and my cum isn't wasted down the drain any longer. It rests deep in her pussy right where it should.

I jump out of the shower, style my hair, and trim my face so it's not clean but just more than a five-o'clock shadow. I'm ready for the day and it's not even seven a.m.

Mum is sipping on a cup of tea in her usual spot on the bench in the bay window that looks over the pool. I grab a cup and make my tea before joining her.

"How did you sleep, sweetheart?"

"Fine, you?"

Mum flicks her gaze to me with a look I saw many times as a kid. The *I know when you are lying* look.

"Ashley," she warns.

Sighing, I take a drink from my cup and set it onto the small table in front of me. "I keep having a dream where I don't save Payson." To put it lightly.

"Oh, sweetie."

"But last night it wasn't just Payson I couldn't save. There was also a little girl . . . our *daughter*." The heaviness I felt during the dream multiplies tenfold when I think about the little girl, an equal mixture of Payson and myself, calling me dad. *Daddy* actually, but I'm doing my best not to think about how conflicted that makes me feel. Payson hasn't called me that since being here, if I'm remembering correctly, she hasn't since she woke up. Our relationship has changed since, and she must feel it too. Like we are on a whole new level than that.

I'm not saying I'd never enjoy hearing that title slip from her lips when I'm balls deep inside her. But with marriage, kids will be on our radar at some point. Won't they call me daddy? And if they do, I can't imagine wanting to hear the same title from my wife. I certainly feel different about it now after hearing our fictional daughter cry it.

"And what happened with your daughter in the dream?"

Huh? I blink the fog from my thoughts, and my eyebrows dig into my forehead. I remember exactly, but this is a heavy topic to discuss with my mum over morning tea.

"Ashley."

"I don't know. She was crying and no matter how much I ran I couldn't catch her." A lump forms in my throat, and I do my best to swallow it but my voice still comes out strangled. "Then a large cut appeared out of nowhere across her throat and they both disappeared."

I didn't expect a reply because what do you say to that? She slides closer, and like I'm four years old, she pulls me into her loving arms and pats my back.

After a few minutes, I pull away. "Thanks, Mum."

"I'm sorry I don't know what to say."

"Not sure who would," I joke.

She flattens her lips, and I'm guessing she does. I'm also guessing I won't like who she says.

I dread this hideous brown-brick place. The smiley face on the door is to distract you from how mind-numbing inside is. Or who's inside, I should say.

The little bell on the door jingles, alerting anyone inside of my entrance. Dr. Howard pops his head around the computer, and it takes everything inside me not to turn around after seeing his goofy ass smile. Like he was expecting me or some shit, but that's impossible because I didn't call. I was hoping he would be busy and wouldn't be able to see me, then I could at least say I tried.

"Just in time to be my first client today."

Bloody hell.

"Great."

He laughs like someone who has smoked for years, but I doubt this man has even held a cigarette in his life. From the purple-and-orange bow tie around his neck, to his neon-blue glasses I told him not to wear around me, or the way he walks like there is a fucking song in his head constantly, this bloke beats to his own drum, that's for sure. Mum says it's because he works with children as well as adults and it can be intimidating for them, so he wants to look friendly. Whatever the reason is, it's not good enough.

"Come on, then."

He leads me back to the spare office with only an old desk, an office chair, and a plastic chair for me to sit. His main office is decorated and welcoming—to most. But it looks like Barney the fucking dinosaur threw up in there. I told him if he wanted me to relax enough to talk, we needed a new space. So, here we are.

"What brings you into my office this morning?"

This is why I hate therapy. It's not Dr. Howard, no matter how weird I think he dresses, it's not that his office is obnoxious, it's talking. The only thing you have to do at therapy? Yeah. I bloody hate it.

I'm Ash Pearson. I pretty much grew up with a silver spoon in my mouth. I am a three-time Olympic gold medalist and a retired professional athlete. What the fuck do I have to complain about? I have also gone through enough knee surgeries that will eventually make it impossible to crawl around with my future kids and grandchildren after a certain age and will lead to complete knee reconstructive surgeries before I die. I spent years of my life questioning if my relationships with people were because they liked my company or my bank account. Because I have been an athlete for most of my life, my body aged quicker than the average thirty-three-year-old.

None of those issues require therapy. There are people—like Payson—who have had it way worse than me, so why am I here?

Because, just a few months ago, I sliced my girlfriend open because I believed I was doing her a favor. And weeks later, I held her as she bled out from cuts right next to where my scars laid.

I'll never forgive myself for what I did to Payson. Dr. Howard can say whatever he wants, but I was a huge factor in Payson's attempt. If I would have gotten her help sooner, done what I knew was the right thing and not what she wanted from me, there never would have been the hospital stay, and I would have never had to watch her die. I'll never forgive myself, and I don't deserve to.

The fact she is even here is something I don't understand. How can she stand to be around me? Allow me into her life after everything I did. How did she accept my proposal so easily? Somehow, she still trusts me, and even though she's spent months in therapy that allowed her to heal in certain aspects of her life, she still wants me just as before.

Her eyes still dilate when she looks at me. I feel how easily she relaxes when I'm around. Wouldn't a good therapist tell her to avoid me at all costs? That seems like the smart option. Not that I would let her, but I'm an asshole; we've been over this.

I don't want Payson mentally healed if it would cause her to question our relationship, I just wonder why she doesn't, and if she's as good as she seems.

"Ashley?" Dr. Howard asks, his voice light.

"If Payson were your patient, would you tell her to stay away from me?"

My question catches him off guard, but like always, he recovers quickly. I guess that's what he was trained to do.

"If you heard the same story I told you, but from her perspective."

He thinks for a moment. "The same story?"

I nod.

"No. I wouldn't tell her to stay away."

Shock rips through me, a little anger too. "Why?"

He places his notebook on the desk and folds his hands together on his lap. "Are you not pleased with my answer?"

"Yes. No. I don't know. That is the issue."

"What's the issue?"

This man is infuriating. My blood simmers. I knew I shouldn't have showered this morning because like every time I get out of this hellhole, I will need to blow off some steam and I'll need another shower. Usually I workout, or go for a run, but with Payson here . . . I can think of a different way to work up a sweat.

"What if I told you Payson wasn't my twenty-two-year-old assistant coach and was a player? Then would you tell her to?" I harden my eyes and tighten my fists. "Hypothetically."

I fibbed a little when giving him the information at our first appointment. Looking back, I'm not sure why I lied, but I think subconsciously the age gap is bothering me, or maybe always has, but I'm so blinded by lust I didn't care. Not on her end but mine. What kind of man am I to be in love with a seventeen-year-old? Nothing will change, it's too late and my fate is set, but I wonder if I'm the best option for Payson.

"Well—" He blows out a sharp breath. "If I had Ms. Payson in here telling her side of the story, and it matched yours . . . I still think my answer would be no, I wouldn't tell her to stay away. Hypothetically, of course."

"Why?" I growl.

"Can I ask you something first?"

"You're going to anyway," I grumble. My fists are cramping.

"Why are you so persistent for me to tell her she needs to stay away? Do you want her to stay away?" That goofy therapist look filters onto his face. A cross between curiosity and like he already knows the answer before you say it. *Wanker.*

No. I don't want her to stay away. I've lived a life without Payson, it's not one I enjoyed, and life is much better with her in it. "I just wonder if she should want to. Is it normal for a teenager to want someone my age?"

"Normal is subjective. To Payson, yes, it obviously is normal for her, but I would bet she has some peers that disagree." *To say the least.* "If what you told me about her is true, then yes, it is quite common. The younger partner looking for the void left behind in a partner. So, if your dad abandoned you at a young age, you could—"

"Look for that in a partner." My stomach twists, and my head begins to swim.

"Yes, but it is only a problem when you don't know that is why you are doing it. If you are aware of the reasoning and can make a legitimate decision without pressure that it is not the reason for your attraction, then, in my professional opinion—there is nothing wrong with it. Older men have a lot to offer to anyone of any age. Within reason, of course, I would not suggest anyone underage ever get with anyone older. But sometimes, women are just interested in the gray hair and it's nothing more than that." He laughs but I don't. I don't have gray hair.

"What it sounds like to me is you are wondering if Payson is with you because of her feelings, or her trauma. My suggestion? Ask her."

"Simple as that." I laugh humorlessly.

"Yes, it is."

Great, just ask the love of my life if she loves me for me or if because her dad left her when she was four and her stepdad molested her after. *Easy fucking peasy, Doc.*

I go to push to my feet but stop. "Can dreams be related to real life?"

"Oh, yes."

Fan-fucking-tastic. "What would it mean if you dreamed up your daughter and her crying about her dad not being able to save her like he couldn't save her mum?" I have discussed my dreams before, and he knows about her attempt. He knows everything besides her real age.

Leaning back in his chair, he crosses his arms and he leans back, completely at ease. Unlike me. "Do you have a minute to talk?"

Do I? Yes. We are not heading to London until tonight. Do I want to? No. But I am curious about what he will say about the dream, so I lean back in my chair and wave him on.

"Go on, Doctor. Do your thing."

I go on explaining the dream and everything that happened, he asks me my feelings and then discusses what each part could mean. The storm could represent what is happening in my head, apparently. The battle between my thoughts, or something. And according to him, the daughter is my wants being represented—he's right on that. One day, I want children with Payson. As far as the cut throat and Payson being covered in blood, it's just PTSD from that night.

The bell sounds, and even though he tells me we can keep going, he has given me enough to think about for one day.

"Thank you." I shake his hand.

"Of course. Anytime. And I meant what I said about Payson joining you for a session. I would love to meet her."

"She just spent months in therapy, doc. I don't know if she wants to go back so soon."

A knowing grin splits his face. "Very well. Have a good day and enjoy the city. Be sure to take her to see the British Museum. It's very interesting."

Yeah, okay. I'll get right on that. Of all the things to do in London, taking Payson and Janelle to a museum isn't on the top of my list.

32
Payson

"WHAT ABOUT THE BRITISH Museum?" I ask.

"I think that is a brilliant idea." Beverly smiles, genuinely meaning it. William on the other hand is quite obviously holding back a smile, and when Janelle boos me, it breaks out.

"Pay, we are going to London. You want to see the museum?"

"I think history is cool!"

She leans forward and grabs the "Things to do in London" pamphlet from my hands. "You are not in charge of the itinerary."

If his parents weren't here, I would call her a bitch, but I'm trying my best to be on my best behavior.

"Oh, you girls are very entertaining." Beverly laughs. "Whatever you decide, will be lovely. You can't go wrong with much in London."

"I can think of a few places that would be a waste of time," William tells us as he pulls up his booklet like he's about to read us a list.

The front door slams, and Ash steps into the room, his eyes immediately finding me. I don't know where he's been all morning. I've only been awake for about an hour, but he's been gone longer than that because his side of the bed was cold.

"What is a waste of time?" He drops behind me and pulls me against his chest, laying a firm kiss on the side of my head.

"Payson is trying to make our trip to London lame, your dad is trying to save us from it."

Ash's dad chokes on his tea, obviously disagreeing, but Janelle is paying no attention.

"What are you wanting to do, baby?"

I drop my head onto his shoulder and look up. "I thought the museum would be nice."

Dumbfounded for a moment, he groans loudly. More than I would have expected, but he doesn't even get a real word out before Janelle is shouting, "Told you" in my direction, like we are eight again.

"No, Payson. This isn't a school trip."

My mouth drops. "You're meant to be on my side!"

He smiles, but it doesn't meet his eyes. "I'm always on your side."

"Then say yes to the museum."

"I cannot in good conscious agree to that."

Oh, now he has a conscience.

"How about we compromise." William offers, like the good business-man he is. "We don't do the museum this time"—ugh—"but we do the entire bus tour."

That's actually a good compromise because Janelle doesn't have to do the museum and I get the full bus tour. We planned on only going to a few stops, but this way, I'll get to see the full thing.

Eyeing Janelle, I know she is thinking it over, and when she comes to a decision, I drop to my knees and hold my hand across the coffee table to her. She gives it one large shake.

"Deal."

"Brilliant!" William claps like a happy dad who stopped his daughters from fighting. Something tells me it took more than that to settle debates between his kids when they were younger.

The room clears, everyone heading in different directions, but Ash's arm around my stomach keeps me rooted in place.

"Where were you?"

He peppers kisses across my jaw and down my neck, and a wave of goose bumps breaks out across my skin. "I went for a walk."

That doesn't seem very believable. "Ash."

His kisses pause and he sighs, blowing his hot breath against my pebbled skin. "Sometimes, I have nightmares of that night. It can make it difficult to sleep."

That night? What is he . . . oh. *That* night. A deep-rooted guilt I hadn't felt before makes itself known, tugging my insides until I worry they might never go back to normal.

I never considered what that night did to Ash. I've dealt with the repercussions. I wear the scars on my arms as a constant reminder of a place I never want to be. But in the midst of all that, I never once considered Ash, really considered him and his feelings. Selfishly, I believed he would simply move on. Like my death would be something he would mourn for a few months, maybe a year, and then he would meet someone new and forget all about me. Now that thought hurts more than cutting ever did. Not only did I not consider how my death would make him feel but seeing me die is a whole new ball game. I could argue I didn't expect him to come when I called, there's a sliver of that being true because we were fighting, but I know Ash more than that. I knew he would look at my location and come to me. I wanted him to because I didn't want to die alone.

Selfish.

He was meant to just hold me and watch me die . . . and then what, Payson? Go on with life like nothing happened?

Nightmares have interrupted my sleep as long as I can remember, only Ash keeps them at bay and yet, I have caused him to have his own.

"Shh, baby," he coos. He is talking about how I gave him nightmares and still he is the one holding me.

I bury my face into his chest and wrap my arms tightly around his neck. "I'm so sorry." My voice shakes, but I will not cry. I spent years not crying, I can do it now.

"Don't apologize, babygirl. I don't want your apology."

He might not want it, but he deserves it. "I'm sorry."

"Please don't apologize."

I've viewed Ash as a big indestructible being for so long, it's sometimes hard to remember he's human as well. He does such a good job protecting me I never considered he deserves the same.

I pull away and cup his face like he often does mine. His stormy eyes scan my face.

"I never considered your feelings during all of this. It's selfish, but unfortunately true. You're Ash Pearson, the man I used to pray to like a god. Sometimes it's hard to remember you're not actually one."

That earns me a panty-wetting smile. "You can pray to me anytime you want, babygirl. I'll even let you drop to your knees while you do."

Some things never change, and Ash's dirty mouth is one of them. But I have a feeling he is deflecting the conversation, and that's not okay with me.

"I'm sorry I gave you nightmares. Do you want to talk about them?"

"No."

"Okay . . . well, if you ever do."

Ash grabs my hands, holding them between us with one hand and pushes some hair behind my ear with the other. "You're here. That's all I ever need."

That's not true, but if it makes him feel good, that's all I care about right now. I curl into his chest and focus on the steady beat of his heart.

London is the prettiest city I have ever been to. Not that I've been to a lot of cities, but there is something so magical about this place.

It could be the company alongside me, though. Ash's parents are the best tour guides. We are doing our big exploring tomorrow, but they are making sure to point out things as we pass.

Ash hasn't let my hand go once, and it's so nice getting to act like a real couple. We don't have to worry about who might see us or what anyone thinks. I look young, but no one would know I wasn't eighteen if they were looking, but they're not. Ash and I totally fit in here. There are couples of all kinds, so our age gap means nothing. I think Ash has noticed and is enjoying it just as much as me. He's in much better spirits than he was this afternoon. I've asked him repeatedly if everything is okay, which he continuously promises it is. I'll need to ask more about his dreams, get him to open up, or go see someone if he doesn't want to tell me, but I'll save that long conversation for when we are back home.

"You made it," Beverly cheers. Henry saunters our way, and his suit makes my biker shorts and cropped shirt look like pajamas.

"We were worried you would miss seeing the Eye." His dad claps him on the back.

"Nah, I had to make some calls before I left the office." Henry stops, his eyes bounce around the group before locking onto Janelle.

I flick a look her way only to see her with her face in her phone. I don't know what she's looking at, but she seems highly interested in it. The slight amusement that seems to always be dancing behind Henry's eyes faulters for a moment, but he quickly recovers. Not quick enough. I saw the disappointment when Janelle wasn't paying him any attention. Ash says his brother sleeps around, and Janelle is looking for a commitment. If he is interested in Janelle and thinks she will be a quick bone, then he better look elsewhere. Ash's son broke her heart; I'm not letting Ash's brother do the same.

I wrap my arm around Ash's neck and pull his ear to my lips. "Tell your brother to find someone else to focus on."

Ash checks out what I mean and grins. "I think you underestimate your friend's abilities to tell him herself."

Janelle lowers her phone and their eyes meet, a beat passes, then another and a protectiveness fills my system. "I think you underestimate how horny she is."

Ash barks out a loud laugh, grabbing the attention from the people around us, including Henry and Janelle.

Who knew a giant Ferris Wheel would be this popular. We've been in line for the London Eye for nearly an hour and just now getting to the front. There's a place to pose for a photo, and then we are able to get on. A few other families join us in the egg-like tube.

Todd is back at Ash's parents' with a dog sitter. I wanted to bring him, but Ash warned me this may not be a very dog-friendly trip, even with him being a service animal. I was still wary until Ash's mom told me the dog watcher was Ash's cousin who is also a vet. I guess there's no one better to care for my boy.

I rush to the front so I can get a good view. It's already so pretty, but as the wheel turns, it gets even prettier. Ash steps up behind me and points various buildings out. Some popular enough I've seen them in movies, others not.

"It's so beautiful," I say as I look out over the city blanketed in artificial lighting. Seeing the world from this high up and knowing there are millions of other people living their life, makes everything seem so small.

"I've always loved London at night. The day is pretty, but it's a completely different world at night."

We move toward the middle on the way down to allow others to see, and when we get there, I find Janelle bent over and Beverly rubbing her back. I crouch down in front of her. "What's wrong?"

"Apparently, I don't like heights," she croaks, a weak smile on her face, mostly for my benefit, I assume.

"You didn't know?" Ash asks.

She shakes her head. "I've never been on anything this high. The carnival around us is microscopic in comparison."

"Shit, Jay."

"I'm good. You go look . . ." She lifts her head, eyes fleeting to the window in front of her. Her face turns a shade of green I've never seen on a person before. I look around for a garbage but there is none. What kind of place like this doesn't have a garbage?!

"Are you going to throw up, sweetheart?" Worry pinches Beverly's face. She is such a mom, and I love it so much.

Hearing her question, the other families and couples disperse from the middle, basically hovering to one side and watching in horror as they wait for the inevitable. But she doesn't throw up, not on it. Somehow, she held it long enough for us to jump off and run to the nearest bathroom. Which, by the way, takes a freaking quarter to use?! This country is wild.

I'm holding her hair back and doing my best not to hurl, but hearing her, it's not easy.

"On a scale of one to ten, how embarrassing was that for me?"

"Uh, like a two. Hardly embarrassing at all. I bet like a hundred people get sick on that thing a day." Thinking like that, it doesn't seem as romantic as it felt when we were on it anymore.

She groans into the toilet but makes sure not to actually touch it. "I think I'm fine."

Slowly, she stands, and I wait until she is up to let go of her perfectly curled hair. Her blue eyes are watery, and her skin is flushed.

"You feel okay?"

"No. But not like I'm going to throw up so." She shrugs. "I really need a toothbrush now, though."

Oh right. And our luggage was dropped off at the hotel already which is across town . . . shoot.

"We can head back to the hotel. It's probably pretty late anyway."

She agrees, and we head for the sink where she does as much cleaning as she can manage in a public bathroom. Everyone is waiting outside when we get out, and they all ask her if she's okay, which I think is sweet. Well, everyone besides Henry, but even he looks struck with worry.

"Can we head back? She wants to brush her teeth and stuff."

Ash grabs my hand and kisses my knuckles. "Of course, let's head to the tubes."

"My office is right here. I have hygiene products in the toilet." Henry points to a large glass building. The largest glass building around, actually. And sure enough, down the side is the name of Ash's parents' law firm.

"Do you want to go to the hotel or clean up here?" I ask, making sure she knows either option is okay. I don't know what time it is, but it feels late. You wouldn't know by how busy the streets still are. I'm starting to believe no city has ever slept.

Janelle takes a while to decide, but eventually, chooses to just use Henry's stuff. I offer to come with, but she assures me she's fine. The only reason I don't go to ensure Henry behaves himself is because Beverly and William are tagging along to show her around at the same time. Apparently, this isn't even the main building. This is an outpost where they deal with smaller cases, I guess, and is the one Henry runs.

We were told to give them an hour and we would meet up after, so for the next hour, Ash leads me around various parts of the city. In retrospect, we don't get all that far from the Eye because the city is just so big and I was making him stop off at any cool thing I saw, which was a lot. I'm not a picture taker but some sights deserve to be photographed. Besides, the photos from the Eye, my favorite so far is from the bridge that overlooks the Eye and the clock tower. Seeing these things only makes me more excited for the red bus tour tomorrow.

I lean against the edge of the bridge facing Ash.

"I'm having the best time. Just thought you should know."

He beams and places a chaste kiss on my nose. "Me too, babygirl. I've been to London more times than I can count, but this is my favorite to date."

My heart warms with his confession. "I'm glad to be a part of it, then."

"You are the reason, Payson."

Swoon.

Emotion swirls behind my eyes as I hold his. "I hope you know how much you mean to me. I know I am not easy to love, but somehow you find a way to do it."

He crowds into me, and I have to crane my neck to see his face. "You don't know how bad I needed to hear that right now, babygirl."

"I'll tell you every day for the rest of our lives if that is what you need." I giggle, but I mean it too. We all know I require more assurance than nearly anyone. If Ash is struggling and needing the same, then that is what I will give him. It's the least I can do.

A shit-eating grin splits his face, and his eyes fill with excitement. He grabs my arm and drags me to the center of the walk bridge. Some people curse after being cut off, but he pays them no attention. Only staring at me with wild eyes.

"What is happening?" I look around us for something that would have set him off on whatever mission he is on, but there is nothing.

"Give me the ring."

Confused, I tilt my head. His eyes drop and I follow, now realizing what he meant. I've only been wearing it on my finger a few days full-time, and forgot it was there.

"Why?" I frown. "I don't want to."

He pokes my nose, a distraction so he can grab the ring with his other hand and slip it off my finger.

"Ashley." I stomp my foot like a bratty kid who had their favorite toy stolen from them. Because that's exactly how it feels. "You can't take it back after you gave it to me. It's mine."

"I know." A mischievous grin grows on his face. "Just trust me, okay?"

Fine, but I better get it back soon.

He leans closer, cups the back of my neck, and presses a deep kiss against my forehead. "Don't forget your line, baby. Just one word—*yes.*"

One word? Yes? What the—*no.* My eyes blow wide, and I squeal, but not in a good way, as panic surges through my system. "Ash, don't," I beg, and it only makes his grin bigger.

He wouldn't do this to me. He can't; he knows I hate this kind of attention. But he does. "If you do this, I'm saying no." But it's too late.

Ash Pearson lowers himself onto one knee in front of me. This is a sight I always dreamed about, but my annoyance is so loud I can't focus on that.

People are already noticing what is happening, and it doesn't help the embarrassment burning its way up my neck.

"Ashley," I hiss. "Stand up."

He glances around, and unlike me, the crowd only fuels him. "You stumbled into my life a short time ago." I can't believe he is doing this. "Our story hasn't been perfect. There were a lot of odds against us, but we paid them no attention and continued to do as we pleased. Some bad decisions were made, but the bad, good, and between are just a part of our story now.

Something we will one day tell the grandkids." He winks, and my aching stomach flutters with the flaps of a thousand butterflies. "Before you, I was searching for what we have without even knowing what I was looking for. Beginning to believe true love didn't exist, but you turned those gorgeous eyes on me and suddenly, the wait made sense."

His voice shakes. *I've never heard his voice shake before.*

"Love isn't an emotion. It's a promise, despite everything you lead to believe before me." A real sob rips through me, and he squeezes my hand as if to say just hold on. He holds the ring up with his other hand.

"I promise to love you on your good days and even harder on your bad ones. Because there will be bad days, baby. But take this ring and I promise we will go through them together, side by side, hand in hand. I will love you forever and always. You and me, until the end of time.

"Marry me?"

Tears flow freely down my face, but I don't bother wiping them away. He did it, he actually proposed. I want to be mad at him for embarrassing me and doing the exact thing I said I didn't want. Also, for making me cry in public, but I can't after everything he said.

"Answer him!" a voice shouts from somewhere in the crowd.

"You're up, baby. You're one line."

The easiest thing I have ever said. "Yes."

The crowd cheers, and I think I see a few flashes go off, but I pay no attention. Ash places my ring back where it belongs, then picks me up and spins me around, exactly like a cheesy rom-com, and I love every single part of it. I wrap my legs around him, and he squeezes me tightly to him.

"I'm still pissed you did that," I hiss into his neck.

It vibrates against my lips with a deep belly laugh. "Be pissed, baby, but I just nailed that bloody proposal." He turns his face and traps my ear between his teeth. "Won't be the only thing I nail tonight either."

I can't help it, a laugh bubbles up inside me because leave it to him to mention sex right now. Most people have left, but there are still some watching us. "Please never change."

"Never, Jailbird."

I pull back and tilt my head. "You haven't been calling me that much lately."

"Do you miss it?"

I'm not admitting it out loud. But I don't need to because he knows I do. He kisses my forehead and lowers me back to the ground.

"Don't worry, you'll always be my jailbird, attempting to hide that little monitor from me. Seducing me and me caving, even when I knew it was illegal." His eyes sparkle, and he tips my chin so our lips can meet. "My little jailbird and soon-to-be wife."

33

JANELLE RUNS UP AND pulls Payson out of my arms. They jump around squealing even though she's been engaged for months, this is exactly what she needed. Whether she knows it or not. My pride booms knowing I caused that. My plan was to propose as a joke, but then I got down on my knee and the words just came out.

I got to thinking that Payson hasn't had many traditional things in her life, so I might as well start now.

Mum wanders up beside me, a tissue in her hand and dabbing at her face.

"Beautiful, Ashley. But you could have warned us, we had only just walked up when you got on your knee."

"Then you didn't miss anything."

She slaps the back of my head while squeezing me. "Nearly, and I would have made you do it again."

She would have, and if she didn't, Janelle would've.

Dad claps me on the back, and Henry congratulates me with a bro-hug. "You're doomed now, bro."

"Fuck off. Some of us actually want to settle down at some point in our lives." I ruffle his hair because I know he hates it, but I've been doing it since we were kids to piss him off. It's a tradition now.

"Aye." He swats my hands away, then straightens his suit and cufflinks. "Some of us enjoy the freedom of not being tied down."

This is a never-ending disagreement between us. He knows I've had that "freedom" for a long ass time. Eventually, the *freedom* feels less like freedom and more like a dead end. Hookups lead you nowhere, but with Payson, I have a whole future to look forward to. Something Henry doesn't understand, not anymore anyway. There was a point when I was the wild one and he was the respectable fiancé, seems like a lifetime ago now. But as he looks around the group, there's a distant look in his eye when he lands on a certain blonde. A look I haven't seen on his face in a long time.

I know what Payson said about keeping him away, and if I knew his intentions were to be a dickhead, I would agree, but something tells me maybe that's not his intention, at least not the only one. He's never argued with a woman like he does Janelle because he doesn't think they are worth his time.

I shake the thoughts from my head. I have my own relationship to worry about; I can't be in charge of Henry's too, that is up to him.

Payson's eyes close as she is hugged by my mum and dad, and my beating heart settles.

"You know, I'm not about all this shit, but"—a dusting of a smile relaxes his harsh features as he watches our parents hug my girl—"I think you made a good choice with that one."

"I know I did."

"Seems she might need this more than you." He glances in my direction.

"You have no idea." I've not told a soul about all of Payson's history, they know some, but not everything. Not even my mum, and I plan to keep it that way. She can tell whomever she pleases, and I'll be there to support her, but it's not my place.

"Can't wait for your Stag. It's going to be wild." He claps me on the back. "I'm thinking Zante."

I don't care that he is my best man, he's not getting the opportunity to plan my Stag. I don't know if we will do a Stag or Hen parties; the thought of Payson seeing a male stripper is not a nice one, and I can imagine she would feel the same about me and female strippers, given our past and her jealous tendencies.

Marriage to Payson isn't the end of anything I'm going to miss. I'm not celebrating my last day of freedom, I will be celebrating a future with my favorite person, and that can be done at our reception. She mentioned not having a wedding, but there's not a chance I'm missing out on seeing her in a wedding dress and fucking in the bathroom during our reception.

"Think about it," he says as he backs up toward our parents and Janelle.

Payson saunters my way, a huge smile on her face. "Think about what?"

I pull her against my body. "A Stag do."

"Huh?"

Right, American. "Bachelor party."

Her face screws up. I chuckle and kiss her forehead. "I had the same reaction. Don't worry, he's not planning it."

"Good because if there are strippers—"

I slant my mouth over hers, cutting her off. This isn't even something that needs to be chatted about.

"Come on, love birds! Time to celebrate!" Janelle shouts, and Payson pulls away. Her cheeks heat at the people around.

I tug on her hand, concealing my smirk at her embarrassment. "Come on, future Mrs. Pearson."

"I might keep my name, you know. That's becoming more popular."

Over my dead body. If she wants to hyphen, fine, we will discuss it, but Pearson will be somewhere in her name.

"How do you feel about purple, like a lavender? Oo! Or maybe sage dresses? The guys are wearing black? You know that blue is totally in right now. Blue would bring out Ash's eyes. But he has a warm undertone so brown would also look amazing. Oh my gosh, I was looking for inspiration and saw the cutest center pieces. Remind me to send them to you.

"Oh my gosh! What about your dress?" Janelle has been nonstop with the wedding talk since I proposed. It was about a ten-minute walk here, and since we've sat down. I'm not sure she has taken a breath. I appreciate her excitement, but with each passing moment, the excitement dwindles in Payson. I'm not sure what is eating her, but it's obvious, to me at least, that she's not in the wedding-planning mood. I would prefer we marry tomorrow, but I also don't want to rush her, *much*.

"Janelle." I keep my voice low.

She stops midsentence, her mouth hung open.

Without wanting to draw too much attention, I flick my eyes to Payson. She's not paying any attention. Her eyes are glassed over, and she's picking at her thumb.

Janelle's eyebrows knit with worry, and she places a hand over Payson's. "You okay?" she asks softly, but Payson quickly looks around the table, and her tanned cheeks pinken.

"Uh, yeah. I just, uh. What were you saying?"

"Um . . . I was asking what kind of dress you think you'll want."

I can't see Payson's face with her looking at Janelle, but her voice wobbles. "Oh, I haven't thought about it."

A heavy silence settles, and a pregnant pause later, Mum looks at me with a pinched face. She is on that side, so she can see Payson's face, meaning whatever is happening, isn't good.

"I, uh, need to use the bathroom." Her chair drags across the wooden floor and she stands.

"I'll come with." Janelle throws her napkin onto her place and stands, but Payson is already walking away.

"No, no I'll be right back."

I catch Janelle around the wrist, stopping her from following, and she frowns at my hand on hers.

"I'll do it."

"I didn't mean . . . I'm just excited."

"It's okay. You know how Payson is, she doesn't enjoy this kind of attention, that's all."

She slowly nods a few times and lowers back into her seat. Wanting to get to Payson as fast as I can, because I watched her head the opposite way of the bathroom, I shoot a *help me* look to Mum, who nods, understanding what I want.

"Can you tell us again what you are going to school for, Janelle?"

Thank God for my mum. I give Janelle's shoulder a quick squeeze because I don't want her feeling bad. I understand her excitement.

I think I saw Payson head toward the front doors, but when I break into the warm evening air, I don't see her. Like always, people crowd the streets, but there is a bigger crowd surrounding a street performer singing something by Queen. After a quick look around and getting nowhere, I head toward the crowd. She's short, it's not like I could easily see her, even at my height. I circle the crowd once and when I come up empty-handed, my blood pressure is through the bloody roof and I'm wondering if I missed her inside. Then my eyes catch on a head of curly brown hair and a sad face across from me.

Hurrying back around, I push through people until I'm directly behind her. She's unaware of my presence, lost in watching the performers. They are good, I see why she wandered over here. A guy on guitar and a woman singer. They are one of the best street performers I've heard in my time.

They start playing a new song I recognize as "Stand By Me," and I take the moment to wrap my arms around Payson. She jumps but looks down and must recognize my hands because she relaxes against my body.

I'm in no rush to move, and neither is she, so we stand like that through two more songs before she turns and hugs my center. The guy walks around with a cap flipped, and I dig in my wallet and drop a twenty in. I really should start carrying smaller notes.

I use their break as the perfect time to drag Payson back toward the restaurant but stop off to the side where no one is. She's refusing to look at me, and when I take her chin and tilt her head up, I see why.

She's crying.

Fuck.

"I'm sorry."

"Don't apologize. What's wrong?"

It's breaking my fucking heart seeing her crying like this. Crying on her proposal night, no less. If I knew what she was feeling, I would have never agreed to come here. We could have spent the rest of the night in our room, and if she needed to cry, she wouldn't be embarrassed because we are surrounded by people.

She keeps looking around at the people walking by, and knowing we are a tube ride from our hotel, I know I can't wait that long to talk. I crowd into her space, blocking anyone from seeing her.

She lets out a thankful sigh. "I'm sorry."

"What did I say, Jailbird?"

"Sor—I mean, okay."

I cup the side of her face. "Tell me what's making you cry."

"I miss my grandpa. Every day I pretend like he's back in Bayshore since I haven't been there to believe any different, but the only person I want to call right now is him, and he . . ."

"He'd so happy for you, babygirl. I know it."

"How do you know, though?" The sadness in her voice is fucking destroying me.

"Because no one wanted to see you happy more than him, and I like to believe I make you happy."

"You do. No one else makes me happier."

I take her hands in mine and bring them up to kiss each one. "Then he's happy."

"I know it's been months since it happened and you just proposed and I shouldn't be crying about my grandpa, but all I keep thinking about is how he won't be there. I never thought about my wedding, but I always thought if the time came, he would be there, no"—she shakes her head—"he would officiate it. That was always the plan but now." Her lips wobble and she slices her eyes to the side, avoiding me. Thankfully, because I don't want her to see how my eyes are watering. "Now, now what? Who is going to marry us? Who is going to walk me down the aisle?

"I have no one, Ash. I know you want a wedding, but your side is going to be full and I'm going to have to look into the audience and see my side empty."

Fuck. *Fuck*. I was so focused on her in a dress, I didn't think about the other stuff. But of course she did, and these are very legit and real worries for her.

"Hey." I clear my throat and force her eyes to mine. "We don't need to have a big wedding. Just you and me. If I remember correctly, Colorado doesn't require an officiate or witness."

But she's already shaking her head. "No, your mum would be so disappointed, and I think Janelle would end up crashing anyway." A sad smile graces her lips.

"My mum would understand, and we won't tell Janelle."

She snorts. "She would find out. Besides, I want you to have a wedding and everything that comes with it, you deserve that."

My selfless little Jailbird. If I could love her any more than I do, I would. "You breathing is the only thing I deserve. It's the only thing I need, okay? We don't need to think about the wedding for a good while. Okay?"

"Okay." She sucks in a breath and blows it out. Then again. And again.

"That something you learned at therapy?" I know it is, because Dr. Howard told me to do the same bloody thing when I get overwhelmed. Which I will not be doing. It's nice to see Payson listening to her therapist though.

"Yeah, he was pretty smart."

"He?" This is the first she's mentioned his gender.

She giggles, and even though I plan to ask more on *him* later, it's such a pleasant sound after seeing her cry.

"He was like, over fifty."

I level my stare and cock an eyebrow. "You realize how old I am, yes?"

"Yep. Twice my age."

Fucking hell, when she says it like that, it's worse. "Do you ever wish our gap wasn't so big?"

I brace myself for whatever she's going to say but she doesn't. Instead, she slips out from under my arms and grabs my hand, dragging me back into the restaurant.

"Are you not going to answer me?"

She shrugs, not bothering to look at me when she says, "No. Stupid questions don't deserve answers."

This girl. I've spent the entirety of the day, and more so recently, thinking—worrying about our gap and she's acting like it's not even a big deal. I guess that's her answer, she doesn't. I pull my free hand back before letting it crack onto her ass and enjoying the ripple and her yelp when I do.

"I'm so looking forward to having you on your knees with my dick in your throat, babygirl."

She shoots me a flirty smile over her shoulder, and I know she's looking forward to it too.

34
Payson

IS SOMEONE PLAYING THE drums or is that pounding coming from inside my head?

I look around but—wait, my eyes aren't even open and no matter how hard I try, I can't get them to open.

So slowly I move my hands until I touch something hot. Ow, what the—Ash. He runs like a furnace.

I poke whatever body part I'm touching. "Ash."

Something that sounds like an alligator dying comes from behind me.

"Asshh."

"Yeah?"

"I think I'm dying."

"You're hungover. Not dying, don't say that."

Hungover? Oh yeah. After we ate dinner, Ash's parents told us to go out, celebrate, have fun. So, we did. I guess. I actually can't remember much. I remember drinking . . . something. Ash had to go up and order since I'm not eighteen.

Janelle was there. Did she drink? Does she feel the same as me?

"Are you hungover?"

"Yes."

"What the hell did we drink?"

"Fuck knows. Everything."

I try and move but my body weighs a million pounds. Eyes first, then we will work on the rest.

Oh my God, it's so bright. "Ashhh," I whine. "Help, everything hurts, and I can't even open my eyes."

"Payson, I love you. But shh." Something heavy falls onto my face, not mouth, my entire face.

Wait, am I naked? I drag a heavy hand up my stomach, and yep, sure enough, I'm naked. "Are you naked?"

He groans and the bed under us squeaks. I think he's moving. "Yes."

"Did we have sex?"

His hand slips between us, I squirm away but he puts his fingers between my ass cheeks. "Stop it."

"Payson." I squirm more because I can't believe he wants to have sex right now.

"Payson."

He's inside me. When did that happen? I can feel the heaviness, but I don't remember him slipping it in.

"Ash, get your fingers out of me. Do you want me to throw up on you? Because I could."

"It's not my fingers."

Huh? I force my eyes open and cringe against the light to see both of his hands in the air.

"I think we fell asleep having sex . . . and my dick is still inside you."

"Did we at least finish."

"I do not know."

What the fuck. "Is it stuck?"

"No. I don't think so." A pause. "I do not know."

What if his dick is stuck? We will have to call an ambulance, or whatever they call them here, and everyone would know that his dick is stuck inside of me.

What if when they pull it out, my insides fall out?

What if they can't pull it out and they have to cut it off? Then my husband will be dickless. I love him for more than his dick . . . but his dick is really nice. That would be a huge bummer to lose.

"I'll love you even if you lose your dick."

"Do not even talk about that."

"If it's stuck—"

"It's not stuck." His hands drop to my ass, and he pushes. Not hard, but when he does, I fall to my stomach and the heaviness, that I now know what his dick, slips out. No insides fell out and he's not screaming, so I'm guessing it's still attached.

Unless he died. My head is like a cement block, but if he's dead, I need to know, so I force it that way and open one eye.

Ash is easily the hottest person I've ever seen in real life. I've never seen a single bad angle from him. Until right now.

His eyes aren't closed, or open, kind of in the middle, and his mouth is wide open. If his chest wasn't moving, I would assume he was dead, that's how bad he looks.

"It's nice to see you look like ass for once."

His mouth snaps shut and he scowls at nothing because he's still not looking at me—or anything. "Remember how nicely I asked you to be quiet?"

"Mhm."

"Yeah? Shut up."

My stomach shakes with a giggle, but I quickly stop because that hurts too. "I'm never drinking again."

"Everyone says the same but then the opportunity comes up to drink and you do, and then you promise you'll never drink again. It's a cycle that everyone must go through until death."

Fantastic.

I'm drifting back to sleep when the worst sound I've ever heard blares through the room. Groaning, I shove my knee into Ash's side until he grunts awake.

"Damn woman, what?"

"That noise." I nearly cry. "Make it stop."

"What noise?"

It happens again, and I bury my face deeper into the pillow.

"It's the phone."

"Answer it."

"It's on your side." He pokes at my side.

"Answer it!" I shout into the pillow and immediately regret it when the smell of my breath smacks me in the face. It's almost fruity, but the strong alcohol scent hits my stomach, and the nausea rolls.

Either the roof caved in or Ash rolled on top of me. Since I can feel something sitting perfectly between my ass cheeks, I think it's Ash.

"What?" He barks at . . . something. Oh, the phone, that's right.

"No—did you still want to go on the bus tour?"

"Oo!" I whip my head up only to smack into something equally as hard. I'm guessing Ash since he is cursing up a storm behind me.

When his weight leaves, it takes everything inside of me to push onto my hands and knees. Ash lies on his back, the phone now discarded onto the floor, and he's holding his nose.

Not wanting whoever is on the phone to hang up, I lie on top of him and grab it. He grunts at my weight, and I scowl at him. I'm not that heavy.

"Hello?"

"Payson? Everything okay in there?" William, I think, asks.

Ash groans, and now that both my eyes are open, I can see the blood. *Shit.* "Yeah, we're good."

"Uh-huh. Well, the bus tour is starting soon if you still wanted to go."

"Yes, I do!"

Ash reaches for the phone while shaking his head, but I slip off the bed, stopping him from grabbing it.

"Brilliant. If you two would like to get ready, we will meet in the hotel café in an hour."

"Payson, no," Ash growls.

"Perfect." I smile and say goodbye before letting the phone drop to the floor.

"You're a pain in my ass." The bed squeaks as he rolls to the opposite side of the bed, and after a couple seconds, he pushes onto his feet. I drop my eyes to his ass, and a giggle rips out from my lips.

"What?" He stops his stumbling to glare at me over his shoulder.

His hair is a mess, his face and chest are covered in blood, and Pays-n's pr-perty is written across his ass in black marker, upside down—and the missing o's are where his crack is. I completely lose it and fall to my side, laughing until my sides hurt. I don't know how long he leaves me on the floor but eventually, I'm hauled over his shoulder, and after my uneasy stomach settles, I burst out laughing again. Now reading my writing right side up.

My ass burns when he spanks me, but I still can't stop laughing. My stomach hurts, but I don't know if it's from laughing or from his big shoulder digging into it.

He drops me into the hotel tub with a thud.

"Owww, my ass."

He leans over and flicks on the water, freezing cold pelts at my front.

I scream and he laughs. I fill my hands with water and throw it at him as he pisses in the toilet.

"You're making a mess, stop it."

"Don't be a dick!"

He narrows his eyes. "Stop laughing at me."

His ass is to a mirror, and I start to giggle again. He follows my eyes behind him. It takes a second but eventually his eyes drop to where I'm looking and his jaw locks. "Your ass is getting fucked tonight, princess."

Promises, promises.

"That's it?" My eyebrows inch up my forehead. *This* is the Buckingham Palace? It's so . . . boring. "Big Ben is more impressive."

I turn to Ash's family. Each one of them is doing their best not to laugh, but I don't know why, it's true.

"It looks like a library."

William is the first one to break, and one by one, they fall into a fit of laughter.

"Easy, babygirl. You'll offend the king."

William grunts something under his breath that earns him a slap to the chest from his wife.

Beverly herds us into a group in front of one of the gates. She insists on taking photos at every stop. The poor lady she suckered into taking our photo stands a few feet in front of us, ready to snap a photo.

"Everyone say, Henry is more impressive than the castle."

No one says that.

I have a brother, but Henry is like the older brother I never had. He's never serious and picks on me constantly. I pretend to be annoyed, but secretly, I'm glad he treats me like family. All of Ash's family has accepted me as their own, besides one. I heard William and Beverly murmuring about Grace the days after she stormed out. I think they were trying to call her, but besides that moment, no one has mentioned her. I can't say for sure, but I think it's bothering Beverly that she's not here.

"We will have to Photoshop Janelle into these," Beverly says while scrolling through the photos we've taken so far on her phone.

I giggle to myself. Janelle refused to get out of bed for "a stupid bus ride" when I knocked on her door this morning. I would blame the hangover, but I think she's just avoiding the bus tour, and I'm sure she will be fresh as a daisy come the fancy dinner tonight. I've never heard of the place, but when Beverly mentioned it last night—before we were all drunk out of our mind—Janelle gasped like she'd been told we were going to Disney World.

The bus tour has been amazing so far. It'd be better if my head wasn't thumping, but that's not the tour's fault. We started in the museum, which Ash claimed made his headache worse, but he was just being a baby. I saw how interested he looked during some parts.

Since we didn't make it to the souvenir shop last night, thanks to my impromptu proposal, Beverly made sure we stopped at three today. I have a whole bag of stuff and a brand-new sweatshirt. Ash made me promise I wouldn't wear it while in the UK. Apparently, he doesn't want me making him look like a tourist, which I think is a lost cause, especially when I speak. At least I'm not the only one with an accent around, I've heard so many languages since we've been out.

I will admit, by the time we are heading back to the subways to get ready for dinner, I'm dog-tired. I didn't think the tour would be so long, but holy, was it long. Basically the entire day. We got off at nearly every stop, much to Henry's and Ash's dismay. When they are together, it's so easy to imagine them as two whiny children because that's exactly how they act.

These past two days have been the busiest I've probably ever had, and all I want to do is curl up and sleep for the next two hours. We have four until dinner, and since I don't take that long to get ready, that's exactly what I plan to do.

Apparently, Ash has a different idea on how we will pass our time.

35
Payson

"ON YOUR KNEES, BABYGIRL."

I swallow hard. "Ash, I'm tired."

"You should have thought about that before you wrote 'Payson's Property' on my ass."

I have to bite my lip to stop myself from laughing again. "I was drunk!"

He flips the lock on our door without taking his eyes off me. "It doesn't matter."

"You have to admit using your asshole as the o is so funny."

His lips twitch but he doesn't let it surface. "Not as funny as it will be when I use *your* asshole how *I* please."

Last time he used my ass how he pleased, my mind let me believe it was Fred behind me and I blacked out. That was the first day Ash cut me.

He prowls forward and places his hand on my shoulder, then shoves me to the ground and hooks my chin so I'm forced to look at him. Since I woke up from my coma, sex with Ash has been gentle, loving, good—but right now, I'm getting a look at the Ash before, and it's bringing up old feelings. Good feelings, like so good my pussy grows wet with the thought of what's to come.

"Fuck, seeing you on your knees again makes my dick fucking hard."

His words cause a shiver to rack my spine. "Seeing you like this makes me wet."

His eyes roll and he growls. "Show me."

I make haste stripping and tossing my clothes away. Back on my knees, I drag my hand seductively over my body until I reach the v between my legs. His eyes are so hot watching me. I put on a little show, spreading my legs and moaning when my finger slips past my opening.

"I said show me, not play with yourself." Ash wraps his hand around my wrist and lifts it into the air. The sun peering in through the window glistens off the tips of my fingers.

A groans rumbles from deep inside of him as he bends down and wraps his hot tongue around my fingers and sucks.

"I love watching you taste me."

He sucks up the rest and pulls away, pushing back to his full height. "Take me out, return the favor, babygirl."

"Yes, Daddy."

We freeze as the word dances around the room. I can't get a read on his thoughts, but his jaw is locked tight. My ears burn with uncertainty. We haven't talked about not using that word, but I think we both came to our own conclusions it's not healthy. Probably should have voiced our opinions, but now it's out there.

"I'm so—"

"Hurry up, babygirl. Daddy's waiting to have his dick sucked."

A relieved breath blows past my lips. I eye him for a second longer, making sure he is actually okay with this and not just amusing me.

His eyes soften, and he cups my face. "Even the healthiest of people have their weaknesses. You calling me daddy is mine."

Thank God.

"We can go back to being healthy versions of ourselves tomorrow." He bends at the waist and gets in my face, but he doesn't kiss me.

"Tomorrow you can go back to being my future wife. Tonight, I'm going to treat you like my dirty little slut while you scream for your *daddy*."

Ash

Payson's throat is like a fucking hoover. I don't know if it's because we agreed to throw all our therapy to the wind for one night, or what, but she's had my dick in her mouth for two minutes and my balls are already tingling with the need to come.

With eyes half-mast, a dick in her throat, and spit dripping from her chin—she looks like a bloody masterpiece.

I bury my hand in her hair and squeeze. Her eyes pinch shut, but she doesn't stop sucking.

Fucking hell. "You suck me so good, Jailbird."

Her eyes blaze with that nickname as she works her hand around my shaft harder, tighter, and—

"I'm going to come, babygirl. Open that throat nice and wide."

I push as far as I can, and she sputters around me. With the fluttering of her throat, I come fucking hard.

"Take it all. Take all of daddy's cum like the good girl you are."

With my balls empty, I pull out of her mouth. She falls forward, hands out in front of her, coughing, and I head to the bathroom to grab a few things I will need.

She's still on the floor when I come back but she's finished choking. She lifts her head after hearing the thud of the bottle I set on the nightstand.

"What is that?" Her voice is hoarse, and if I hadn't come thirty seconds ago, it would make me hard knowing I did that.

"Lube."

"Uh, for what?"

"Anal."

She scrambles to her feet, wobbling but steadies herself on the bed. "I don't think I'm ready for that again."

"I will make you ready."

She licks her lips while her eyes dance from me to the lube and stack of towels. "Ash."

I lift a single eyebrow.

"Daddy." Her embarrassment when she's not full in the mood when she says that is bloody intoxicating. "I don't want. . ." She pushes out a hard breath. "I don't want what happened last time to happen this time."

Me either. "It won't."

"How do you know?"

"Because I am prepared this time. I should have never taken your ass the way I did for the first time. I apologize, and I promise you will enjoy it."

Unsure, she twists her lips into the cutest worried pout.

I walk around the bed, and she turns so I'm able to step between her legs. Her eyes fall to my half-flaccid dick. "It's soft."

"I just came," I deadpan. "I need a few minutes."

"Because you're old?"

"Be nice." I squint. "The integrity of your asshole depends on you and your smart mouth, babygirl."

She crawls back onto the bed, crossing her legs, but I am quick to uncross and settle between them, my head level with her pussy. Payson's pussy is fucking beautiful. Especially when she's wet like she is right now. I lean forward and suck in a huge breath through my nose. Her headiness pulls me closer, and I lazily lap my tongue around her pussy, not focusing on any certain area.

Once she's wet enough, I slip two fingers inside her and curl them up.

She moans the sexiest little sound. Making sure not to stop my slow thrusting, I reach over and grab the lube. Keeping my eyes on her, I pull the butt plug from my pocket. First sliding it through her folds, and she gasps at the cool metal touching her.

"What is that?" Her voice is breathless.

I hold it up, twirling it between two fingers so she can see all the sides, including the blue diamond top.

Her eyes round, and her mouth pops open. "That's meant to go in my ass?"

"Mhm. Trust me?"

She takes longer than I'd like to reply, but I think it's because she's nervous. At least that's what I'm choosing to believe.

"Yes."

"Good. Scoot your ass down and spread your legs, wide."

She's shaky, so I don't attempt it right away. Dropping my head between her legs again, I get her worked up, so her head drops back. Her back arches, pushing her beautiful tits into the air. My hands are preoccupied or I would grab one.

My dick is once again full mast and ready to feel her tight walls. I reach for the lube and squirt a bunch on the plug before running it through her own wetness and smearing it on her puckered ass. She squirms when my fingers press, but I hold her close.

"Relax, babygirl."

She settles but keeps her eyes closed. With a hand flat on her stomach, I use the other to slowly push the tip of the plug into her.

"Ash," she whines. It's not a painful whine, she's scared. If I want Payson to like this, I need her to relax, and what's the best way to get my girl to relax? Dirty words spoken by her daddy.

I reposition us with me behind her and her body half on me, half on the bed so I'm still able to reach every part of her.

The power imbalance between us is one of my deepest desires; Payson being naked while I am still dressed, teases that need. I play with her pussy long enough to work her up again, then I lift her leg and wrap it around me, opening her to the room, and I slip the plug between us, not entering, simply teasing her hole. She's plenty wet enough between the lube and her natural wetness, she just needs to relax.

"You're so wet for Daddy, babygirl." I tug her earlobe into my mouth and breathe harder, knowing she loves it. Her back arches, and she pushes on the plug.

Such a good girl.

"You make me so proud when you open your legs for me."

"Yes, Daddy." Her voice shoots straight to my dick, now probing her.

"You going to be a dirty little slut for me and take my big dick up your ass, baby?"

She whimpers, and the animal inside me loses his fucking mind, clawing at the surface, begging to break free.

The plug is basically inside of her, so I push more, meeting her thrusts until it's seated inside. Her hips shake and she whimpers louder.

"Oh, fuck."

"That's my girl. Does it feel good?"

She turns her head and wraps her arm around the back of mine until our lips are touching. "Yes, Daddy," she pants.

I roll my hips with hers, not yet inside but letting her get used to her ass being filled before I enter her pussy. I can already tell this time is going better than the last. One, she's moaning and not crying, and two, she's rocking her hips, already craving an orgasm. Her trying to get herself off without me seated inside of her is simply not going to happen.

I grip her soft hips, hard, halting all movements.

She lets out an exasperated breath and fights against me.

"You're not going to come without my dick inside of you. I was going to fuck your pussy first, let you get used to the plug, but if you are that greedy for your ass to be filled. . ."

"Please, Daddy."

I drag my nose up her jaw and kiss her throat, leaving behind a love bite I know she will complain about later. "Tell me what you want, baby. Be specific."

I lick up her throat, tasting the slight saltiness from the day.

"Fuck my ass." Her words are so quiet I almost don't hear her over her thumping pulse. *Almost.*

I grab the lube, apply it to me before slowly pulling the plug out, and lube her ass again. Aside from the time I made her squirt, I've never seen her this wet, so I don't know if lube is necessary, but I am taking every precaution this time.

My head slips in, and we both hiss. Fuck, she's wet but she's *tight*. "Relax so I can slip it in."

Wild eyes meet mine filled with needy lust—and worry.

I run a hand down her face, hoping to soothe her. "Trust me, babygirl."

She nods, and her legs fall open. I pull out and roll her hips up before slipping back in. Inch by inch, she takes all of me until I'm completely settled inside the most intimate part of her.

Fucking. Hell. Her pussy is gold, and her ass is fucking diamonds.

"Good girl. Good fucking girl taking all of daddy's dick in your ass. Look how you take me, Payson."

I pull her to sit just enough she can watch the beautiful sight. Her ass clamps and I grunt.

"Your ass is so greedy for daddy's dick, isn't it, baby?"

She gasps, and I fuck her harder. Relaxed now, she takes every thrust I give her, and even meets a few. Her moans are loud, and if my parents' room wasn't on a different floor, I'd have to cover her mouth.

I know when she comes because her ass squeezes me hard, and I fall after her. Moans, skin slapping, and our heavy breathing fills the room until we're both drained, figuratively and literally.

I drop on top of her, still cradling her head so I don't actually crush her, and place a kiss to her swollen lips.

"That was amazing," she says.

I grin, feeling proud and satisfied.

"Trust me, babygirl, Daddy will always make it feel amazing."

36
Payson

"I AM NOT WEARING that to dinner, Ashley." I place my hand on my hips, they're still damp as my hair continues to drip water from our shower. What the hell is he thinking telling me I will wear a butt plug to a fancy dinner with his parents?

"You misunderstood." Did I? His normal cocky glint in his eye sparkles. "I wasn't asking. Now we can do this the easy way and you can bend over, stick that ass nice and high, and let me place it inside of you. Or—" He licks his lips and its obvious which option he is wanting. "I can pin you down and force you to take it."

I don't move, keeping my stubborn stance even though my legs are wobbling. I hope he can't see that.

His eyes blaze, and he bites the corner of his mouth. "Very well."

He steps forward and I step back. In one movement, he has me around the waist and bends me over his knee. No matter how much I struggle, he doesn't let up. I'm upside down and can't see what he's doing, but cool air breezes across my ass, then he spanks me, and I nearly cry at how much I've missed this side of him.

See, there's no reason we can't have both versions. Anal was fucking amazing, no hallucinating, no crying. It was good. Amazing—mind-blowing is more like it.

"Stop it, please!" I beg, but when he pushes, I arch. The want inside quickly turns to need.

His chuckle is low and mocking. "Such a good little slut who likes things up her ass."

He lets me up, and I shuffle a few times, getting used to the feeling. It's good, not great, more like pressure than pleasure, but I like it. I like that he is the only one who will know I have a plug up my ass. Like a dirty secret between us.

"Turn around and let me see."

I listen, only because I want to see the way his eyes roll when I bend over.

"Fucking beautiful." He growls when I do.

I shake my ass in his face, loving how he is watching me. He drags his tongue over his bottom lips, slowly, seductively, then his eyes flick to mine.

"Keep it up and I'll be having your ass as my dinner."

As much as I think I would now enjoy that, if we don't show up, I know people would come looking for us, and I do not want to get caught with Ash's face in my ass by his mom or dad. Well, by anyone—but especially them.

"I need to see if Henry has a tie I can borrow. Will you be okay?"

Always a worrier. "Yes, I'm fine."

He presses a kiss to my forehead. "I'll be right back."

The door clicks behind him, and I fall back onto the bed. The plug in my ass makes me shift, but eventually, I'm able to just lie here and think without worrying about my asshole's integrity.

So many things come to mind. And I get lost in them until a heavy weight comes down on top of me. His familiar scent stirring a deep feeling in my lower belly. I shouldn't be horny, but Ash has always had that effect on me. I wonder if he always will or if eventually, we won't feel the need to rip our clothes off as soon as we are alone. I hope the feeling never goes away.

"Did you get your tie?"

"I did."

My body erupts in goose bumps as he nips at my neck. "You need to get dressed because I am certainly not letting you out of this room naked."

Exhaustion from the late night last night is taking over. "Give me like five minutes."

If he continues kissing, biting, and licking me the way he is, I will not mind if we miss out on a fancy dinner with his family. His mom was so excited about it earlier today, and I'd like at least one female in his family to continue to like me.

I push up so I'm sitting. Ash follows, still not letting up on his kisses.

"Do you think Grace is going to be upset that she isn't there?"

He pauses, groans, and pulls away. "Let's not ever mention my sister when I am ravishing your body. Okay?" He rolls his eyes and sighs. "But maybe. Grace did it to herself the moment she raised her voice at you. I don't care if she's upset."

"I think it bothers your mom though, she seemed to miss her today."

Ash sighs and presses a deep kiss to my forehead. "You care too deeply sometimes, Jailbird. I love it about you, but sometimes, you can't care. Grace acted like a cunt and yelled at my girl. I need time to get over it before I see her again."

Why must he always be so annoyingly sweet?

37

Ash

PAYSON SEEMS JUST AS surprised when we walk into the restaurant and Jethro is sitting at our table with his arms crossed over his chest.

"Why is he pissy now?" I ask her.

Her throat bobs before her face shifts from surprise to something like a child who knows they are about to be reamed. "Uh, probably because I didn't tell him we were coming here."

"Here, as in . . .?"

"England."

Fuck *me*. I bet he will be a dick about it and blame me. For once, I'm innocent in this whole thing. I won't throw her under the bus, though. I don't care if he hates me, but I know she cares about him. Unfortunately.

"Uncle Jet." Payson's voice is wary when she stops in front of him, but his eyes are locked onto me.

"Nice to see you too," I grumble before pulling out Payson's chair, then my own and falling into it.

"Took you long enough, big guy." Janelle slaps his shoulder on her way to her seat, but he pays her no attention, still glaring at me. Maybe he is used to intimidating people this way, but it affects me less than none. "I'm surprised you weren't here when we landed."

"Me too," Payson squeaks. "I kind of thought Blue Gate would have called you."

"They did."

Her mouth snaps shut, and she lowers her eyes to the table in front of her. I fucking hate how he is making her feel. Standing, I mock his stance with my own.

"She's been with me the entire time. Safe. So, you can either sit down and enjoy a nice meal, or you can leave, but I won't have Payson cowering all of dinner because her uncle is a dick."

Anger, and maybe even some respect, burns in his eyes, then he lowers himself into the seat across from us.

"I knew the moment you left," he says. "I knew where you were going, and I let you be. Until"—he shoots a disapproving look in my direction—"you proposed publicly."

"You saw?" Payson gasps.

He gives her a curt nod. "Yes. Now I'm wondering why Ashley didn't contact me first."

"Excuse me?"

"To get my permission."

I think Janelle is the first to snort, but then Payson giggles by my side, and I snap a look at her. *This is not funny.*

"I'm not bloody asking permission."

"Well, I'm not giving it." He challenges.

He cannot be serious. Even if he is, I don't fucking care. I do not need permission to marry Payson from anyone. If Paul were here, sure, I would ask, but even if he said no, I think I would still do what I want. Throw caution to the wind and all that. I'm marrying Payson Murphy one day, either people accept it, or they don't, it makes no difference to me.

"I've been wearing the ring for a while, Uncle Jet. That was just a public proposal. It's not a big deal."

Finally, he drags his eyes from me and turns to her. Something like love, Jethro's version of it anyway, warms his face when he looks to his niece. I kind of hate that he is the family member she clung to after everything. He's just such a dick. I know she says she can see us becoming friends, but I do not see that happening anytime soon.

He leans forward and lowers his voice. "It doesn't mean I wouldn't have liked to be a part of it."

Payson's lower lips puffs out, her hands come together, and she picks at the skin on her thumb. "I didn't know you'd want to."

Neither did I. I knew he cared about Payson, but it seems they are closer than I thought. *Great.*

"Invite me to the wedding."

"We're not—" But Payson cuts me off.

She lays a soft hand on my lap, a new almost excited look in her eye that I don't understand. A faint smile pulling on her lips, then she turns to her uncle.

"Actually, I have a better idea. Think you'd want to walk me down the aisle?"

My mouth drops, as does Janelle's, and Jethro's parts. He is quick to snap it shut, and his jaw works overtime. Then, he dips his chin. "I would be honored."

They share a smile, or she smiles and he doesn't scowl, at least, but then she settles back into her chair and leans into my open chest.

"I thought you didn't want a wedding."

She turns her head to look up at me, a new softness in her eyes. There was one point I looked into Payson's eyes and saw only sadness. It's still there, as I'm not sure it will ever go away. But more prominent now is ease, peacefulness, and it has to be my favorite look yet.

"His daughter is a bitch; I doubt she will ever get anyone to agree to marry her."

He's busy chatting with Dad, so he doesn't hear, but when I bark out a laugh, he glances our way and rolls his eyes.

I drop a kiss to her forehead. "Fuck, I love you."

She doesn't reply, and when I look down, I know why. She's looking at something over our shoulders. "Uh, remember that. Okay?"

What—

"Gracey," Mum cries. My spine steels, and Payson sits up but keeps her hand on my lap.

"I invited her. Please be nice."

"When?" I growl. When would she have had the time?

"When you were getting ready. That's why I asked to have dinner pushed back, give them enough time."

Grace stops on the edge of the table, next to Payson, and looks down at her. I can see the apology before she even says it, but I'm still not happy. She can apologize until she's blue in the face, but I saw the look on Payson's face after she yelled at her. Knowing my sister, my own flesh and blood, caused that look of embarrassment and discomfort doesn't sit right.

"Thank you for inviting me." Grace places a wary hand on Payson's shoulder. I can't see her face, but her cheeks round as if she is smiling. How Payson forgives so easily after everything, I'll never understand. "I am sorry for the way I acted the other night. I have no excuse."

"Do you mind if we speak alone for a moment?"

Grace agrees, and before I know what is happening, Payson stands and walks away with my sister. I could smirk because Payson is walking different than normal, and I know why, but what the fuck is going on?

Will falls into Payson's seat and turns to me after our girls disappear out the door.

"Grace was surprised when Payson called."

"Her and me both." My jaw locks.

"Did you not know?"

I shake my head. Why would she invite her? Because my mum might have hinted that she wishes Grace were here? That doesn't seem like a good enough reason. But I guess that is the issue. To me, it's not, but Payson isn't me. She's not selfish, she's caring and simply wants everyone to get along. I wonder if that goes back to her childhood. Maybe the arguing scares her. This is something we will need to work through for her sake. We don't argue a lot, but me and my siblings are known to get pissed at each other, ignore it for a few days, and come back together like nothing happened. Maybe it's not something Payson needs to work through but me.

Fuck, I hate therapy. It has me thinking about a deeper meaning to everything.

Families fight, that's just want happens. But in Payson's family, it wasn't just an argument, it was abuse in more ways than one.

"You got yourself a good one, Ashley." Will slaps my shoulder before standing and moving to an empty seat.

I stare back at the doors they walked through knowing just how true that statement is.

It takes longer than I like, but eventually, the door opens and Payson saunters through, with the small train of her tight sexy black dress trailing behind her. The neckline dips low enough to show off a classy amount of cleavage. Her hair is down in her natural wave, a light amount of makeup, and she is easily the most beautiful woman to ever grace this place.

I stand and meet her halfway, only to steer her back outside with a hand on her ass.

"Where are we going?"

I lead her to the side of the second floor where I know there is a balcony. We're not alone but enough. I turn and pin her against the side of the building, crowding her space so the only thing she can see, think, or hear is me.

"That was a naughty thing you did, not listening to me and inviting Grace."

She looks up to me and licks her lips, already anticipating whatever I will throw at her. I press a gentle kiss to her lips, and she sags against me.

"Thank you," I mutter while still kissing her full lips. I'm glad she isn't wearing lipstick, just a simple gloss.

"Are you thanking me for being naughty?"

This girl. I nip at her lip and pull away just enough to drop my forehead to hers. "Yes. Do not get used to it."

She giggles the sweetest sound and wraps her arms around my neck. "Your sister was worried about my age, and the possibility of me being a gold digger, but I think I helped."

I'm sure she was. "Your age?" I pull back, forcing a look of confusion. "Why? It's my favorite part."

Payson's big eyes pop open, then she scowls. A laugh bubbles in my chest, but I don't let it out. "You don't mean that."

"Oh, but I do. Young." I kiss her cheek. "Innocent." Move over and kiss her nose before hovering over her lips. "Forbidden pussy." I make a groaning sound deep in my throat. "Irresistible."

She turns her head, and my lips connect with her cheek instead of her lips. I try and hold my grin off, but it comes out anyway, and she swats at my chest.

"I was rethinking our entire relationship, Ashley Pearson. Don't you do that to me ever again."

She shoves me away and storms to the doors. "I cannot believe you right now." She throws it open, but I wrap my hand around the back of her neck and tug her back into my arms, facing me.

"While your innocence is one of the things that my darker side relishes in." Her scowl deepens. "Your heart has to be my absolute favorite part about you. First broken, now bandaged, but not quite healed. A journey so beautiful it hurts." I poke her cute button nose. "Just like you."

Again, she swats at my hand. "You are being so cheesy lately. I don't know if I like it."

She does. She loves it and she knows it.

"Get used to it, babygirl. You have a lot of years to deal with my *cheesiness*."

She chews on her lip, and I bring my thumb up to drag over the newly wet area. "Years is a long time, are you sure you'll still love me when I'm not jailbait." Her voice is sassy and makes me smirk.

"I will probably love you more when there is not the risk of my arrest any time I touch you."

She turns, grabbing the door again, and this time I let her go and prowl after her. "Somehow, I think you like the risk."

This girl knows me too well.

"Maybe. But there are other risks we can take after your birthday." I glance down to her swinging ass and watch as embarrassment creeps up her neck when she remembers what is planted inside of her right now.

"I can't wait."

Me either.

38
Payson

Months later. . .

I WAKE WITH AN intense pressure between my legs. My eyes flutter open to find Ash guiding his dick in and out of me painfully slow.

"Happy Birthday, Jailbird."

I stretch my arms above my head and wrap them around his body, tugging him down so his entire weight is on me. "You can't call me that anymore. I'm no longer jailbait."

He nips at the side of my face. "You're always going to be jailbait for me, little girl. Every day I struggle to not lock you up in my basement and throw away the key."

So romantic.

I giggle and push on his chest so I can climb on top. Facing away from him, he slips back inside me with ease. Ever since he showed me this position, it's been my new favorite. I love how he watches me take him so intently.

He reaches across the bed toward nightstand, and my stomach clenches. I also love when he does *this*.

"Arch that back, baby. Stick your ass nice and high for daddy."

He teases my opening with the lubed butt plug. I'm embarrassed to admit since the last time we did anal, I've begged for it on a handful of occasions. Sometimes Ash fucks me, and sometimes he uses the plug to satisfy the need to be filled *there*.

It slips in, and I let out a shuttering breath and a whimper.

He drags his big hand down my back in a loving way, then lands on my ass. "Fucking you from behind is such a beautiful fucking sight, you would think it was my birthday."

"Not yet." I smile over my shoulder. "But I can't wait to show you what I got you for yours."

He bucks his hips and grips mine. "If it's anything remotely similar to this, turning thirty-four isn't going to be as bad as I think."

Ash is so worried about getting older. The other night we were having dinner with Uncle Jet to celebrate my birthday, and Ash had a bit too much to drink and was going on about how getting older is a trap and other crazy things. I didn't expect age to be his weakness, but everyone has to have one. Even the great Ashley Pearson.

"It just might be." Ash's gift actually hasn't come yet, and I'm just praying it fits. I ordered some lingerie and some edible underwear. Ash doesn't want many things, and anything he could want, he buys himself. The one thing I know he always wants—is me. I might as well wrap myself up like a gift.

The sun beats down on what's not blocked by the surrounding trees. It's finally starting to cool down, but today is one of the nicest days we've had recently.

And I think I know why.

"Look for me in the sun."

I glance down at the card from Grandpa that Ash had sent me so many months ago. I didn't know it at the time, but Grandpa gave Ash a few cards to give me on my important days. Knowing he thought about me during his most difficult time is the only thing keeping me afloat today. Maybe most people wouldn't want to spend their birthday at a cemetery, but Grandpa has never missed a birthday before, and I don't want to start now.

Ash pulls up next to a familiar headstone. Everything inside me crumbles reading the newly engraved death date next to his birthday that's been there since we buried Nana.

My two favorite people, buried under one stone. At least they are finally reunited; I just wish it didn't hurt so much.

"I don't know if I can do this."

Ash wraps his arm around my body and tugs me across the bench seat, so I'm pressed to his side. "We can sit here all day without leaving the truck. As long as you need, babygirl. It's your day, and I'm here for you, and if you want to go out for lunch instead, we can do that as well."

Tears pour from my eyes, down my cheeks, and onto my lap when I look down at the second envelope in my hand.

The sun peaks through Ash's windshield, highlighting the stark white envelope. *I see you Grandpa, I see you.*

Ray-Ray

Happy Birthday, my sweet granddaughter. Eighteen! I can't believe it. It seems like just yesterday I held you in my arms for the first time. You were so small back then. Now you are a beautiful woman. I'm not there to see you, but I hope you can feel my love all around.

A lot of things change now that you are eighteen. I hope one of those things is your capability to love.

Sometimes those we fall in love with don't fit the mold of the world. Don't be ashamed of it. Love is beautiful, and the best love is unexpected. God's greatest gift is the gift of love.

So, break the mold, sweetheart. Love who you love and <u>be happy</u>.

I believe Ashley will care for you the way you should be cared for. He will love and cherish you because I warned him what happens if he doesn't. (Hell. I'm kidding of course, but what he doesn't know can't hurt him. A little fear might do him good.)

I look up and meet Ash's watery eyes, and we smile.

"Your grandad was a smart man."

I drop my head on his chest to continue reading the last small bit.

Enjoy your day today a little more than every other day. And remember, look for me in the sun, because I'm there.

I love you. Eat a piece of cake for me.

Ash shifts, leans over me to the cooler at my feet that he packed a picnic in. Or so I thought. He pulls out a cake identical to the cakes Grandpa would get me every year. My throat closes.

"The bakery remembered your grandad's order. I hope it tastes the same."

Big tears burst from my eyes; Ash is smart enough to set the cake on the dash before I crush it from climbing onto his lap. I bury my face in his chest and let out shaky breaths.

"I can't believe you did all this for me." Ash has gone above and beyond for me since he walked into my life. I keep waiting for the day he stops, but he hasn't yet.

He squeezes me tightly. "You and me, babygirl. Remember? I would move mountains for you."

I pull back, grab each side of his face. "I love you so much, Ashley Pearson. And I can't wait to marry you."

We officially set a date. Well, we always had a date, but it's officially official now. Invites will go out after the volleyball season when Ash is not my coach anymore. Uncle Jet had to pull some strings, basically get Ash fired from the school and hired as a private coach so he wouldn't get in trouble for our relationship. The photos from our engagement started getting around a few weeks ago, given Ash is sorta famous and all, *which I forget often.* Thankfully, none of the news articles that got ahold of the photos had my face in them and weren't able to look me—or my age—up.

Our timeline is dicey, and sometimes I have panic attacks worrying about Ash getting in trouble and taken from me. He always promises he's not going anywhere, which helps, but knowing I have Uncle Jet and Ash's family of lawyers on my side if anything does happen, helps a bit more.

Everything is mostly planned for a small wedding in his parents' backyard next April. Thanks to his mom, sister, and Janelle. I've approved decisions, but I know they enjoy this stuff more than I do, so I am letting them have creative freedom. The one thing I get to pick is my dress, which I plan to go shopping for during Christmas break. Uncle Jet offered to fly me to London to shop—as if I would ever turn down that offer. I'm not a big shopper, but shopping in London is going to be so fun. Janelle and Abby are coming along as well, and I can't wait to see Abby again. We keep in contact via video calls and texts, she's even joined a chat with me and Janelle and that chat is constantly blowing up; I often come back to over three hundred messages because those two are chatty. Uncle Jet asked if I wanted to invite anyone else, I think he was hinting at Ronni, but the answer was and still is no. I don't know what ever happened to our relationship, but I am trying not to focus on the past. It hurts, and it hurts more because I thought we were better friends than what we are, but sometimes people come into your life who aren't meant to be there forever, and that's okay. I just never considered Ronni would be one of those people.

"Do you think he would be proud of me? Like really?"

"If I know anything, it's that Paul was beyond proud of you, Payson."

I was able to work up the courage and move from the truck to a blanket on my grandparents' grave. I tilt my head up against his chest, and he kisses my nose.

"I wish I could talk to him, both of them, honestly. I feel like it's been so long." It's only been months since I lost my grandpa. The wound is still so fresh, but from that moment I watched him die, to sitting in my fiancé's arms right now, it feels like it's been years. I'm a much different person than I was back then. Do I have bad days? Of course, I think everyone does. Days when Uncle Jet or Ash have to keep a closer eye on me than normal, yes. But healing isn't a destination, it's a journey. One that I will probably be on my entire life. Thankfully, I have Ash to walk with me during it all.

"I never told him I loved him."

"He knew."

Maybe, but that may be my biggest life regret.

A few hours and pieces of cake later, I sit up from Ash's chest, ready to move on with the rest of my day. There's a heaviness in my chest, this is the first time I've actually said goodbye.

He might not be here in front of me, but this is the last worldly connection I have to him. I kiss two of my fingers and press them to the cool stone.

"I love you." My voice is a whisper. Just then a single cloud passes over the sun and I imagine it's my grandpa winking.

A huge smile splits across my face, and I look back at Ash. He's smiling too.

"Told you."

"Are you ready for volleyball to start?" Ash glances my way from his side of the truck.

"Yes, I'm ready to get back to normal. This summer—no, year, has been a whirlwind of emotions and just a lot. It'll be nice to only be a high school volleyball player"—I shoot him a sideways glance—"at least for the next few months."

He squeezes my thigh in his hand. "I agree."

Ash has it in his mind that when the season starts, we will take a break while we are at practice. Pretending to be only coach and player and *not* engaged. "*No more sex in his office,*" he said. I snorted then and I could snort now. We both know he is going to be the first one to break on that.

When he mentioned wanting to let me focus on just playing for a while, I asked if he was going to start wearing a condom because a baby would really affect my '*just playing.*' The next day he had birth control ready to give me. I have no idea where, or how he got it, but I've learned it's better to just not ask sometimes.

He would do anything to not wear a condom.

But the birth control has been nice too, it's given me a normal period which doesn't seem like such a great thing, and I really hate having to remember it now, but at least my body is doing what it should.

"So, what else do you have planned for my birthday, future husband?" I grin from my seat, nearly bouncing. It's been the best day already. I don't really need anything else, but if I know Ash—and I do—he's booked the entire day with plans.

"You'll see."

Ash drives for a while before he is pulling onto a familiar road. I sit forward, eyeing the field in the distance and glance at him. *Why is he bringing us here?*

"This is the place that started our downfall. I have no good memories with you here." He pauses, his eyebrows pull together like they do every time he remembers *that* night. He still won't talk about it much, but he did tell me about his therapist in England. At first, I didn't believe him, but then he took me with him to meet Mr. Howard for a few sessions. I think it's great Ash is getting therapy, and now that I've had a good experience with therapy, I think everyone could benefit from talking to someone.

But it doesn't leave my head that I caused the great Ash Pearson to seek therapy.

"I do not want to have any places where our memories are not good, so." He grabs my hand and pulls me from the truck. "I'm going to fuck you—properly. The way you should have been the first time we were here."

My stomach flips, but I'm not sure it's in a good way.

After he gets the bed of his truck set up with the blankets and pillows I didn't see before, my anxiety is sky high. He stops in front of me and tilts my chin up.

"I love you, Payson. I am sorry I haven't always treated you like it. But I will never make you cry again."

"Unless you're crying out my name, or tears of joy." He flashes a smirk and a laugh bubbles out of me. "A sad tear will not leave your eye with the thought of me in your head."

And just like that, all the bad feelings I was having about what he wanted to do here disappear. I lean in his arms, looking toward the spot on the field. There's no sign of what happened here. Washed away from the seasons, but like Ash, that's not an easily forgotten moment in my life. I remember how I felt so vividly, but it's like I'm looking at it from the outside now. No matter how hard I think about it, I can't bring myself to go back to that point in my life. Which isn't a bad thing, just a weird thing.

At one point, I wanted to die, now the only thing I want to do is live. Fully, happily, and freely. I want to live my life the way I should have always lived it.

Starting with making love to my future husband in the back of his truck like we are in some kind of country Hallmark movie.

39
Payson

I THROW MYSELF INTO the team huddle, not giving a shit that I'm covered in sweat like the rest of the girls because we just won nationals! The crowd is loud, singing our school song, and confetti falls from the ceiling above us. It's a surreal feeling. On one hand, I've never been more excited in my volleyball career, on the other, I know this is the last time I will ever play high school volleyball. The last time I'll play with these girls.

The start of the season was rocky, new girls trying to figure out how we would work together. Ash didn't cut as many girls this season, which was nice for the most part.

He wasn't here at the start of the season, still back in England making sure Parker was settled before he came over. There was a lot of back and forth on whether he would come back at all since Parker had decided he didn't want to. Ash obviously didn't want to leave Parker. I wanted him as my coach, but I would have understood. Luca did a great job for the weeks Ash wasn't here, but ultimately, Parker told him to go.

He will move back now that the season is over, and I know he's excited, but I also know he is dreading having to say goodbye to me.

After the medal ceremony and so many pictures, we are released to go. Uncle Jet wanders up, unsure what to do, so I throw my arms around him and squeeze. After I came home from England, he "grounded" me, but it didn't last long because volleyball started and he couldn't keep me from that. He's a hard-ass, but I've gotten used to him.

"Good job."

A man of few words.

"Thanks."

A silent moment passes between us, then he sighs. "I'm going to miss having you as a roommate, you know?"

"I'll come visit."

"Still."

I am sad to be leaving Uncle Jet. I enjoyed my time with him. Getting to know him has been challenging, as he's a private man, but he's nice to hang out with once you get past the intensity. Some of my favorite nights are when I throw a movie on and he finishes work and joins me. He says he's just there to keep me company, but over the last few weeks, we have been making popcorn and setting it right next to me and getting into the movies equally as much as I do. Even putting on sweats and a tee instead of a suit. I could have moved with Ash after my eighteenth birthday, and I think Uncle Jet expected it, I know Ash did, but I decided to stick around with Uncle Jet a bit longer. He was quiet leading up to my birthday, and when I said I would be staying, he bought me a car. Well, him and Ash. Ash refused to not be a part of that purchase; something about not letting another man buy me things. I don't know, all I know is I love having two grumpy men love me in such different ways yet still find the time to fight over who loves me more—that's how it feels anyway.

"If he ever mistreats you—"

"He won't."

He nods because he knows I'm right. "Still, if he does, you know my number."

"Yes." A laugh-sigh mixture spills from me. Him and Ash are . . . okay, especially now that I'm legal, but I think Uncle Jet is waiting for a reason to punch him. Again.

Speak of the devil. Ash wanders up, shooting me a heated look before snapping his eyes to Uncle Jet. "I get her for the night. Do not even think about challenging me about it."

He doesn't touch me, but I can still feel the weight of his claim, it warms my insides. We eventually agreed that when it came to volleyball stuff, we needed to be professional for the team. It wasn't easy. Especially when he would remove his shirt at practice because he's a dick and likes to taunt me. But then I would bend over right in front of him, arch my back a little, and taunt him back.

It created some very heated arguments that quickly turned into the hottest sex. His whole "no sex in my office" was dropped after the third practice. And by the sixth, he was waiting until all the girls went home to sneak into the girls locker room and fuck me because I guess I was taking too long. I was, I hung out in there as long as I could on purpose to wind him up.

"Actually." I interrupt whatever they are saying. "I think I want to hang out with Uncle Jet tonight, if that's okay." I try and attempt my best puppy-dog eyes, but Ash locks his jaw.

"No."

"Hear me out."

"No," he says again. He steps toward me, grips the back of my neck, and angles my head back. "I get one more night with you, so, no. You are mine tonight. You can hang out with him tomorrow."

"What if this wasn't our last night together?" I wanted to do this in a more fun way, but leave it to Ash to get me to blurt it out.

His bushy eyebrows drop, and he releases my neck. He doesn't care that the entire team and their families are around anymore, I guess the season is officially over and he's no longer my coach. "What are you saying?"

I lick my lips quickly. Here goes nothing. "I'm saying that I'm coming with you."

"Where?" His voice is sharp, as if not believing me.

"To Engla—"

Ash smashes his lips against me. I hear a few gasps but ignore them all and enjoy kissing my fiancé. Until Uncle Jet shoves him off and mutters something about wanting to kill him, but Ash pays no attention.

"Are you serious?"

"Yeah, at least until I start school. I can do all my high school work online, and college doesn't start until the fall." I was lucky enough to get accepted into the same school as Janelle, so I will bunk with her and my roommate from Blue Gate, Abby. I'm beyond excited. When I first got accepted, I was nervous to tell Ash because I know he hates being apart, but I blurted it out a few weeks back that I got the call they wanted me to be their libero, did my research, and he was more supportive than I could have ever asked. I wanted to go to Colorado for so long that I didn't think much about this place, but being with Janelle will be nice, and their volleyball program, while brand new, is the fastest growing in the country.

I think Ash had something to do with them reaching out to me in the first place, but he won't admit it.

Ash pulls me against his body and drops his mouth to my ear "If you say sike right now, I'm going to tan your arse."

"I promise I'm not. I'm yours until August."

He squeezes me again before pushing me to arm's length and lifting a cocky eyebrow. "You are mine forever, babygirl. Not just until then."

Payson

Epilogue One

I always loved the rain, so I guess I was destined to live in England where it rains pretty much daily. I'm sad to be going back to the States in a few days, but I know where my home is, and eventually, I will get to live here full-time.

Lightning strikes in the distance, and a few minutes later, thunder booms, rattling Ash's windows ever so slightly. When we were looking at places, he wasn't sure about this place since it needed a lot of work before he got to it, but I convinced him. The rest of the apartment or—flat, as his family calls it, is renovated now. It's our room that needs a bit more work. I wanted to make sure we got Parker's room done first so he was comfortable living here since he and Ash will live here full-time. What really sold me is the fact it is just across town from his parents. Ash says when I move over full-time, he will buy us a house we can fill with kids. He's still all about the baby making, and asking him to wear a condom wasn't even in question, so he pulls out and hates it every time. Says it's *wasting his cum*. I discussed my worries about being able to conceive, and he took me to the doctor who basically said stress is the leading factor of my lack of periods, which would make sense, considering. She also said that with my stress levels low, we should be able to when the time comes, but until then the birth control should help regulate me. So, I'm hopeful and so is he. I don't think it ever occurred to Ash that there could be complications, he's untouchable but forgets everyone around him isn't.

I follow a single raindrop down the window until it combines with the rest of the water at the base.

For so long, I only focused on the storm and never gave much thought to what comes next. It's easy to get lost in the loud thing, but it's important to pay attention to the after because after . . . just might be the best part.

Like right now. I could have lived in the past, got stuck on what was and not what could be, but I'm glad I didn't. Ash doesn't realize it, but he's the reason I'm here today. He's the reason I am the person I am today. Those moments in my childhood I would pray to him and look at him when things were bad, to the long days in Blue Gate, the only constant was him.

He's my lifeline.

It's a lot of pressure for one person to have, but he takes it in stride.

I have bad days. Days when I remember things I don't want to and they cripple me. Days when I miss my grandpa more than the day before, and days when I hate the sight of my scars. Those are the days Ash loves me the hardest, like he promised when he proposed.

He has days when his memories and dreams bother him more than usual, those are the days I love him hardest—like I promised in our vows.

Our wedding was beautiful, on April fourth like we once agreed. Small, probably smaller than he wanted, but to me, it was perfect. His parents hosted it in their backyard, and it was beautiful. More than I could have ever asked for.

Sometimes I wonder if it will be weird, going into college a married woman, but I'm sure weirder things have happened, and just because it's not the path others would have chosen for themselves, doesn't mean it's not the right path for me.

Speaking of the devil. The floor squeaks and he steps behind me, wrapping his warm arms around my body, a nice contrast to the chill of the room, but not before giving Todd a few pats. We agreed that Todd should stay here with him while I go to college. He's a service dog, but the dorm life isn't fair. Ash says that way he knows I'll come back to him, but he's delusional if he thinks he will ever get rid of me.

"What are you thinking about, Jailbird?"

That nickname. He likes to switch up, depending on his mood, from *Jailbird*, to *babygirl*, and now to *my love*, which I think is my new favorite. Jailbird usually means he's in a goofy mood and wants to tease me.

"You, us, I guess."

"What about us?"

"Everything."

He spins me to face him and gives me a heartfelt smile.

"What?"

"You're beautiful."

I feel the blush already creeping up my neck, and I swat him. "Stop, you're being cheesy again."

His laugh is deep. "It's true." He presses his soft lips against my forehead. "Happy birthday, babygirl."

My stomach flutters. "Thank you." I had it in my head that when I turned eighteen a year ago, he wouldn't be as into me because I wasn't forbidden fruit, but that was a silly thought. I was never forbidden; I threw myself at him on that first day and never looked back.

Ash regards outside, and his lips flick up.

"What?" I turn in his arms to face the window to see what he is smiling about.

"A rainbow."

In the break of the clouds, a faint rainbow arches across the sky.

Like I said, *always wait for the end of the storm.*

I drop my head onto his chest and release a peaceful breath. I don't know what the future holds for us. We are still so young, yes, even Ash even though he is almost thirty-five. So many unsure variables and unanswered questions. The one thing I'm not unsure about is my husband. I know many people probably look at us and our relationship and think that because of the distance we will never last, but they don't know how stubborn we are. How in love too, but mostly stubborn.

Epilogue Two

As I stare down at my teary-eyed wife breathing hard, I can't help but allow my own emotions to rise.

"One more time, Mum," the doctor tells Payson. She squeezes her eyes closed, pushes, and a few seconds later, the best sound I've ever heard fills the room.

The doctor holds up our baby, and all I can do is stare. He's perfect. A thick head of dark hair, crying, and so fucking small compared to our two toddlers. I'm worried about touching him. Payson falls back, exhausted, but smiling with wet cheeks.

"I'm a mom." Her lips wobble. I slant my mouth over hers, tasting the saltiness of her tears and sweat.

"Again."

"Again," she repeats, crying even harder.

The nurse passes Payson our newest son, and my heart fucking aches in my chest. I have loved Payson through so many stages over the years, and she has looked more beautiful than I thought possible in all of them. But mum Payson nearly knocks me on my ass every time I look at her playing with our two oldest, and now while feeding our youngest.

I stopped trying to get her pregnant for a while when she left for college. I was still pumping her full every chance we were together, but the birth control stopped it from leading anywhere. It wasn't until she announced that she was done playing professional ball that I thought we would start trying seriously; it turned out she was done playing because she was pregnant with our first, Murphy.

I thought Payson had years left of playing, but she stopped taking her birth control—without my knowledge—and two months later she was pregnant. It worried me, for a while, her not having volleyball in her life like she's had for years, but I remember so vividly her grabbing my hand and pressing it against her small stomach where our only weeks old baby lay and saying, "I love volleyball and I thought it was the dream, but this is it, Ash. This is my dream—a family with you."

I fucked her hard after that, surprised she didn't become pregnant a second time.

That was four years ago now, and I think she's been pregnant ever since. We're taking a break after this one. Give her body a rest, and just enjoy the family we have.

Hours later, I'm holding our son while his mum rests. He's so perfect and big. A whole nine pounds four ounces, so not nearly as small as he looked when I first saw him. He's nearly two pounds bigger than his eldest brother was when he was born. I've watched Payson give birth three times now, and I don't think I'll ever not be amazed at how beautiful she can grow a baby. Most people say our boys look like me, but they don't see how Murphy scrunches his nose when he doesn't like something we made for dinner, or how Franklin's eyes hint at green when they hit the sun. Our boys might favor my looks, but their mum is everywhere throughout them in small ways.

There's a knock on the door and then small footsteps are sprinting inside.

"Frankie," I say in a whisper, but it's pointless because as soon as Payson hears her son's footsteps her eyes are fluttering open. Frankie is named after my dad, but since we already have two Williams in the family, we went with his middle name, Franklin.

"It's fine." She laughs while she pushes herself to sit up and greet him.

"Where's Murphy?" I ask.

Jethro stops by her side and kisses her forehead. "With Parker, they had to stop off at the vending machine. He was hungry despite just eating breakfast and a snack before coming here.

"Payson giggles. "They have their dad's appetite. I don't stand a chance keeping enough food in the house when they are teenagers."

Franklin crawls onto the bed and I open my mouth to tell him to be careful, but she shoots me a murderous glare before pulling him onto her lap and kissing his face all over.

"I missed you."

Franklin's two, and doesn't talk yet, but I swear they communicate in their own way.

"How is mom?" Jethro asks, taking a seat beside her.

"Tired." Her smile is lazy. "But good."

His eyes flick up to me and I nod. Answering his unasked questions. Payson was right after all, I wouldn't say we're friends, but we're not at each other throats anymore. Usually.

He looks to the baby in my arms and his harsh face softens even more. "And the little, er, big guy. You sure you're okay, kid?" He flicks a worried look to her, as if wondering how this chunky baby came out of such a petite woman. Payson's not changed in looks much since we met. Stretch marks across her stomach and ass from the pregnancies, and her tits are even bigger and so fucking sexy when I'm pounding into her. But other than a few hints where small wrinkles will rest in her future, she's still the same seventeen-year-old that jail-baited me into loving her. She says I haven't changed much either, but I know at almost forty-two my hair is grayer than ever, and my wrinkles have settled.

Payson grins at me and our son. "Yeah, I'm good. Isn't he beautiful?"

"He is." I walk over and pass him to his uncle. "Here you go Great Uncle Jet." He hates it when I call him great uncle.

He huffs but grabs the baby and tucks him into the crook of his arm. "So, what's the little guy's name?"

Payson smiles at me and I grab hold of her hand. "It's Jet," she tells him, excitement bubbling on the inside.

It takes a minute for him to react, but eventually his sharp eyes snap to her, then me. He looks between us for a moment and each passing glance his eyebrows sink. He looks down to the sleeping baby, I swear I see a single tear fall from his nose. I bite back any comment I might have and give this one to him. I'd cry too.

Payson's eyes fill with tears, and she grabs ahold of his hand. "Just like his uncle."

The moment is interrupted by the loud voice of our eldest, and his brother. I wasn't sure how Parker would deal with me having more kids, but he loves his little brothers more than I could have ever asked. He's around as much as he can be with his football career taking off. Moving to England was the best choice for him and me. His career kicked off almost immediately, and our relationship became even stronger than I thought possible.

Parker stops just inside, carrying Murphy upside down. "Anyone order a four-year-old?"

"Ooo! Me! I did!" Payson cheers, making our son burst with laughter. He also has his mum's smile.

I grab Murphy from him and blow a raspberry onto his tummy before sitting on the bed next to Payson and his brother so she can squeeze both of them.

Parker slaps my shoulder and bends to kiss Payson's cheek. "Congratulazioni, Mamma and Papa."

"Grazie," she beams, so proud of her ability to speak Italian now. She's been working so hard to learn for Parker. "Wait"—she narrows her eyes at him—"are you calling me mom or a mom?"

I snort and she scowls. Parker and Payson's relationship is odd—to say the least, with there only being a year difference in age between them—and they argue more like brother and sister than anything, but I know when push comes to shove, they got each other's backs. Payson is just about his biggest fan, next to our sons, and me of course. When we can't make it to a game, which isn't very often, but with her being pregnant, we missed a few this season, she makes sure to put it on the TV and to call him after with any comments on his playing. She might be American, but she loves English football. When she's not pregnant and Parker is home for a visit, I'll often look outside and catch them doing some kind of pepper drill where she will bump, set, and spike to him while he kicks to her. She says next to volleyball it's the most entertaining sport, and I thought I couldn't love her anymore.

We're currently in the middle of adding an extension onto our gym—a football extension. I was even able to convince Luca to come and coach. After we left Bayshore, he stuck around and coached a few more years with Coach Maddox, but eventually he got antsy being in one place. Probably because he ran through all the single women, but I digress. Besides a few visits on both parts, we've hardly seen each other, so it'll be nice having him around.

"Guess you'll never know." He teases her.

"Parker," I warn. "She just gave birth, give her a break."

He rolls his eyes playfully and drops into the couch across the room. "A mum," he says and she relaxes.

That was her one rule when we married. Parker is not allowed to call her mum. No one disagreed with that, but he likes to tease her about it anyway.

Everyone sticks around until I can tell it's becoming a lot for Payson, and I boot them out. Lovingly, of course.

After the door closes, she drops her head back and sighs a longing sound. "I don't remember our boys being so energetic."

I chuckle as I take my seat next to her on the bed. I pull her into my arms, and she leans back against my chest. It's not often we get time alone anymore. Our lives are so busy with the boys and the gym, but I am able to convince her to drop the kids at my parents' for a night, two if I'm lucky, so we can spend some one-on-one time together.

"They are always energetic, but usually you're not recovering when they are." I kiss her temple, and she hums a happy sound.

Jet stirs, wanting to eat again. He's living up to his size and is eating more than every two hours, but Payson takes it in stride, like she does everything with motherhood, it never fails to amaze me. I pluck him from the bedside basket and gently pass him to her.

I shouldn't get hard seeing her breast when she's about to feed our son, but the moment I stop getting hard for Payson's naked body is the moment I don't want to live anymore.

She strokes his cheek as he feeds. "He's perfect. All our boys are so perfect." Her voice shakes, and I give her shoulders a squeeze. "I can't believe how lucky we are, Ash. I know I say this a lot, and cry about it even more, but I feel so lucky when I think about the life I could have had—or not had and the one I do." She hiccups. "I am just so lucky."

I think about the same thing more often than I'll admit. Payson thinks she is the lucky one, but she doesn't realize how much joy she brings to our family. How our boys immediately seek her out in a room, how they wake up and can't wait to tell their mum about any dreams they had, or how my heart takes an extra beat anytime she looks at me.

Like she's doing right now. I once went too long without seeing her big, beautiful eyes on me, so I never take it for granted when her attention is on me. I lean down and press my lips ever so gently to hers.

"We are the lucky ones, babygirl."

She sighs against me and says, "You think our next one will be a girl?"

Bloody hell this woman. Gave birth less than twelve hours ago and is already thinking about having another.

"Let's enjoy this one for a while before we consider another, yes?"

"I don't mean right now." She swats at my chest, making sure to not disturb our feeding son. "But eventually. Don't you want a little girl?"

I still have never told Payson about the dream I had of our daughter, but I've had it more times since that first. Usually after Payson's had a bad day or there's been a lot of stress in our life. It shakes me up every time, and each time we fall pregnant and Payson wants to wait to find out the gender until birth, my anxiety is sky fucking high. But I'll never let her know that. I love seeing how she is excited each time to find out, and if that brings her joy during such a traumatic moment for her body, I can push my feelings aside.

The truth is—no. I don't mind if we never have a daughter. Of course, I will love her more than life just as I do all four of my sons, but I know I would end up smothering her even more than I do the rest. Probably something similar to how I smother Payson. Worried that as soon as I let her out of my sight something would go wrong.

Knowing I've taken too long to answer by the little worry line between her pinched eyebrows, I slap on a smile—not that it's difficult—and poke her nose.

"I already have a little girl who calls me daddy."

Her eyes blow wide. "Ashley Pearson. Ew, gross. Don't talk about that when we are discussing having a daughter. And if we do have a daughter, I can't call you that anymore. Even during our weak moments."

Our weak moments refer to the times when we have to let out our deepest desires. Our sex life is better than ever and more times than not, Payson is full of my cum, but we don't roleplay much anymore. We don't miss it, usually, but there are sometimes I know she is champing at the bit to call me daddy, and I'm equally ready to hear it from her pouty lips. So, to stop either of us from going without our wants, we will tell the other that we are having a weak moment, and we can say and do whatever we please during that time. The only hard line I have is no knives.

There was once when she was in college, after an incident with Fred, that knocked her on her ass for a long while. I was on a flight on my way to her immediately and stayed with her until she was in better spirits. Jethro and I already hired the best security we could find to follow her around after the fact even though Fred was then gone. She wasn't aware of the security until after the incident, then there was someone to take her to and from school, from practice, anywhere she went. She was never alone. But during those first few weeks, she broke down and told me she wanted to cut, breathing was too difficult, and she was suffocating. She asked if I would do it, I refused. After some extra therapy sessions, she apologized for ever putting me in that position to ask—again. I held her and told her she didn't need to apologize.

"Then absolutely no, I don't wish we'd have a girl." I smirk.

"Seriously, Ash." Her eyes fill with worry.

I drop a kiss to her forehead and suck in a deep breath, enjoying Payson's natural scent filling my nose. "No, babygirl. I don't wish for a daughter. I love the family we have. If we have a daughter, eventually, I will not be any more or any less happy than I would be if we had all boys."

"Okay, me either. I love being a boy mom. They keep me on my toes."

That, I can agree to.

We stay like that for a long time. Jet has long since gone back to sleep, drunk off his mum's milk.

Mum and Dad will be down in the morning to meet their newest grand-baby. We didn't want to overwhelm Payson too much on the first day. Payson loves my family, but I know being around everyone at once can sometimes be a lot for the little girl who was so often alone.

I believe tomorrow is also when Janelle finally makes the move over here to start her job at my parents' firm. I wonder if Payson told her she would be working under Henry, and not my parents like she thought. If not, that should go over well. I'm nearly positive something happened after our wedding between those two, but it was never brought up and I never asked.

"I can't wait to be home with all three boys."

I tuck into Payson's side. "Me either." I always dreamed of having a house full of love, and I can honestly say we have it—thanks to her.

She curls into my chest and plays with my chest hair.

"Thank you," I whisper, unsure she's awake. She shifts closer and kisses my collarbone. She doesn't need to ask what I'm thanking her for. I often randomly thank her, so she knows it's not anything specific, just our life because without her, I wouldn't have the life I do today. I don't know what it would have been like, but I know it wouldn't be anywhere near as satisfying if I didn't have her and our boys.

"I love you." Her voice is soft, tired from the long day.

"And I love you. Always."

And forever.

The End

You made it! Welcome to the end where I just ramble and thank you for reading. No, but seriously. Thank. You. For. Reading. It's a surreal feeling, you know? You set out to write a story with zero expectations and before you know it you have people messaging you for the next book. Excited about the next book. Cussing me out because of the book(s) (hehe)

When I started writing I didn't know where this journey would take me. I just knew that I liked coming up with stories, so I began writing them down. I have to admit, I've been blown away from the support for my babies. I care for them so fiercely—even though they are fictional—they feel so real for me and to see you love them (or hate them) as much as I do is a super great feeling. I know this won't be the last time you hear from Ash and Payson. Ash has been bothering me to write their wedding scene, so maybe keep an eye out for that in the future. I'm most active on my Instagram @authorkb.row so follow along for updates!

Whether you liked, loved, or hated this series, thank you for being here. You guys are the real MVPs.

I have some things I'm very excited about coming out in the near future, so I hope you stick around for that. If not, thanks for being here as long as you were!

Also By

Standalones:

Reap3r

Crew's Night (Available until Nov 31st, 2023)

Him For Christmas

Series:

<u>Broken Series</u>

Break For You (Book one)

Leave Me Broken (Book two)

Heal For Me (Book three)

About The Author

I know these are meant to be in third person, but I loathe third person so, here we go. I'm originally from the Mid-west, USA, meaning I put ranch on everything and say "ope" far too often. I grew in a very small town in rural American where I met my loving husband. It was love at first sight... at least for me. Eventually he agreed. In the eleven years we've been together, we have added the cutest pup and an even cuter son that keeps us on our toes constantly. When I'm not writing you can find me probably thinking about writing. Peace!

Printed in Great Britain
by Amazon